Too bad they hadn't started shouting five minutes sooner.

Cautiously, Noelle felt for the stairs. Before her first step had fallen, the man in the basement crossed the distance between them, covered her mouth with his gloved hand, and flattened her body with his against the wall behind her.

A scream bubbled up in her throat, but he prevented the noise from escaping.

His mouth brushed against her ear. "Be quiet and I'll get us out of here alive."

Noelle gave a tight nod. Satisfied, he lessened the pressure against her mouth. A deep breath brought her closer to her captor. The heat from his body seeped through her clothing. She felt his military gear against her breasts and belly, and smelled the distracting combination of leather, warm male skin, and cordite.

Another weary floorboard gave away the location of the intruder above. He was in her bedroom, and she could tell by the slow creak and groan that he was searching for something. Or someone.

"Stay put," the man with her commanded in a low, gruff voice. "I'll come get you when the coast is clear."

From the floor above, she heard a pop and the heavy thud of a body collapsing . . .

Don't forget to turn to the back of this book for a preview of Shannon K. Butcher's next sexy suspense novel, *No Control*.

NO REGRETS

SHANNON K. BUTCHER

NEW YORK   BOSTON

Copyright © 2007 by Shannon K. Butcher
Excerpt from *No Control* copyright © 2007 by Shannon K. Butcher
All rights reserved. Except as permitted under the U.S. Copyright Act of 1976, no part of this publication may be reproduced, distributed, or transmitted in any form or by any means, or stored in a database or retrieval system, without the prior written permission of the publisher.

Warner Forever is an imprint of Warner Books, Inc.

Warner Forever is a trademark of Time Warner Inc. or an affiliated company. Used under license by Hachette Book Group USA, which is not affiliated with Time Warner Inc.

Cover design and art by Dale Fiorillo
Cover photo by Ian Sanderson / Getty Images
Book design by Stratford Publishing Services

Warner Forever
Hachette Book Group USA
1271 Avenue of the Americas
New York, NY 10020
Visit our Web site at www.HachetteBookGroupUSA.com

Printed in the United States of America

First Printing: February 2007

10 9 8 7 6 5 4 3 2 1

For Jim Butcher, my amazingly talented husband, who taught me how to write even though it looked like a hopeless cause. Thank you for your unfailing patience and unwavering belief in me. I could never have done this without you. You are my inspiration.

ACKNOWLEDGMENTS

I want to thank all the people who gave me feedback and insight and helped me make this book better: Nephele, Michele, Deidre, Julie, Jayne, Dyann, Darla and Tonia. If I've forgotten anyone, I apologize, and you know where to find me.

No
Regrets

CHAPTER ONE

David Wolfe's past caught up with him in the parking lot of a small-town grocery store in the Rocky Mountains. Late-November sun warmed his dark hair but did nothing to rid him of the chill of foreboding that sank into him with every step he took toward his former commanding officer.

Colonel George Monroe lounged against David's Jeep, blocking his escape.

"What are you doing here, sir?" asked David, his tone sharp with displeasure.

Colonel Monroe regarded David with a steady stare that would have made a less confident man go pale. Monroe's once-black hair was shot steely gray with age, and he had the emotionless eyes of a man who'd seen too much suffering in one lifetime. But in his white knit shirt and khakis, he looked more like a retired golfer than he did a commander of the world's most elite, secret fighting force.

"You're a hard man to find, Wolfe," said Monroe.

"I wasn't wanting to be found, sir," replied David. "I'm surprised that you got this far."

"We traced the money you sent your sister for her son's surgery."

David spat a searing curse. He'd wired the funds from over a hundred miles away under an alias of an alias of a man who didn't even exist. Monroe should never have been able to find him.

Unless he'd really been working at it.

Ripples of unease slipped down David's spine. Whatever Monroe wanted from him, it couldn't be good. Powerful military leaders like Monroe didn't ambush former military men in grocery store parking lots just to catch up on old times.

"What do you want?" demanded David.

"We need you, Wolfe. There's a . . . situation."

"I don't give a damn about your *situation*," said David, purposefully adding a belated, "Sir."

Monroe's mouth twitched with a hint of a smile. "I see you haven't lost your respect for authority these past two years."

"No, but I'm about to lose my temper, so you'd best move away from my Jeep and find yourself another man for your situation. I quit Delta Force two years ago, remember?"

Monroe didn't budge and David was quickly beginning to think that he was going to have to show Monroe just how much he'd learned in all those years of being under his command—training to fight with whatever was at hand, and when nothing was at hand, fighting with nothing. His body tensed as he sized up Monroe for a quick, efficient takedown.

"I wouldn't do that if I were you, Wolfe," said Monroe as if reading David's violent thoughts. "I'm not stupid enough to think I could take you on in a fair fight, so I brought backup. There's a sniper a hundred yards behind you in the trees. He's not as good as Grant, but he's good enough." A brief, feral smile flashed over Monroe's face.

David froze, suddenly feeling the weight of a lethal rifle aimed at his skull. If he touched Monroe, it would be the last thing he did.

"You're a bastard, sir," said David.

"So says my wife, but then she doesn't know me like you do." Monroe flicked a hand signal at the sniper and David recognized the command to wait—on alert. "I need you to take on an assignment and I'm not taking no for an answer."

"Yes you will. I don't owe you anything. I walked away with a clean slate. The only favors I owe are to Grant and Caleb, and they're not the ones asking." David suppressed his guilt as he mentioned his two closest friends—the men he owed his life to countless times over. The men he'd walked away from two years ago, leaving them to carry on the fight for freedom without him.

Monroe tilted his head and looked directly into David's eyes. He was one of the few men David knew who could really look at him and not flinch. "You're wrong. You do owe me."

The sudden softness in Monroe's voice worried David. Men like Monroe were never soft—not with their wives or children and certainly not with the men like David, who they ordered to the most hellish places on earth to kill some of the most vile people ever to draw breath.

"What the hell are you talking about?" asked David.

"I was the one who ordered the rest of Delta to stand down on your last op."

Pain seared David's chest at the mention of that failed operation and just how much it had cost him. His body shook and the groceries crunched under his tightening grip. Against his will, his eyes shut and he was forced to face the horror of his two-year-old memories, still painfully fresh in his mind.

"You were the one who gave that order?" The lack of air in his lungs made the question come out as a thready whisper.

"I did," said Monroe. "And I'd do it again today if faced with the same choice."

Had David not had the small outlet of revenge Monroe had given him, he wouldn't have lasted this long. The guilt would have eaten him whole.

"Were you court-martialed?" asked David.

Monroe looked away, his gray eyes sliding uncomfortably to the woods behind David, where the sniper waited for a sign to kill. "It doesn't matter now. What does matter is that I need your help. I never meant to call in that particular favor, but I don't have any choice. I need you to come back for this op. Lives are at stake."

Bleak, painful memories flooded David's head and he fought to hold them back—to stem the flow of blood, death and pain all cloaked in shades of nightmares.

"I won't go back," growled David, unfamiliar with the raw sound of his own voice. "I can't. I lost too much working for you to ever go back."

Monroe's mouth flattened into a grim line. "The Swarm has resurfaced. They've started killing again."

David was so shocked it rocked him back onto his heels. "That's impossible. I killed them all. I torched the building and watched to make sure not one of them made it out alive."

David relived every single moment of his last op in the

space of a heartbeat. He felt the blind rage that had gripped him as he killed, felt the grim satisfaction of knowing that the Swarm would never hurt anyone again, felt the hollow emptiness of knowing that no matter how many men he killed, he couldn't bring back the dead. Revenge changed nothing.

After several tense moments, David was able to rebuild the barrier on the part of his mind that was a tempest of chaotic nightmares—images that beat at his sanity until only a bubble-thin film remained.

"Four civilians are dead and the life of a young woman is at stake. I need you. *She* needs you."

"You want *me* to protect her?" asked David in disbelief. "You must be desperate."

Monroe pulled in a deep, weary breath. "You know the Swarm. You know their tactics. You also know what will happen to her if you fail."

Seething, violent rage billowed up into David's throat, leaving behind the acid taste of bile. For two years he'd thought that he'd taken out every one of the Swarm's members. Before he quit Delta Force he'd made sure that they could never harm an innocent again.

He'd been wrong. For two years, he'd been wrong.

"Tell me where the Swarm is now," demanded David in a near growl. "I'll kill every last one of them myself."

"We don't know where they are. But we know what they want."

"The woman," guessed David.

Monroe nodded. "Dr. Noelle Blanche. Stick with her and you won't have to find the Swarm. They'll find you."

A slow, ferocious smile curled over David's lips. "Where is she?"

"We need to talk."

Noelle Blanche started, and she turned around to see who had interrupted her concentration.

Professor Joan Montgomery, Noelle's longtime mentor and friend, stood in the doorway of Noelle's cramped office, looking worried and slightly nauseated.

Joan had been one of Noelle's undergraduate professors at the University of Kansas. She had given Noelle her first taste of Latin and, because of Joan, Noelle's educational destiny had changed. Her career path to mathematician had taken an exit toward linguistics and she'd ended up at some wacky rest stop called Assistant Professor of Applied Mathematical Linguistics.

Noelle forced a welcoming smile on her face, pushing aside the intriguing, vaguely Cyrillic script she'd just received in an e-mail from a colleague in Russia. "I'm teaching linear algebra in fifteen minutes, but I have until then."

Joan's expression twisted with discomfort. "I've been sent by the dean to find out your final decision about that grant. He's tired of waiting."

Noelle stifled a resigned sigh. "I already told him I won't accept any grants funded by the military."

Joan tucked her graying, chin-length hair behind one ear, pulled out the orange, 1970s cast-off office chair and sat down. "Why not? You're the only one in the department who can do the work. Hell, as far as I know, you're the only one in the country who can do it."

Noelle shook her head and shoved a hand through her red curls to untangle them from the hinge of her glasses.

"That's not true. There are at least four other people who know more than I do about that particular flavor of cryptology and two of them live right here in the States. It's just a hobby for me. They do it full-time."

"They weren't the ones the government offered oodles of grant money," Joan reminded her. "Apparently, you're a lot more valuable than you think."

Noelle made a rude, snorting noise. "My sister's the smart one. Let them ask her. Or anyone else. Just not me."

"Why won't you do the work? It sounded fairly tame to me. It's not like they're asking you to build a bomb or something."

"They want me to develop a mathematically based encryption system for military use."

"So?" asked Joan, frowning at Noelle in confusion. "Don't you think you can do it?"

Noelle waved a pale hand, almost knocking over the Leaning Tower of Paperwork. "Of course I can do it. I'm already halfway finished with the algorithms because I couldn't stop my brain from working on the puzzle while I was sleeping. I'll have the solution in another two months, whether or not I want to know it, but that's not the point."

"Then what is the point? Because I'm not seeing how turning down easy money is going to help solidify your position here at the university."

"If I give the military a tool, they will use it. Eventually, they will use it offensively. When that happens, people will die and I'll be partially responsible. I can't do that."

"If you don't, someone else at some other university will," said Joan, her face softening with understanding. "You're brilliant, and it will probably take someone else five years to do what you can in two months, but eventually, someone will figure it out. Eventually, someone will give the military their tool."

"But it won't be me," replied Noelle. "I won't have that blood on my hands, even if it means I get fired."

"Downsized," corrected Joan with a grimace.

"Whatever." It all meant that Noelle would be out of a job.

Silence filled the room, broken only by the faint buzzing of the cheap fluorescent light overhead.

"Not whatever," said Joan. "Downsized."

The apologetic tone of Joan's voice caught Noelle's attention. "They sent you to fire me, didn't they?"

Joan's dark eyes met Noelle's green ones. "If you don't accept this grant money, you're going to be let go at the end of the spring semester."

Let go. Noelle felt like her outdated chair had fallen out from under her. She probably shouldn't have been shocked, but she was. It was one thing to think about the possibility of losing her job; it was entirely different to know it *will* happen. And when. "Are you sure?"

Joan nodded, making her short gray hair sway along her chin. "That's why I was sent here. The department doesn't want to lose you and your freakish brilliance, but we just can't afford the additional expense right now. Since your salary comes out of the Linguistics Department budget, we had the final say. I'm so sorry."

Noelle closed her eyes. What would she do now? Finding a job that didn't require her to say, "Do you want fries with that?" was going to be nearly impossible. It wasn't as if she had employers beating at her door, begging her to come to work for them. Mathematical linguistics wasn't exactly a booming field. Someone in an obscure career like hers would need months, if not years, to find another suitable position—likely one that would have to be built specifically for her. What would she do until then?

She had racked up tons of debt in student loans just to get her Ph.D. The loan payments by themselves were more than her other living expenses combined. She could hold off the bill collectors for a while, but she was going to need a decent income—not the kind she could make flipping burgers.

Noelle swallowed past the panic that clogged her throat. It was just money. She'd find some way around this obstacle.

"You could always take the grant," suggested Joan.

Noelle wished it was that simple. She was sorely tempted just to give in and make her life a whole lot easier. But for someone who started college at sixteen, easy clearly wasn't her modus operandi. "I can't do that. It's blood money."

"Don't be so dramatic," scolded Joan. "No one's asking you to hurt anyone. In fact, it's entirely possible that doing this could save lives."

"And if you're wrong?" Noelle stood and shoved her laptop into its black nylon tote. "I can't take that chance. I wouldn't be able to sleep at night wondering if my work cost the lives of innocents."

"This is your career we're talking about—your entire future rests on this decision."

"Now who's being dramatic?" scoffed Noelle.

"I'm serious. If you walk away from this grant, chances are you won't find another position anytime soon. If you take the job, then you stand the chance of becoming famous in academic communities as the woman who revolutionized mathematical linguistics."

Noelle rolled her eyes. "I'm sure they'll write that on my gravestone, right next to the part about how I helped kill thousands of innocent civilians in some country where the children don't even know what math is."

"I can't let you do this to yourself," said Joan. "You're too brilliant to slaughter your career because of something that *might* happen."

"It isn't your choice to make. You've been by my side, supporting me when everyone else pointed fingers and laughed at the scrawny kid with more brains than social skills. You are more than just my mentor, you're my friend, but you can't ask me to do this. I won't be a part of killing, no matter how necessary some general thinks it may be."

Noelle shoved students' homework into her bag, refusing to look at the woman who had given her nothing but good advice and steadfast support.

"I'll call you this weekend, after you've had some time to think," said Joan.

Noelle didn't bother to tell her that she'd already done all the thinking she needed to. Her mind was made up. And just to be sure she wasn't tempted to change her mind when the financial panic truly set in, Noelle pulled her laptop back out from its case and typed the command that would kill every trace of data on her hard drive tied to the project. There was no going back now.

She'd be out of a job come spring, but at least she'd be able to live with herself and that was something no amount of grant money could buy.

Fired or not, Noelle still had a job to do until spring, and she had just settled in for a wild Friday night of grading clumsily executed Calculus I homework when the lights in her tiny rental house went black. With a sigh that came all the way from her toes, she pulled open a drawer that held one of many flashlights in her home. She'd always been told that old houses possessed great amounts of charm and character, but in her experience, they simply possessed noisy plumbing, abundant drafts and faulty wiring. It was the third time this week that she'd blown a fuse in the house's ancient fuse box.

Making her way to the basement more by memory than sight, Noelle descended the bare wooden stairs. With the speed of much practice, she unscrewed and replaced the same fuse she'd put in just two days ago. Mentally, she made a note to speak to Mr. Hasham about this problem when she paid him next month's rent.

Even with the new fuse in place, the lights didn't come on. That had never happened before.

Above her head came the crash of breaking glass, followed by the muted tinkle of brittle shards falling to the hardwood floor.

Noelle jumped, then froze, listening. The sound had come from her back door.

Someone was breaking into her house.

CHAPTER TWO

Noelle's heart slammed around inside her chest as she fumbled to switch off the flashlight so she could hide in the dark basement. Overhead, she heard the slow, methodical step of at least two people walking over the floor.

She prayed that they'd just take whatever they wanted and go. As silently as she could, she tiptoed over the dusty floor toward the stairs. The basement was relatively empty and the only hiding place was behind the creaky stairway.

Noelle held her breath until her lungs burned, listening as the footsteps came near the top of the stairs. A beam of light flashed into the basement, falling on the spot where she had been standing only seconds before. In the center of the white pool of light sliding slowly over the floor was a tiny red dot—the kind cast by a laser pointer like she used when lecturing.

Or like the laser sight on a weapon.

Noelle sucked in a silent breath as the realization hit her. These weren't just some punky kids out to make a few bucks off a stolen TV. Whoever was in her house was armed in a serious way.

Noelle heard the faint rattling of the batteries against the plastic case of the flashlight held in her trembling hands. The white spot of light swung to her left, casting the shadow of steps—like jagged black teeth—onto the floor near her feet. The red dot glowed brighter and she could see the streak of laser light bouncing off the dust particles floating about in the grimy basement air.

A soft gasp escaped her mouth against her will and blood pounded loudly in her ears. Noelle watched the white light, saw it gather and grow smaller and brighter as the wielder stepped onto the stairway.

The old wood of the top step creaked under the man's foot. She could see his heavy combat boots through the open back of the steps as he descended.

Noelle tried to catch her breath as she shrank back into the smallest space possible. She clutched the flashlight knowing that it was her only weapon. She knew also that it was going to be a poor match against men armed with real weapons.

A sharp pop, followed by a muffled thump sounded from what Noelle thought was her living room. The foot on the step moved, pivoting as if the man had turned around to look behind him. The column of light disappeared for an instant. She heard a grunt and the sickening crunch of breaking bone, then the body of the man at the top step slowly tumbled down, bouncing limply off the hard edge of each wooden step.

When he landed at the bottom of the steps on the dirty floor, his dark eyes were open, staring right at Noelle.

She froze with fear. It took her several frantically fast heartbeats to realize that the man was dead. Most of his face was covered with a black knit ski mask, but she could see his eyes, glazed and fixed in death.

The small flashlight mounted to the top of his rifle cast

a brilliant cylinder of dusty light against the wall immediately to Noelle's left. The dust kicked up by his body's landing on the dirty floor swirled in the air, clawing its way into her lungs. The need to cough strained her chest as she fought to remain silent.

The groan of old wood sounded directly above her head and her chin shot up in time to see a new pair of boots land stealthily on the top step.

This time the boots were larger.

The man moved down the steps, staying to the outside edge so that the wood made as little noise as possible. Noelle forced herself to remain quiet, pressing a hand hard against her mouth and nose to keep herself from coughing. He moved with caution and a practiced grace that told her he'd done things like this before. A lot.

No flashlight was mounted to this man's weapon, but now that he had descended the steps far enough for her to see him through the wooden slats, she realized that he was wearing headgear—likely the Starlight scopes the military used for night vision.

He knelt before to the dead man at the bottom of the steps and pressed two fingers against the side of the fallen man's throat. Even as he checked for a pulse, his eyes never lowered.

He plucked something from the dead man's head and fitted it into his ear—probably some sort of communication device, she guessed.

He scanned the room and as soon as he spotted Noelle through his night-vision goggles, his body went still.

Cold sweat slid down between her breasts. She clamped her fist around the plastic flashlight, gripping it as she would a baseball bat. Slowly, she forced her trembling legs to straighten and began inching her way to the only escape—the steps.

"Dr. Blanche?" asked the man in a near whisper.

He knew her name. That had to be good, right?

"I'm not here to hurt you. I'm here to get you out before the bad guys can." He extended a gloved hand. His body was entirely encased in black. Even his face had been smeared with black paint behind the eyeholes in his mask. He held the rifle with the unconscious confidence of a man who had spent a lot of time handling weapons.

She prayed he wasn't lying. She wasn't used to running on instincts, so hers were rusty, but they told her that he was telling the truth. He was here to help.

Intellectually, her best option was to make a break for the stairway to get out and let the police sort out good guys from bad. It was a good plan. Her only plan. But as if he anticipated her moves, his body shifted so that if she wanted to get to the stairs, she'd have to go through him. She'd taken enough statistics classes to know the chances of that happening were almost as bad as her chances of winning the lottery.

Painful, ragged heartbeats punctuated her scattered thoughts. Above the thud in her chest came the faint creak of aging floorboards. Someone else was up there.

Noelle's heart did a flip-flop and settled low in the pit of her stomach.

The man in front of her didn't even flinch. He raised one gloved finger to his lips for silence and knelt to switch off the dead man's flashlight.

Instantly, the basement was plunged back into dusty blackness. Noelle's eyes widened, but there was simply no visible light available. She was blind.

Noelle resisted the urge to flip the small plastic switch on her own flashlight and sweep away some measure of terror with the brush of light. She knew that would give away her position not only to the man here in the basement, but also to the one above.

Those rusty instincts screamed at her to get out of the house. Too bad they hadn't started shouting five minutes sooner.

Cautiously, Noelle reached out a hand to feel for the stairs as she stepped forward. Before her first step had fallen, the man in the basement with her had crossed the distance between them, covered her mouth with his gloved hand and used his body to flatten hers against the brick wall behind her.

A startled scream bubbled up in her throat, but his hand prevented the noise from escaping.

He bent his head down so that his mouth brushed against her ear. His words were a mere breath of sound, almost too quiet for even her to hear. "Be quiet and I'll get us both out of here alive."

Noelle had no idea what this was about or why these men were in her house. But one thing was for sure, no matter how much she wanted to flee, there was no way she was moving until he was ready to let her. Her body was pressed so tightly against the wall that she could feel the tiny serrations in the bricks behind her.

Noelle gave a tight nod to let him know that she would comply. Satisfied, he lessened the pressure of his fingers against her mouth. She pulled in a deep breath, which expanded her chest, bringing her closer to her captor. The heat from his body seeped through the knits of the multilayered clothing she wore to combat her drafty house. She felt metallic bits of his military gear against her breasts and belly, along with the hard edges of a bulletproof vest. Her nose was level with his collarbone and she could smell the distracting combination of the leather of his glove and warm, male skin and cordite.

Another weary floorboard gave away the location of the intruder above. He was in her bedroom, and she could tell by the slow creak and groan, the intruder was searching for something. Or someone.

It was completely black in the basement, but Noelle could feel his steady, even breathing mingling with her own frantic, rapid breaths. If he was nervous, he certainly hid it a lot better than she did.

She found his confidence oddly comforting.

His body shifted, and she could feel the warm press of his mouth against the top of her ear. His wide, gloved hand still hovered directly over her lips. She didn't doubt for a second that he'd be able to stop her from yelling before she even pulled in enough breath to make a squeak.

"Stay put," he commanded in the low, gruff voice. "I'm going to clear a path to get you out of here."

"But —"

His fingers sealed off her mouth, preventing any more words from escaping. "I know what I'm doing. I'll come get you when the coast is clear."

Before Noelle could argue anymore, he was gone, and she was left alone in the darkness without even the faintest whisper of footsteps trailing behind him.

Noelle wasn't about to be trapped in the basement again with an armed stranger. Her gut told her that this man was telling the truth—that he really did want to help her. Logic told her that he was just one man against multiple armed men. If he failed to clear a path, as he put it, she might well be left to her own devices to escape.

Using only memory to guide her, Noelle shoved the flashlight in her jeans' pocket, held her hands out in front of her, and began to inch slowly across the basement floor. The dry, splintery surface of the wooden stairs scraped her fingers, but she refused to let go of the only object that could safely lead her to freedom. The toe of her tennis shoe bumped into something limp and heavy. The dead man.

She shivered in revulsion as her stomach clenched and she ground her teeth together to keep from vomiting onto the basement floor. Pushing the thought of corpses out of her mind, she knelt and felt around the body until she touched the cold, smooth surface of his rifle. Being careful not to pull the trigger accidentally, she positioned her hands so that she could use the weapon as it was intended. Her fingers trembled and her skin was slick with the sweat of terror. She wasn't sure that she could actually shoot someone, and she prayed that anyone looking at her wouldn't instantly know that was the case.

From the floor above, she heard a pop and the heavy thud of a body collapsing. Fear slithered along her spine as she wondered which of the men had fallen.

She prayed it wasn't the man with the commanding tone and the smell of leather on his skin.

David picked up the weapon of the man he'd just killed. A quick glance through his NVGs confirmed his suspicion that the ammunition they were using was nonlethal. Tranquilizer darts.

The men after Dr. Blanche were not here to kill her. They wanted her alive.

The thought should have made David feel better about the situation, but then again, the Swarm had wanted many other hostages alive. At first.

Bitter memories churned in his head, making his gut clench. He'd failed one woman and it had cost her her life. He wasn't about to make the same mistake twice.

He looped the strap of the confiscated weapon over his shoulder and headed back down the hall toward the main living area.

The door to the basement was open, as was the shattered kitchen door that led to the backyard. Cold, black air swept over the ancient tile floor and curled around David's legs. The scent of burning leaves and woodsmoke wafted on night wind, reminding him of campfires and countless frigid nights spent on frozen, enemy soil.

So far he'd taken out three men. The comm unit in his ear buzzed with another voice, frantically trying to locate his buddies. If David had been running their mission, there would be at least one more silent participant covering the outside of the house on the off chance that the woman would be able to escape the trap they had made of her home.

A shadow fell across the concrete slab just outside the kitchen door, giving away the presence of another man right outside. To David's left wooden stairs creaked, and he knew that Noelle was heading right into the line of fire.

David crouched low, down to the right so he could cover her entrance into the kitchen. The matte black coating of his weapon and silencer blended into the shadows.

If anything was going to give him away to his enemy, it would only be that he was a darker shape than the night that surrounded him.

Slowly, the enemy pivoted around the doorframe, making himself a clear target. Before David had time to squeeze the trigger, Noelle stepped out into the kitchen directly between David and his target.

With a silent curse, the muzzle of David's weapon jerked toward the ceiling. "Get down!" He shouted.

The man in the doorway ducked and fired, hitting Noelle with a dart.

Noelle jumped and the rifle in her hands fell in a metallic clang on the tile floor. Her file stated she had no combat training, but, to her credit, it only took her a split second to respond. She spun around toward the sound of his voice and ducked low, covering her head with her arms.

David heard the hollow thud of the second tranquilizer dart as it exploded from the end of the rifle and sank into Noelle's flesh.

She yelped in pain and reflexively ripped the dart from her arm, tossing it on the kitchen floor as if it were a live snake. Clumsy fingers swatted the remaining dart from her arm, but it was too late. The damage was already done. Her body wobbled unsteadily as the drug began to take effect. David rose from his crouch, leveled the gun, and squeezed off two rounds in a double-tap. The bullets hit the target one-half inch above each eye socket.

Even before the dead man had landed on the ground, David lowered his weapon and went to Noelle. Her fingers were pressed over the injuries on her arm. A dark spot spread out over the thin pale fabric of her sweatshirt—likely more drug than blood considering how quickly she'd shed the second dart. The first one, however, had stayed in long enough to do its job, and the drug was already coursing through her system.

David didn't dare remove his NVGs to check her injury. There wasn't much time before she'd be unconscious, and he needed her awake to complete the second part of his mission.

Noelle's eyes rolled around loosely in her head, which she moved as if it were too heavy to support.

None too gently, David took her by the shoulders and gave her a shake. "Don't leave me yet, Noelle," he commanded in a quiet growl. "Where is your research?"

She squeezed her eyes shut and opened them wide, trying to focus on his face. "My laptop," she managed, jerking a hand toward the small desk in the living room.

"Where do you store your records?"

Her eyes shut and David reached for the hypodermic pen that contained a stimulant powerful enough to keep her awake for a few more minutes—long enough to get the information he needed. He'd had the pen dosed for someone lighter than himself, but his hand wrapping around her slender upper arm told him that the dose wasn't small enough. He'd seen surveillance photos of Noelle, but he hadn't expected her to be so slight under her baggy clothing. Even the reduced dose could make her OD.

Save the woman at all costs. We need her alive.

His orders had been crystal clear. Had they left even a shadow of a doubt that he'd have to be responsible for another woman's death, he would have walked away from the assignment and not looked back.

David stowed the drug and gave Noelle's slim shoulders another shake. "Where are your papers? Your records?"

Clumsily, her mouth worked to form words. "No paper," she mumbled. "Here." Noelle tapped a limp finger against her temple.

Her eyes glazed over and her face went slack. She was out.

"Shit," David cursed, hoping she wasn't just bragging about having her work in her head. It would make his job a hell of a lot simpler if he didn't have to go on a search and destroy mission as well as a rescue mission.

Before any more visitors appeared, David scooped her up and positioned her over his left shoulder in a fireman's carry so he could still fire a weapon. He ripped the laptop cords from the wall and shoved the whole octopine mess into the travel case nearby.

As soon as his burden of limp woman and laptop were settled, he raised his weapon and headed for his truck.

Only one enemy remained, guarding a getaway vehicle. When David's arm jerked slightly as he fired two silenced rounds into the man's throat, Noelle didn't even stir.

Owen lifted the edge of the lacy curtain and watched Dr. Blanche being carried away. From his vantage point, in the house across the street, he'd listened over comms as his men were killed off one by one.

Pity. He'd put considerable effort into their training.

As Owen watched the soldier carry the girl away, something nagged at his memory. There was something familiar about the way he moved—the way he killed.

Owen frowned, feeling the thick burn scars along his forehead wrinkle. Perhaps it wasn't so much that he knew that particular man as it was the fact that he knew men like him—dedicated to an ideal they would never see realized.

Such a waste of talent.

It was almost a shame that someone with so much to offer would be dead in a few hours. And the girl he'd spent his last hours protecting would soon be convinced to become quite helpful. Or she would join her dead colleagues.

All very simple and neat, just the way Owen liked it.

In the distance, he heard the wail of approaching sirens. The authorities would be here any minute and he wanted to be long gone before they arrived.

Owen let the lacy curtain fall back, accidentally knocking over a framed photograph that had been prominently displayed on the table next to the window. He picked it up and carefully put it back in place, marveling that the photographer had managed to get an open-eyed smile on every one of the seven young grandchildren. They were lovely children, with chubby cheeks and bright eyes.

As Owen stepped over the bloody remains of the old woman who used to live here, he wondered if one of those children would be the one to find her body.

CHAPTER THREE

———— ❧ ————

David sped down the highway until the lights of Lawrence, Kansas, were only a faint glow in the night sky. The road was mostly empty and after several lane and speed changes, he was fairly sure that no one had followed them out of town. Kansas, however, was flat, and in the clear autumn air, a tail wouldn't have to be close to be following him.

He flipped open his cell phone and dialed Monroe's private number.

"Monroe," answered the colonel on the first ring.

"I've got her, sir. You'll need to send a cleanup team to her house."

"What kind of mess?"

"Five bodies and one van. Still running."

"Did you get all her research?" asked Monroe.

"Think so. Do a sweep to be sure, but she said it's all in her head. She didn't have any notes."

"Damn. I knew she was smart, but that's a little spooky, even for an egghead."

David glanced at Noelle's limp form sleeping in the passenger seat. She didn't look spooky, but he hadn't exactly spent a lot of time talking to her, either. Right now she just looked vulnerable and he kept stealing glances to make sure she was still breathing.

He had no way of knowing what kind of tranquilizer they'd hit her with or how much was in her system. The only comfort he had was the fact that he knew that the Swarm had wanted her alive. If they hadn't, they'd have been using real bullets. He just prayed that their intelligence had been better than his and that the man who had shot her had dosed the tranqs for her small build.

If not, she might never wake up. And if they lost her, they lost their last, best chance for breaking the most complicated bit of ciphertext that had surfaced since the end of the Cold War. That was why both the Swarm and Monroe wanted her alive.

"I want to get her to a hospital," said David.

"No. She'd be too vulnerable there. You've been trained to deal with this situation, so deal with it."

"I don't like this. She'd be better off with professional medical attention."

"You take her to a hospital and she'll be dead before sunrise. You, too. You have your orders, Captain. No hospitals."

David resisted the urge to tell Monroe to shove those orders up his ass and glanced at Noelle. Her red curls had spilled over her eyes, but he could still see the clean line of her cheek. Her skin was too pale and it worried him. If he couldn't take her to a hospital, he needed to get her tucked away at the closest location he'd scoped out during his quick preparation for this op. Not far up ahead was a little motel where he could take the time to check her out more carefully and work on reviving her and getting the drugs out of her system.

"I'll call you when I'm settled and check back in," said David.

"Where are you going?"

David had no idea if anyone was listening to this conversation, so he didn't dare give anything away. "I'll let you know soon. Have a different vehicle ready to switch out with ours, just in case we were followed."

"Is that likely?"

"No, sir. I took out all the Tangos I saw. I think we're clear, but I'd rather be safe than sorry."

"Right. Report in as soon as you can."

"Yes, sir."

David drove until he was a mile away from the closest car behind him on the highway and pulled off at the next exit. After turning off the headlights, he pulled around the corner and waited to see if anyone else took the obscure exit into Nowhere, Kansas. While he waited, he wiped the greasepaint off his face with some wet wipes he'd brought along for just that purpose. When his face was relatively clean and he was satisfied that they were not being followed, David drove down narrow, poorly kept roadways until he reached a cheap, cash-only motel that catered to the desperately horny or the hopelessly lost.

The flashing neon VACANCY sign buzzed a lazy rhythm as David pulled into the parking lot and slid the truck up close enough to the office window that he could keep an eye on Noelle while he went inside to get a room.

The man in the office turned away from his staticky black-and-white TV and pressed his nose to the glass to look outside into the darkness.

Daniel glanced at Noelle, who sat slumped in the passenger seat of his Ford truck. He'd seat-belted her in, but during the drive she'd slid down so that she looked more dead than asleep.

There was no way he was getting her into a room without carrying her, which could well raise suspicion on the part of the motel attendant, even if he wasn't the brightest of men. David had picked this location because of its relative privacy and the last thing he needed was to have the local police knocking on his door in a half hour, wanting him to answer questions about why he was toting around an unconscious woman.

Though he had fake ID in his wallet that would fool even the best-equipped police station, his CO wouldn't take kindly to having to cover up the trail of a soldier who bumbled something as simple as finding a place for Noelle to sleep for a few hours.

David slid across the bench seat and lifted Noelle so that she sat more upright. She let out a soft moan and her head lolled forward and landed on his shoulder. Her mouth pressed against his throat and warm breath swept over his skin like a caress.

David's body responded like the man he was—one who hadn't had a woman in two years. After his last operation with Delta Force, he'd gone into isolation—complete isolation. His lust wasn't going to cause another woman to be harmed—not even one he was simply using for sex.

He clenched his jaw, squeezed his eyes shut and mentally began to field-strip every weapon he'd ever used.

With his eyes shut, the faint scent of strawberry shampoo and sleeping woman filled his nostrils, scattering his thoughts. His body hardened in a maddening rush of blood—all of it leaking out of his brain.

David cursed as sweat beaded along his hairline.

Why couldn't it have been a man he needed to rescue? Why did it have to be a soft, pretty woman who smelled like spring and felt even warmer?

The motel attendant gave David a curious stare and cupped his hands on the glass to get a better view.

Fitting in with the man's expectations was the only way to keep him from getting suspicious. David's choices were to look horny or lost. He knew without a doubt which one he'd pass for easiest.

With a prayer for strength, David leaned over and made a show of nuzzling Noelle's neck. It sure as hell wasn't the worst thing he'd had to do in his career to look inconspicuous. Her skin was soft and even though it was just pretend, he couldn't keep himself kissing the skin just below her ear.

She tasted as good as fresh strawberries and cream.

David stifled a searing oath and forced his hands to loosen their hold in her hair. He had no idea how they'd gotten there, but the soft, springy texture of her red curls sliding between his fingers made his hands burn. He wondered if all of her hair was so soft and fiery and whether or not she'd sigh his name as his fingers slid through it.

Noelle let out a contented breath and slumped heavily against him. Her gold-rimmed glasses sat crookedly on her face, the hinges hopelessly tangled in her hair.

With an effort of will, David commanded himself to remember that she was unconscious and what he was doing now—even though it was at least in part done to protect her—was taking advantage of her. Her file confirmed that she wasn't married, but for all he knew, she had a boyfriend, or even a fiancé. He had no right to be tasting a woman who surely had to belong to a man—a man who wouldn't get her killed just by sitting next to her in a truck.

That thought was like ice water down his pants. He pulled away from her, adjusting her glasses, then her head so that it was leaning comfortably against the seat, touching her as little as possible in the process.

The man in the window scratched at his stained undershirt and gave David a lecherous grin meant to cheer him on and a thumbs-up sign. He stood there in open anticipation, waiting for the show in the truck to go on.

David moved so that no part of him was touching Noelle. He could still smell her skin, but he was pretty sure that he would remember that scent even if he was halfway around the world.

After several long seconds, he managed to slow his breathing to a normal pace and don the loose jacket that would cover his weapons. He got out of the truck and locked Noelle safely inside—away from him.

Flashing neon light and the smell of strong coffee forced Noelle's brain to reboot. Her head felt as abused as the floor at a Metallica concert and her mouth tasted even worse.

She reached unsteadily for the cup of water she kept on her bedside table, but her clumsy fingers barely moved before they encountered something hard and warm instead.

Panic sparked the residual adrenaline in her system and streaked through her like fire through a fuse. Her eyes flew open and the meager light in the room stabbed her skull and made her groan in pain.

"Easy," said a quiet, deep voice close beside her. Too close.

A wide hand wedged itself under the nape of her neck, helping her to sit up. The cool edge of a glass pressed against her lips.

"Drink."

Cold liquid touched her mouth and she parted her lips to keep it from running down her chin.

She forced her eyes to open again and accept the strobe of a neon sign that flashed through the small slit between dingy hotel drapes. With each flicker of the word VACANCY, her temples throbbed.

"The headache will ease off in a bit. These pills will help."

Hard, bitter pills were pushed into her mouth and began dissolving against her tongue. When the cup was once more offered, she welcomed the cold wave of water that passed her lips and washed the pills down.

Noelle squinted against the light of the bedside lamp and the man shifted his body so that his shadow fell across her eyes. Her vision was fuzzy without her glasses, but she could easily see his wide shoulders and the short spike of his military-issue haircut breaking up the sharp light behind him. He sat only inches from her and his arm was still supporting the weight of her shoulders so she could drink. The heat of his hand burned through all three layers of clothing and she could feel his casual strength flowing through his arm—the ease with which he held her up.

Strangely enough, she recognized his scent—leather and man and cordite—and knew without a doubt that he was the one responsible for getting her out of her house alive.

The whole night came flooding back to her in a heartbeat and she barely stifled her panic. With an effort of will, she forced herself to think logically, rationally. If she was in some kind of danger, she needed her wits about her now more than ever.

Slowly, she became calm enough that she could manage a clear thought. She was alive. No one was shooting at her anymore.

Noelle swallowed hard in an effort to find her voice. "Who are you?" she asked first.

"David." His voice was deep and quiet and she wondered if it was in deference to her headache or if he always talked like he didn't want to be overheard.

"Okay. David. Where are we? What am I doing here? And who were those men in my house?"

He ignored her questions and eased her back down to the pillow. She felt boneless and weak, like she was on the third day of a bout of stomach flu. She didn't have the strength to sit up under her own power and suddenly, fear began to slink around in her stomach again.

David must have seen the fear on her face because he laid a soothing hand on her forehead and gently kept her from thrashing about. "The weakness will pass in a little while. It's an aftereffect of the tranquilizer they hit you with."

"Tranquilizer?" Noelle remembered the sharp pain in her arm and jerking out the stinger. She hadn't really processed what had happened at the time, but now it was clear that she'd been shot with some sort of dart like the kind they used on animals.

His thumb swept over her temple in a soothing arc,

pausing to lift her eyelids for a brief inspection of her pupils. "I've checked you out and given you something to help clear the tranquilizers out of your system. The weakness will wear off. You'll be fine. I promise."

Noelle shot him a disbelieving glare. "I have no idea where I am or why those men broke into my house. I was shot. *Twice!* And I have no clue why. I'm too weak to move and if more of those men come crashing through the door right now, there's nothing I can do to protect myself. In my book, that's a long way from fine."

Her rant went completely ignored. "How's your head?" he asked in a near whisper.

Noelle felt tears stinging her eyes in the face of her confusion and helplessness, but blinked them back before David could notice. She hoped. "Dancing elephants," she managed to respond.

A faint grin kicked up one shadowed cheekbone. "That bad, eh?"

"I've had worse—4.00 A.M. the morning before Friday finals."

He grunted and went to refill the glass at the cheap motel room sink.

"Where are we?" asked Noelle.

The clink of ice and the hiss of water filled the stale air. "Off I-70 not far from where we started. Before I could get you completely out of town I had to make sure you were okay and find out if there were any more copies of your work anywhere—including electronic format."

Noelle blinked in confusion. "My work? What work?" She'd been working on at least a half dozen projects, none of which would interest anyone without a burning love for Latin, Cyrillic script, or differential equations.

He turned. Her eyes had adjusted to the light and she could now make out his features more easily, though they were still a bit fuzzy without the aid of her glasses. He was fairly tall—maybe just over six feet. He wore black military gear with a many-pocketed vest over the top of his tough, long-sleeved shirt. There was a gun neatly holstered under his left arm and in the mirror, she could see another pressing into the small of his back. His shoulders were as wide as her arm was long and though he didn't have the visible bulk of a professional wrestler, she could tell that his practical clothing hid a lot more than just skin and bones.

His face was shadowed with stubble that was only a little shorter than the close-cropped hair on his head. At his temples, a few gray strands glistened like slivers of moonlight on black water. At some point, he'd lost the gloves and washed the greasepaint off his face, and it made him look more human than he had in the darkness of Noelle's basement.

He had the kind of masculinity that could make a woman who normally didn't notice such things or care about men in general do a serious double take. Noelle did just that.

It shocked her to be looking at him with anything more than idle curiosity. Searching him for clues as to what was happening to her was one thing. Looking at him with thoughts of what he'd feel like pressed up against her was another. Maybe it was just the drugs talking, or maybe it was the fact that he'd pinned her up against that brick wall during a time when her whole adrenal system was going haywire, but she was seeing David No-Last-Name as a man. A very interesting, physically appealing man.

And considering her current situation, that itself was enough to make Noelle question her sanity.

David stepped closer and she watched as a sparkling bead of water ran down the side of the glass, over his tanned fingers and dripped onto the gaudy orange-and-red carpet.

She was suddenly quite thirsty again.

"I've been given clearance to know about your work with encryption algorithms for the military. You don't need to hide it."

Noelle struggled to sit up, but her numb muscles refused, and she wanted to scream in frustration. "I'm not hiding anything," she snapped. "The truth is I'm not doing any encryption work for the military. I gave it up once I found out the U.S. Army was footing the bill."

"And all the files from before you gave it up? Where are they?"

"What little I did document was deleted. Sent to that great ones and zeros party in the sky."

"Bullshit." His voice was quiet, but his tone was still harsh enough to convey his disbelief.

"Excuse me?"

"I was informed about your work on project Cobweb. You were offered a lot of money to do the work. You wouldn't have just thrown that all away."

"I've never heard of project Cobweb."

"Not the name, maybe, but you were offered grant money to complete your research."

"Grant money? You mean blood money."

He gave her a casual shrug of indifference. "Call it Fred for all I care. My question is, where are the files?"

"I told you. I deleted everything that was on my hard drive—which wasn't much. I don't tend to write things down until I'm finished with them and ready to give the final report, unless they are truly complex, and I was only half-finished with that project."

David stood silent for a moment as if he was trying to determine the truth of her words. He ran a hand over his short, dark hair and shook his head. "The laptop hard drive?"

Noelle nodded.

"Are you sure there are no other backup copies of the work anywhere? Backup files on a network server? Disks? Paper files? Notes written on napkins?"

What did he think she was, an idiot? She knew better than to leave anything that valuable lying around where anyone with half a brain could find it. And use it. Her parents—both scientists—had taught her well. She had a responsibility to make sure no one could use her work to do harm. "I'm positive. When I decided not to take the grant money, I killed the files using a clean sweep deletion program created by some of the guys in the Computer Science Department. The files weren't just deleted, they were destroyed. There aren't even any remnants of them left on the hard drive to be recovered. I didn't want to be tempted to take the grant when the university fired me."

One dark brow rose in surprise. "You were going to be fired?"

She watched another bead of water slip off the glass and licked her dry lips. "The university couldn't afford my salary anymore with all the new budget cuts, so without that grant, I was outta there come spring."

"And even though you were going to be fired if you didn't take the grant money, you were still refusing to do the work?"

"Yes. I refuse to do anything in support of violence—even violence condoned by the U.S. government."

"Why?" He seemed genuinely baffled.

"Because I was raised by people who know what it's like to have their work twisted into something violent. They never wanted that to happen to my sister or me, so they made sure we understood that we have to be careful of what we create and whom we trust. It was a lesson I learned before I was able to walk."

David regarded her for a moment before nodding and sitting down on the bed beside her. The firm mattress dipped with his weight, but her body was too heavy with drugs to adjust to the movement. She rolled into his side until her hip rested against his. Having devoted herself to her education even before she hit puberty, Noelle wasn't used to the feel of a man's body against her own. Especially not a man as . . . manly as David No-Last-Name.

Her one and only boyfriend, Stanley, was an unimaginative toothpick of a man who generally preferred his PlayStation to sex with Noelle. After a couple of romps in bed with him, she preferred the PlayStation as well.

David made Stanley look like a child by comparison, which made Noelle wonder what sex with a real man might be like. Probably a lot better than any video game if her guess was right. There had to be a reason so many babies were born each year. If she lived through this, she was going to devote some of her soon-to-be-copious free time to researching her theory.

David slid his arm behind her and propped her up in the V between his arm and body. He held the cup for her to drink, but a little spilled out the side of her mouth and ran down her chin and neck.

The cold water made her gasp as it slid down into her modest cleavage. David grabbed a tissue from the bedside table and followed the trail of water until it disappeared under the collar of her T-shirt.

She shivered as long, strong fingers slid just beneath the edge of her clothing.

"Cold?" he asked, moving his gaze to the far wall. "Depressants can sometimes do that. Not to mention shock."

Noelle looked away from his hand to his face and tried to concentrate on his words rather than just his mouth moving. It looked firm and mobile and she wondered if he knew how to kiss as well as he could kill.

What the hell was wrong with her? This was not the time or the place to be developing hormones. It had never happened before, so it must have something to do with the drugs she'd been given or maybe just her own personal reaction to over-the-top danger. Whatever it was, it was damned inconvenient.

"Shock?" she mumbled, staring at the way his tanned fingers tapered to short, clean fingernails.

He lifted an amused brow. "You don't think that being attacked in your house and shot at is enough to shock you?"

Even as he talked, he removed Noelle's shoes and folded the covers down on the far side of the bed. Without warning her, he lifted her, placed her in the downturned bedding and covered her up to her chin with the cheap, white sheet and thin blanket.

The weightless feeling of being lifted so easily made her head swim, not to mention the fact that she felt every bunch and shift of his muscles as he moved her. Being held by such raw strength was more than enough to muddle a girl's brain.

Noelle watched him with confused eyes. Nothing on his face gave away what he was thinking. For all she knew, this was the kind of thing he did every day. She'd been around military types enough to know that they weren't much for small talk and even less for telling you what's on their minds. They liked to be the one to ask questions while you give short, simple answers that preferably ended in the word "sir."

"Better?" he asked, his gaze shielded with coal black lashes. She could tell his eyes were a pale color, but beyond that, she saw little in the yellow motel lighting.

"I don't know. You tell me. Am I better off now? Can I go back home in the morning?"

This time, he met her eyes and she could see frost gray chips swimming in a cold blue sea. "No, Noelle. You can't go back home in the morning." He pressed a wide palm to her forehead, his rough skin oddly comforting. "You can't ever go home again."

It took a moment for his words to sink in, but when they did, Noelle struggled to breathe through the thick bars of shock that gripped her chest. Never go home again?

"No!" was all she managed to say.

David pressed his lips together in a grim line and nodded. "I'm sorry, but that's the way it has to be. It's best you start getting used to the idea now."

"Why?"

David stared at her for a long minute, his pale eyes scrutinizing every angle of her face. "You really don't get it, do you?"

Fear, confusion, isolation swirled together within her, creating a cold, achy spot in the pit of her stomach. "Get what? All I want to do is go home."

"You're currently listed as the most gifted civilian cryptologist in the country—possibly in the world."

Noelle nearly scoffed at the ludicrous statement. "That's absurd. I don't even focus on cryptology. I just tried it for kicks and enjoyed the challenge. There are at least two men in the U.S. alone who have more knowledge, experience and brains in that area than I do."

"Six months ago, maybe, but not anymore." His voice was so deep and quiet it took a moment for his words to register in Noelle's mind.

"What happened to them?" she asked, fearing she already knew the answer.

"You only need to know that the same thing isn't going to happen to you."

"Tell me what happened to them," she demanded, needing to know but not wanting to hear the bleak truth spoken aloud.

His hand stroked over her mussed red curls and he regarded her with a stare that was fierce . . . determined. "They didn't have me protecting them."

CHAPTER FOUR

David watched Noelle from the corner of his eye as she fell back asleep in the space of a few seconds. The tranquilizer was still affecting her, but not as much as he'd feared. At least the drugs weren't going to kill her. It was up to him to see that nothing else did, either.

She was a small lump under the thin blanket, sleeping off the remaining effects of the drugs. They couldn't stay here much longer, but he wanted to give her every minute to recover that he could. He could tell by the panic in her green eyes just how much it scared her not to be in control of her own body.

David doubted that Noelle had fully grasped the concept that her name was at the top of a terrorist hit list, Four men had been on that same list, and each had been kidnapped by the Swarm because he had a knack for cracking obscure codes. Either those men had refused to cooperate with the sadistic terrorist group or had simply been unable to break the code because all four had been executed. He just couldn't bring himself to tell Noelle she was next. The poor woman had been through too much already today and a person could only take so much fear before they simply quit processing more.

As much as David hated having his isolation ruined, Monroe had been right to call him back into Delta. David knew just what would happen to this young woman if he didn't do his job right. Mistakes were one hell of an effective teacher.

He only wished that Noelle didn't appeal to him so much as a woman. Even with her messy red curls and her baggy clothes and her face devoid of any hint of makeup, she was still alluring. She was so damn . . . cute.

He couldn't forget the way she smelled, all sweet and warm, or the way she made these little, faint noises while she slept. Every time he had to touch her, he felt himself getting excited, anxious like some fifteen-year-old boy who was about to see his first naked woman.

It was pathetic. And it was suck timing. Sure, he'd been more than two years without sex, but he should have been able to resist touching her more than absolutely necessary. Giving her a drink, yes. Feeding her the pain pills, sure. Putting her under the blankets, fine. But stroking her hair? Touching her face? Completely unnecessary.

But really nice.

Maybe it was just his protective instincts on overdrive, but he had to keep fighting off the urge to pull her into his arms and tell her that everything was going to be okay.

The truth was, it wasn't going to be okay. Even in the best-case scenario, she'd have to walk away from her life, cut all ties and never look back if she wanted to live. Either that, or sign on with the Army, or maybe the CIA and live in some compound with airtight security where they would protect her in exchange for her brainpower.

Her comment about blood money had David guessing

that she would rather die than choose any option that would put her at the disposal of the military.

Noelle shifted in her sleep. At least the drugs were wearing off enough that she might be able to walk out of here under her own power. That would keep him from needing to touch her more, which was for the best.

Their new vehicle was due to be dropped off within the hour. The truck he'd been driving would be taken away tomorrow morning and used as a decoy, going in a different direction than they were headed. By then he and Noelle would already be long gone.

With luck, he'd be able to convince her to cooperate with the CIA before they made it to the safe house where CIA agents would no doubt be ready to pounce. Monroe hadn't given David the code they needed Noelle to break, since it was strictly classified, but he had said that the information would lead them straight to the remaining members of the Swarm.

The need for revenge still burned hot in David's gut, even though he knew it wouldn't change the past. He needed to completely wipe out every member of the Swarm from the face of the earth. Only then would he be satisfied.

And for that, he needed Noelle's total and complete cooperation. One way or another, that's what he was going to get.

There were a lot of things that Noelle could handle, but letting David help her use the bathroom was not one of them. She had her pride. That was the drive that finally pushed away the last of the gooey cobwebs in Noelle's brain and got her legs moving. She wasn't completely steady on her feet, but with a wall nearby, she'd be fine.

Noelle pushed herself off the bed, hoping that David would just keep watching out the window through a crack in the plastic drapes and not notice her at all.

She wasn't that lucky. He noticed and strode over the gaudy carpet to her side. "How are you feeling?" he asked, his eyes measuring her body as if he was absorbing every little detail.

"Like I need to pee."

If her bluntness bothered him, it didn't show on his angular face. "Dizzy?" he asked.

"A little. Nothing I can't handle."

His hand gripped her upper arm, not so tight it hurt, but tight enough that if she took a spill he'd be able to hold her up. It was comforting in an odd you're-a-stranger-and-possibly-a-crazed-maniac-but-at-least-you're-here sort of way.

He escorted her to the bathroom door and she gave him a scowl that told him she'd take it from here.

He just grunted, which by the sound of it she guessed was as close to a laugh as he ever got, and leaned against the doorway with his arms crossed over that wide chest of his. "I'll be right here if you need me."

Noelle forced herself upright to her full five feet six inches and gave him her best professorial stare—the one that sent freshmen straight to the library with a burning desire to study. "I won't need you for this," she said as she shut the door in his face.

The effort of putting on all that attitude made her head throb and spin. Whatever it was she'd been shot with had one heck of a wallop. Of course, she'd missed a couple of meals today, which probably didn't help the whole dizzy thing much.

Now that she was vertical and relatively coherent, she took inventory of her situation. She still had no idea where she was, or who David was. She assumed he worked for the U.S. military, but there was a chance that he just wanted her to think that. For all she knew, he could be a foreign spy, sent to pick her brain for the decryption algorithms she'd previously worked on.

She wasn't as freakishly smart as her sister, Lilly, but she wasn't stupid, either. She knew the power her solution would give to any intelligence agency, be they government-sanctioned or otherwise. Information was power. Protecting information was crucial to maintaining that power. As soon as Noelle realized just how far she could take her work, she knew it was too powerful a weapon to develop. Whoever had control of it would never again have to worry about breaking any code, at least not as they existed today. Her solution wasn't just a one-time-only deciphering tool. If she took the time to finish it, she was pretty sure that, given enough computing power, her work would come close to artificial intelligence. Feed it enough ciphertext, and eventually it would have enough data not only to break any code, but actually to predict future codes based on historical information. The system would first learn, then it would *teach*.

Developing something that complex would likely take her years, but the fact that she could almost imagine how it would work, somewhere on the fringes of her brain, was enough to convince her that it was not only possible, it was within her ability to create.

No one knew how far her solution had advanced, and

if she wanted to stay alive, she'd keep it that way. She couldn't imagine a situation in which someone would be able to force her to create such a thing against her will, but she was smart enough to know that her imagination for human cruelty wasn't as well developed as others'. As long as no one knew what she was capable of, there was no risk that she would be forced to work on what she considered the ultimate codebreaker.

The question was, if they didn't know about that—which she knew they couldn't—then why were those men after her? Why had David come to save her?

And more importantly, could she trust him?

Noelle looked around the cramped bathroom. It was nothing special, just a combination of cracked, mildewed tile and water-stained wallpaper. The most noticeable feature was the small, frosted-glass window high above the toilet. One just big enough for her to squeeze out of if she really tried.

The door to the bathroom was locked, but she knew that it wouldn't take David much effort to break it down. She also knew that he'd do just that if he heard her trying to escape. She could tell him she was going to take a shower and get out while the water was running to mask the sound. It might work. Her legs were stronger now than before, though she still felt rubbery all over and moving took a lot more effort than it should have.

She could try to run. She might even be able to make it out. But should she? What if David was the only thing standing between her and whoever had tried to kidnap her earlier? It seemed stupid to run away from a man who had done nothing but help her so far. Maybe it was just a ruse to lull her into a sense of false security, but Noelle didn't think so. There was something about him that screamed of honor. He was a bit gruff and not exactly a gifted conversationalist, but he had protected her. He'd gotten her out alive. Groggy, but alive.

Noelle wasn't one for trusting instincts. She preferred logic and facts and a thick stack of empirical data to make decisions. But right now, she didn't have any of those. All she had was her intuition and it was telling her that David was a good man. Staying with him was a lot safer than shinnying out a window and facing the night alone, weak and unarmed.

Right now, David was her best bet.

When Noelle came out of the bathroom, he was still there, lounging against the doorframe. "I'm glad you didn't try it," he said.

"Try what?"

"The window."

Noelle tried to still her expression before he could see her shocked reaction to him knowing that she'd thought about running. "I don't know what you're talking about," she told him.

A faint flicker of amusement crossed his eyes. "You're too smart not to have at least thought about going out the window. You'd have fitted, but you wouldn't have gone far before I tracked you down."

Noelle rolled her eyes. "If I'd really wanted to get away, I would have, so don't go getting all macho he-man at me."

"No, ma'am. Wouldn't even think about it."

She gave him a look full of challenge, but the fluorescent lights over the sink and mirror behind him made her brain sting.

"Your head still hurting?" he asked, bending his knees so he was on a level to look directly into her eyes.

"Yeah, but I'll live."

He pulled a little penlight out of his vest of stuff, and said, "Hold still."

The light hurt, but whatever he was looking at must have bothered him, based on the serious frown he now wore.

"The tranq should have worn off by now, but your reactions are still sluggish. Are you on any medication? Taking any drugs?"

Noelle's gut twisted in indignation. How dare he accuse her of being a junkie when she'd never touched the stuff in her life? "I don't do drugs, not that it's any of your business."

He put the light away but blocked her exit so she couldn't turn away in a huff the way she wanted. "Everything about you is my business. I've been assigned to keep you alive, so you won't so much as blink without me knowing about it."

"Assigned? By whom?"

His lips pressed together into a thin, silent line.

"I see. So you get to know everything about me, but I don't even get to know who sent you?"

He nodded once. "You got it."

"You *must* be military. No one else would be that full of themselves with the whole secret mission thing." She tried to push past him but it was like trying to swat a redwood out of her way.

"We need to get moving now that you're up," he said as he turned away from her, ignoring her implied question.

"Where are we going? No wait, let me guess. You could tell me but then you'd have to kill me, right?"

One corner of his mouth actually twitched with a smile. "Now you're getting it."

Noelle sighed. She wasn't getting anything out of him. Maybe he was taking her to his superiors, where she would at least be able to ask some questions. She knew that he was here to protect her and that someone had tried to kill her for the work she'd been asked to do for the government. She also knew that as soon as she got to talk to someone with enough rank to make an independent decision, they'd get this whole mess straightened out and she could be back to her old life by Monday.

Not that her old life had much to offer with a ton of freshman homework to grade and the reward for her dedication being a pink slip at the end of the year. But hey, at least it was her life. Her choices. Her pink slip. That's what really mattered.

Noelle washed her mouth out at the sink, trying to rid it of the essence of decaying stuffed animals. From the corner of her eye, she saw David hold out a tiny tube of toothpaste and a toothbrush wrapped in plastic.

Hallelujah!

"We can grab something to eat on the road, but we need to get moving. When you're done there, let's get you geared up."

Noelle raised a questioning eyebrow at him in the mirror. "What gear?"

"Vest, tracking device, a small handgun if you'll carry one."

"Not likely."

"Didn't think so."

Noelle made quick work of her teeth and pocketed the toothbrush for later use. She didn't even have her purse with her. No money, no ID, no nothing.

Except her laptop. David had taken that and only that from her house.

The sleeve of her loose KU sweatshirt was stained with blood and something oily. The darts hadn't left much of a hole, but the blood was going to be pretty notice-able against the pale gray material. Noelle slipped it off, straightening the two T-shirts she wore beneath. Normally, she only wore one, but her house was cold, and every time she wore a jacket, the loose sleeves would send her stacks of papers careening onto the floor.

David watched her as she scrubbed the bloody spot with a tiny bar of soap at the sink.

"Does your arm hurt?" he asked, as if he just now remembered that people could feel pain. He was obvi-ously a real tough guy.

It did hurt, but Noelle didn't like him knowing she was at a disadvantage. "It's fine."

"You're a pitiful liar." He dug in a black canvas duffel bag and pulled out a small first-aid kit.

"Yeah, well it comes from not making a living by it, Mr. Mysterious."

He grunted again and took the bar of soap from her hand. He lathered up a washcloth and cleaned the small holes with a delicate touch for a man of his size who apparently didn't feel pain.

The long, tanned fingers of one hand held her in place while he worked. They were a stark contrast to the milk-pale skin that came along as a package deal with Noelle's natural red hair and scattered freckles. His fingers wrapped all the way around her arm, making her look almost child-ish in comparison.

His eyes slid to where he held her. She knew that he couldn't help but notice that she looked like a scrawny kid. She always had. It hadn't bothered her for a long time. Until now.

Now, she wanted to be beautiful and glamorous with boobs out to here and legs up to her neck. That was doubt-less the kind of woman that David liked. As far as she could tell, all men did.

"You're smaller than you looked in the surveillance photos," he said in a low, deep voice—the kind he might use to calm a child.

The idea that she'd been covertly photographed was an unpleasant violation of her privacy, but she decided that it was best just to let that comment pass without complaint. She had more important things to spend her strength on. "Yeah, well, I like loose clothes. They're more comfortable."

"How many shirts are you wearing, anyway?"

She looked down, wanting to cover her small breasts with her arms. They were just two more things that added to the total immature look of her body. Of course, the bold letters across her chest reading "I left the house for *this*?" didn't help her mature image much.

Noelle looked away, wishing she were anyone but her-self. She was smart and kind and generally liked who she had become. It was stupid and completely insane that her body image would bother her at a time like this, but it did. And that pissed her off.

"I'm wearing two," she snapped. "And before you ask, I'm wearing two pairs of pants as well—jeans over leggings.

But only one bra and pair of panties and pair of socks—all one hundred percent cotton, since polyester makes me itch. I think that about covers my wardrobe. We already covered my drug habit and medical record. Is there anything else of a personal nature that you'd like to ask me?"

He just stared at her, his jaw tight, his hand still around her arm. She didn't think he was going to say anything, that he was just going to do that military silence thing, but then he asked, "You got a boyfriend?"

David wanted to slam his head into the wall for being so stupid. *You got a boyfriend?* What the hell was he thinking? He had no business caring whether or not she was involved with another man—or woman. It didn't even matter. Whoever her boyfriend might be, she wasn't ever going to see him again, so how could it matter?

But it did matter. And that pissed him off.

David finished bandaging her arm, refusing to notice how soft her skin was against the calluses of his fingers, how wonderfully pale her body was next to the dark tan of his hand, how fragile the delicate bones of her arm were compared to the thick column of his arm. She was completely feminine and fragile, and it made every primal protective urge in his body stand up and roar.

She was on a hit list. He couldn't forget that. He was here to protect her, not ogle her.

He wasn't going to let her die because he was too busy thinking with his dick.

So, instead of stripping off those oversized shirts to see if the rest of her body turned him on as much as her freaking *arm,* he turned his back and checked out the motel window while she stripped down to one shirt and fastened the Kevlar vest around her.

"I don't think this is going to fit," she said from behind him.

David cursed his luck and went to help. She was right, the vest was too big, and even when pulled tight, the adjustable fastenings were too long to make the vest snug. If she fell, the heavy material would slide around and do nothing to protect her vitals.

David swallowed a curse and undid the vest. "Put all your clothes back on and put the vest over it."

"Isn't it going to be a little suspicious for me to walk around showing off my fashionable Kevlar vest? I don't have a jacket to cover it up unless you brought one of mine from the house."

David was already stripping out of his vest and long-sleeved shirt. He pulled on a short-sleeved T-shirt from his duffel and handed her the black thermal undershirt he'd been wearing. "We'll put this over the vest to keep you warm and hide everything until we can get you a smaller vest."

David helped her fasten the straps, which fit better over the bulk of the three shirts she was wearing. His black shirt covered her completely. Only someone who was looking closely would know she was wearing a vest. David wasn't going to let anyone get that close.

The long sleeves hung over her hands, and she rolled them up. Even so, his shirt was way too big, swallowing her up and making her look vulnerable.

David told himself that it was okay for her to look vulnerable. She was.

They didn't need to have David get distracted by a hard-on that arose from something as simple as seeing her in his clothes. It was juvenile and stupid that something like that could turn him on.

He was clearly losing it.

"How do I look?" she asked, her cheeks flushed pink with embarrassment.

Like his demented wet dream.

"It'll do," he said.

CHAPTER FIVE

Noelle leaned against the inside of the passenger door, watching the flat countryside slide by. The sun had just broken the horizon, and the sky was washed with pale yellow and rose. The Buick's tires hummed over the interstate pavement with nothing to break the monotony of the noise.

David was still wearing his vest and guns, but he'd covered the whole affair with a loose windbreaker that hid everything beneath it. Including the fact that he was completely ripped.

Noelle had watched him in the hotel room as he'd stripped off his shirt for her to wear. No longer groggy, she had been able to truly appreciate just how fine a body he had. The muscles in his chest and abs were an artist's dream, all defined and shadowed by a dusting of dark hair. Each movement was graceful as he'd checked his guns and gear. He wasn't bulging with muscle, but those he had were plentiful and slid fluidly against each other beneath his skin, bunching and flexing in hypnotic masculinity.

By the time they'd left the hotel, Noelle was shaking. She told herself it was just from low blood sugar, but she knew it was something more. Something girly and ridiculous and . . . exciting.

It was ludicrous. She didn't even know the man. She had no idea if he was married, though he did wear some sort of ring on a chain around his neck. Heck, she didn't even know if he was straight.

"How much longer until we get to this mysterious destination?" she asked, to distract herself.

He glanced at the dashboard clock. It was just after 6 A.M. "Before lunch. Which reminds me, what time did you eat dinner last night? I was thinking that might have been the reason the drug hit you so hard."

"I forgot to eat dinner," she said, looking out the side window.

"Forgot. Okay. When was lunch?"

"Yeah, well I kinda missed that, too. I was teaching a class, then I got this e-mail with these ancient Russian images on them, then Joan came by. . . ."

David let out a sigh. "Breakfast?"

"I'm not really much of a breakfast person."

"You are today," he said as he took the next exit toward a McDonald's. "So, you'd gone the entire day without food. It's a wonder you're not still asleep."

"I've spent a lot of nights working instead of sleeping. Resisting the urge to crash is just one of those things that comes along with an academic career. I like to think of it as a fringe benefit."

He pulled into the parking lot and headed for the drive-thru. "What do you want?"

Noelle shrugged. It had been so long since she'd eaten that her stomach had just turned off. That happened sometimes. "I don't care. Just pick something."

After the old, grandmotherly lady in the window handed them their third full bag of food, Noelle began to think that had been the wrong thing to say.

"The coffee's mine. You get water until that crap is flushed out of your system."

"Yes, sir," she growled, tempted to throw a sausage and egg biscuit at his head rather than eat it.

He just gave her that lopsided grin of his and pulled back onto the highway.

She was asleep again. David wasn't sure if that was a good sign or not.

After eating a decent breakfast, Noelle had curled up against the car door and drifted off before he had a chance to convince her to help out the CIA.

Now they were at the safe house in southern Colorado, where they were to meet up with at least half a dozen others—both CIA and Army—who would pressure her into cooperating.

It was the right thing to do. Hell, it was the *only* thing to do as far as David was concerned. They'd never find the Swarm without some decent intelligence and right now, Noelle was the only shot they had.

David wanted those terrorist bastards dead to a man, but it still chafed him that she would be used in a game where she didn't even know the rules.

He pulled into the gravel drive at the back of the old farmhouse but didn't kill the engine. He'd been tracked by the scopes of at least four sharpshooters before he'd even pulled onto the property. At least these guys were on his side. They were as safe here as they were going to get, but he still felt the adrenaline flood his bloodstream as he shifted his head into the game. There could be no mistakes now.

"Wake up, Noelle," he said as he scanned the area. He could see Colonel Monroe's face in one of the front windows, along with several other suited men. He saw one of the marksmen on the roof and another just inside the tree line. He kept hoping to see Grant or Caleb among them, but hadn't.

Man, it would have been nice to have his old buddies at his back for this op. It would have made him feel a hell of a lot better about moving Noelle around in the open.

She stirred and opened her dark green eyes. "We're here?"

"Yeah. We need to get you inside where it's safe. I don't like just sitting out here."

Noelle yawned and reached for the door handle.

"Not yet. Wait until I come around to open it."

"I'm perfectly capable of opening the door myself."

"I know. You're also perfectly capable of getting shot in the head while standing out there without me to cover you. Instead, why don't you let me come around, okay?"

His tone had been harsh, but he couldn't let himself care about hurting her feelings. He had to care only about protecting her body.

That thought led him on a mental voyage of just how sweet her body might be under all those clothes. He wondered if she was pale all over, or if she had a sprinkling of freckles across her breasts.

Whoa. That was not anywhere near where his thoughts needed to be right now.

With a harsh reprimand for his stupidity, David stomped on his libido until it cowered back in its dark corner, where it belonged.

He moved around to open the car for Noelle, keeping a hand on his weapon. She slid out of the front seat, wide-eyed and trembling with fear.

Shit. He hadn't meant to scare her like that.

Now he had no choice but to offer her what little comfort he could. He put his arm around her shoulders, feeling the fine tremors of fear coursing through her. He shielded her body with his, tucking her head against his chest, making sure that if someone took a shot at her, it was going to go through him first.

He told himself that he was only doing his job, but the predictable tightening of his pants proved he was a liar. He liked the way she felt huddled against him. It was a perfect fit, with her head nestled just under his chin. It was the kind of fit that had him wondering just how well the rest of them would fit together.

As they hurried up the back steps, he leaned close to her ear, drawing in the fresh strawberry scent of her shampoo. He wanted to whisk her away to some secret island where no one would ever find her. He wanted to wipe that look of fear from her eyes and never let it haunt her again. He wanted to go back in time and kill every member of the Swarm before they'd managed to spread like a malignant cancer thought long dead—before they could threaten Noelle's safety and ruin her life.

But he could do none of that. He couldn't change what had happened. All he could do was protect her until she made her choice about whether to give up her current life and live or cling to it and die.

The thought of her choosing the second option was not one David could stomach. There had been enough death of innocents in his life. Standing back and accepting another one was something he simply could not do. If Noelle was going to live, she had to trust someone and he wanted that someone to be him.

She had no idea what she was about to go through in there. She'd be questioned, pressured, manipulated. Whatever they felt they needed to do to gain her cooperation, they'd do it, no matter how slimy they had to get. They needed her, and if David's guess was right, they needed her more than she needed them. She just didn't know it.

The urge to protect her burned strong within him. He had a lot of mistakes to make up for—mistakes so big they could never be rectified. He not only wanted to protect her life, but he wanted to protect her comfort as well. What she was about to go through would not be comfortable, and that pissed David off. He just wished he could take her away from all this and spare her the grueling ordeal of being pressured by the CIA.

But he couldn't do that, nor would he be allowed in the room with her while she was questioned and coerced. This was the last chance he'd have for a while to give her what little support he could offer. The idea of her being alone in that interrogation room with the suited goons did not sit well. He wanted to stay by her side and tell her everything would be okay. He'd make sure of it.

But that was a lie. No matter what happened, nothing for her would ever be the same again. The best he could do was arm her so she could fight her own battles. Her knowledge and skills were formidable weapons—weapons he doubted she even knew she had. The question was, where did his loyalties lie? With the government who needed Noelle's help or with the woman herself? He knew which one Monroe would pick, but he also knew that he had to act with his conscience. Noelle had to be his first priority. It could be no other way. Anything less than total commitment to her safety—even emotional safety—was unacceptable to him. He was more than just a tool of the government. He was a man. And as a man, he had to listen to his heart.

In the end, his heart won. He had to offer her what help he could while he was still able. "Don't let them scare you in here," he told her in a low whisper against her ear. "Remember, you're the one who has something they want. You have power. You're in control."

She looked up at him, shock glowing in her dark green eyes. From that split-second glance, he knew that she'd understood what he'd told her was important. She might not yet understand why or how, but she'd figure it out. He knew she would. He was suddenly relieved that Noelle was a smart enough woman that she didn't need a lot of help connecting the dots.

Before she could ask any questions, they were inside, surrounded by an imposing group of men that nearly smothered her in a sea of black suits as they whisked her away to the interrogation room.

Noelle sat in a hard wooden chair, waiting for the next group of men to come question her.

It was late afternoon and the routine was getting old.

She was tired of answering the same questions over and

over. She was tired of sitting in this windowless, dingy room with a bunch of men who looked at her as either a freak or a tool. But most of all, she was just plain tired. Her arm ached where she'd been shot and her mouth was dry from thirst and frayed nerves.

As she repeated the events that had happened to her last night to the suited men, the reality of her situation started to sink in. She'd been hunted down and attacked. Granted, the men who attacked her wanted her alive, but that really didn't do much to make her feel better about her situation.

The door of the musty room opened again and an older man in a golf shirt and khakis came in, followed closely by David. Her heart jumped with relief when she saw him. She had to keep herself from rushing into his arms for a comforting hug. He was the only familiar face in a crowd of strangers. Sure, she didn't know his last name, or even whom he worked for, but he was a large step above the self-important men who had filtered through this room all day long trying to convince her to give the government what they wanted—something she was not willing to give.

At least her parents would be proud of her for not giving in, for standing by her principles. She only hoped she'd get the chance to see them again and tell them just how brave she had been and that their teachings hadn't gone unheeded.

David placed a chilled bottle of water on the table, taking away the half-empty foam cup of coffee they'd given her earlier. He slugged back the rest of the stone-cold coffee in one long swallow, making Noelle wonder just how badly he needed the caffeine.

He looked tired and his shoulders were less square and straight than she remembered, but he still had the strength to pin her with a demanding stare that ordered her to drink up.

Noelle smiled, happy to oblige as long as she didn't have to face the suits again.

The older man had graying hair and a build that would have once been much like David's—muscled, but not obscenely so. Now, it was starting to soften with time and gravity until he just looked . . . comfortable. Even so, there was an air about him—something about the way that David looked at him with total respect—that warned her not to underestimate him.

"Would you like a break? Perhaps a trip to the bathroom?" asked the older man.

Noelle shook her head. She just wanted this over with.

"I'm Colonel George Monroe," he said, extending a hand in greeting.

Noelle glanced at David, and at his slight nod, she decided to stand and shake his hand.

Monroe lifted a surprised brow as he noticed the exchange between her and David, but said nothing about it. "Please, sit down."

"I'd rather not," said Noelle. "My butt's fallen asleep on that thing."

Monroe shrugged and slid into a seat across the table that had once graced the kitchen of someone with a lot of kids, from the well-used look of it.

"I can save us all a lot of time here, Colonel Monroe. I've already told the men in the matching suits what happened last night at my house. I'm sure David here can corroborate my story."

"I'm not interested in that, Dr. Blanche."

Noelle winced. She hated being here almost as much as she hated her name. Noelle Blanche. White Christmas. Someone should have kicked her parents in the ass for that stunt.

She straightened her shoulders and looked the imposing man right in the eye. "Then to answer all your other questions, no."

"No?" he asked, frowning.

"Right. No. As in, no I won't work for you. No I won't help you decrypt any ciphertext. No, I won't finish developing those encryption algorithms that you wanted. No, no, no. I think that about covers every possible contingency. Yes?"

"Noelle," said David, in a low, coaxing voice. "Don't be so stubborn. Just listen to him, please?"

She looked across the room at David. He looked tired, worried. She realized that he must have been up all night watching out for her. Protecting her. She wanted to repay him for his help, but she just couldn't bring herself to compromise her principles.

With a heavy sigh, she resigned herself to another two hours penned up in this stuffy room. "Fine. I'll listen, but don't expect me suddenly to change my mind because you keep asking me the same questions. I might be tired of answering, but the answers won't change."

Monroe nodded, giving her a look of newfound respect. "Just how far did you get with the encryption algorithms—the ones you were offered the grant to develop?" he asked.

Noelle looked at David, suddenly remembering what he had said. They wanted something from her. She was in a position of power here. She was smart, she could figure out a way to play that to her advantage.

Noelle crossed her arms over her chest and offered Monroe the same look she'd seen David give her when he was stonewalling. "No. First you tell me where I am."

Monroe looked over his shoulder to where David was lounging against the wall, looking bored. The older man's expression was written clearly with a this-is-all-your-fault look.

As he turned back to Noelle, a faint, indulgent smile tugged at Monroe's mouth. "Okay. You're in southern Colorado at a CIA safe house."

Noelle felt a surge of victory, but tried to keep it from showing on her face. "Who were those men who broke into my house?"

Monroe shook his head. "First, you answer my question. How far had you gotten in your development?"

"More than halfway." It seemed like a vague enough answer. Truthful, but holding no real information.

Oh yeah, she could play this game.

"How long would it take you to complete the work?" Monroe asked.

"Who were those men?" she countered.

"They were members of a terrorist group called the Swarm," he answered with a knowing grin, matching her vagueness and raising her an ounce of frustration.

At this rate, they were going to be here all night, and neither one of them would gain any truly useful information. She decided to throw him a bone in the hopes that he would do the same. "It would take me two months, maybe as little as four weeks if that was all I was working on. At the end of that time, I would be able to enter any string of code based on the over three thousand variations possible in the sample ciphertext that was given to me and have a solution." It was a fairly simple code and she was sure she could figure it out in a few weeks.

"And if you were given a different sample of text? How much longer would it take you?"

Noelle shrugged. "I can't say without seeing it."

Monroe opened his jacket and pulled out an envelope that contained a folded piece of paper. He opened it carefully and smoothed the paper out in front of her.

Noelle glanced down at the page and instantly, her heart began to pound with excitement. She'd seen something like this before—from the Russian professor she'd been working with. The symbols were the same, but their use was entirely different. She could already see a complex pattern among the flowing symbols, something vague and elusive, but definitely there.

"This isn't just text," she stated. "It's mathematical."

Monroe frowned. "How can you tell? You've been looking at it for all of ten seconds."

Noelle pointed toward several symbols. "These are Greek, not Cyrillic. Their sequence and placement leads me to believe that the other symbols are variables in some sort of an equation. Or equations. I can't be sure."

David and Monroe shared a guarded look. "Now we know why they wanted her," said Monroe. "The Swarm must have figured out there was a mathematical angle and knew she was one of the few who could pull it off."

Her palms itched to reach out and grab the paper. This was the kind of puzzle that Noelle loved to solve. She could feel it already. This was something she'd never done before. It had weight. Importance.

It was a true challenge, and Noelle loved a challenge.

Before she could begin to see the pattern, Monroe slipped the paper back inside his jacket and leaned back.

Noelle tamped down her disappointment.

"We need you, Dr. Blanche. We've had a team working on this for months and they haven't even gotten as far as you did in a few seconds."

Noelle swallowed and tucked her hands under her thighs so she wouldn't reach out for the paper. "And you think I can do better than your team?" she asked, trying to sound casual but sounding more breathless instead.

Monroe shrugged his wide shoulders. "You already have. This is important. We're talking averting-a-nuclear-disaster-important. This text contains the location of several . . . misplaced weapons from the Cold War."

War. It always seemed to come back to that with the military.

Her stomach twisted as she realized that she wasn't going to get a chance to see that script again. She wasn't going to be able to tear it apart into the right pieces and put it back together so it made sense. Order out of chaos.

Resigned frustration burned hot in her belly, but there was nothing she could do about the way she felt. She'd have to settle for being disappointed.

"I wish I could help," she said, meaning it. "But I won't get involved with military projects. To crack it I'm going to need to develop some algorithms. They'd be specific to this sort of code, but still generalized enough they could be used again. I can never be assured that my work won't be used offensively."

Both men clenched their jaws in frustration and the

room filled with the palpable tension of men longing for violence. Probably against her.

"We need to find out what's on this page," said Monroe.

"Then I suggest you start looking for number six on your list of experts, Colonel Monroe."

"We could offer you a substantially larger sum than the grant," offered Monroe.

"I don't want the money. It was never about the money."

"But you're going to lose your job if you don't do something. At least this way, you'd have a way to pay your bills."

"I'll figure something out. I've worked crap jobs before. I can do it again." She had no intention of telling them that a crap job wasn't going to pay for her monumental student loans as well as her rent.

"Why won't you help us? Do you have something against your government?"

"No, but I have read enough history to learn from it. Over and over there are stories of scientists who discovered or invented great things only to have them turned into something deadly. I won't let that happen to my work. My parents are both scientists, and they taught me that I must have as much responsibility as I do brains because I'll be held accountable for the things that I create and how they are used."

Monroe's mouth twisted with a grimace. "It's ridiculous of you to hold yourself accountable for something that is out of your control. You can't possibly be responsible for the actions of everyone who will use your work, be it for good or evil."

"But that's where you're wrong. I have a responsibility to think ahead and make sure that my work can't cause harm. I may not be able to think of everything, but I have to try, and in this case, it's a no-brainer."

Monroe leaned forward and she could sense a truly frightening quality in him that would make even a man as strong as David show respect. A hard, ruthless cold glinted in his eyes. "If you don't help us, we can't offer you our help in return. You'll be captured within days, if not hours, and the men who take you will ensure that you do this work by whatever means necessary. We can't let that happen."

Noelle felt true fear slink in a cold spiral down her spine. She sensed more than heard the underlying message: If the U.S. couldn't have her, no one could. And he wasn't bluffing.

David stepped forward, but Monroe held out a hand to halt him. "This isn't a game or a way to display your anti-war sentiments. This is a matter of national security and we will *not* let you fall into enemy hands. You're simply too dangerous."

Noelle had to swallow to make room for the words to get past her fear. "But I'd never help them."

"You would. In the end, you would. You're not trained to resist torture. They'd find your weakness and exploit it. And once you served your purpose, they'd kill you. No appeals, no second chances, no remorse. If you walk away from our offer, your life is over. For the sake of national security, before I let you leave, I will order your death." He let his words hang in the air, so cold and thick it was hard for her to breathe.

Noelle didn't want to die. She didn't want to endure

torture and help an enemy of her country. But more than that, she didn't want to be the cause of the death of countless others. She knew that her work could be twisted, mutated into something dangerous. Deadly.

It was the hardest thing she'd ever had to do, but she looked Monroe in the eye and said, "I'm sorry. I can't help you."

CHAPTER SIX

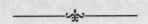

David had never seen the colonel so distressed. For a man who was used to hiding his emotions, it was odd that he would suddenly become so transparent.

David didn't like it when things were odd. That meant that he was being played, or something was really wrong. He just didn't know which. Yet.

"You've got to give her kudos for her resolve," said David, as they watched her over the closed-circuit hidden camera.

Her head was propped up on her arms and her shoulders shook with the unmistakable signs that she was crying.

David bit back a curse and looked away, unable to control the urge to rush back in there and comfort her. He'd gotten soft in his time away from Delta Force. It was the only explanation for his nearly overpowering need to soothe her.

"I'd love to go in there and congratulate her for her stubborn streak, but it seems kind of silly to compliment a corpse," said Monroe.

David's body tensed. "What the hell are you talking about, sir?" he demanded. "You were only bluffing about killing her to keep her out of the Swarm's reach, weren't you?"

Monroe shook his graying head. "This is big, son. There's only so much I can do. The U.S. government can't let her fall into enemy hands. Her knowledge is too dangerous to be let loose. I doubt they'll even be willing to put her in a secure facility if she won't play ball. There's just too much of a risk she'd be captured while en route." He looked David in the eye. "My guess is that they'll give her another day here to cooperate, and if not, then she'll be executed as a threat to national security."

"What?" bellowed David. Rage bubbled just below the surface, along with something else. Something deadly. He wasn't going to let her die. He'd brought her here for protection and he'd kill any man here before he'd let them hurt her. Including Monroe.

A couple of suited agents from the other room poked their heads in the door, offering questioning glances, but Monroe waved them away.

"They can't do that, sir," said David through his clenched teeth.

"They *will* do it if we don't convince her to help. I'm sure of it."

David blew out a string of vile curses.

"I agree. Don't worry. They won't make you do the job. They've got a pool of men who can off an innocent girl and somehow still sleep at night."

Over his dead body, but he didn't offer that bit of information to Monroe. "Where'd they find men like that? The back alley of hell?"

Monroe shrugged. "They serve their purpose. Can't say I'd invite them home for dinner with the wife and kids, but we've used them before."

David looked at the colonel. He respected Monroe

more than almost anyone, yet Monroe sat there, talking about killing Noelle as if it were just another distasteful op that would be full of mosquitoes and cold mud.

David wanted to feel sorry for Monroe and all the shit he must have lived through to make him hard enough inside to be so casual about killing, but instead, he found himself hating the man for even thinking about hurting an innocent woman. David had spent his life suffering and killing to protect the innocent. Yeah, he'd done some horrible things that still haunted him late at night. And yeah, he wished away a lot of days on dreams of a different line of work. But in the end, he was doing the right thing. He killed scum so that the innocent could live.

But Monroe was talking about killing one of those innocents whom David had devoted his life to protecting. Somehow, that put them on opposite sides of an invisible line.

David stepped away from Monroe, unable to look him in the eye without giving away the burning hatred that flooded his gut.

Monroe placed a wide hand on David's shoulder and it was all he could do not to shrug it off and break the man's wrist.

"We've still got time to change her mind," said Monroe.

"You've already threatened her with torture and death, and she still hasn't come around. What the hell do you think will work? Oh, wait, I know. We forgot to say 'please.' I'm sure that was it."

"Don't be an idiot, son. It's obvious that this whole thing is chapping your ass, but the bottom line is that you'd better stop hating me for giving you the truth and start looking for something that will change her mind.

You were with her the longest of any man here. You've got to have some idea of how we can convince her."

David searched his memory for some soft spot in her armor. She didn't have a child, for which David was grateful. Any kid of hers would certainly have been used as a pawn.

Two weeks of intel said that she didn't go out with friends, at least not during the time she was being watched. She went to work and came back home with the occasional trip to the grocery store or library. She had family they could threaten—parents and a sister who lived in Kansas. David could see using them as a last resort, but somehow, he didn't think threatening to kill her family would make her warm up to their way of thinking.

The only thing he could think of was the way her eyes lit up when she looked at that paper Monroe had shown her. David would have sworn she was looking at the Holy Grail of ciphers. Maybe there was a chance they could whet her appetite enough and get her interested in solving the puzzle just for the sake of knowing the answer.

Of course, even if she did break the code, what were the chances of her presenting it in a format that would be useful to the CIA? Just because she knew the answer didn't mean she had to share.

David ran a hand over his chin feeling the stubble of his three-day beard. He was tired. Frustrated. Angry as hell.

He needed some air to clear his head. There had to be something he was missing. He didn't know Noelle that well, but there had to be some way to convince her to help.

That code would tell them the location of several nuclear warheads that had been hidden in Russia during the height of the Cold War. That was why the Swarm was so dead set on breaking that code before the CIA did. Intel had told them at least that much. Word was, twelve good men had died just for that little tidbit of information.

If Noelle didn't help, those twelve lives were wasted. Not to mention the fact that if David didn't know where the Swarm was, he wasn't going to be able to get his revenge. He'd vowed to kill them all, and that was exactly what he meant to do.

But even the need for revenge was not strong enough to overshadow his desire to see Noelle safe. And the only way she was going to stay safe was to agree to work with the military. They'd offer her protection in exchange for her work. It was a symbiotic relationship, and probably not a comfortable one, but the only real option she had.

Whatever he did, he had to think of a way to get her to cooperate and fast. With only twenty-four hours left, there wasn't a lot of time to change Noelle's mind. He had to find a way to weaken her resolve.

In the end, he had only one card left to play, and the thought of using it made him break out in a cold sweat. His past was not a friendly place. If he shared it with her, she'd know just how horribly he'd failed. His biggest mistake would be highlighted in vivid color in all its gory detail. And even if he did it—even if he bared his past and his dishonor, it still might not be enough to convince her to cooperate.

David knew he had no choice. He had to try. Failing another woman was not a sin he was strong enough to live with, and like it or not, he'd gotten himself involved in Noelle's life, tying their fates together. If she died, so would he. He'd do whatever it took to protect her. And, unfortunately, that included facing his past again.

CHAPTER SEVEN

Noelle's arm was aching, but not nearly as much as her head. All she wanted to do was curl up on her old, second-hand couch with a blanket and a good book and pretend that none of this had ever happened.

For the first time in her life, she wished she had been born stupid. At least then she wouldn't be sitting here wondering whether or not she was going to live to see her twenty-seventh birthday. She'd be out at a club somewhere with Muffy and her giggle-gang getting drunk and picking up men.

Man, that was the life.

But instead, she was in this dingy little room, waiting to see how long she had until they executed her.

The bulletproof vest David had made her wear cut into her sides, so she took it off. It wouldn't help if they wanted her dead, anyway. They'd just go for a head shot.

The room was cold, so she pulled David's shirt back on over her others, wishing for a blanket to cover her chilled toes. It was probably some sort of interrogation technique to make her as uncomfortable as possible so she'd be more willing to get out of here by giving them what they wanted.

Too bad she wasn't the type of girl to give in that easily. It sure as heck would have made things a lot simpler all around.

Noelle huddled in the chair, pulling her legs up under her to help keep them warm. The shirt smelled like David, clean, with a faint hint of male warmth and some manly deodorant, and she couldn't help but bury her head in her arms and breathe in his scent for comfort.

In all her dealings during the past twenty-four hours, he was the only one who had shown her even a modicum of humanity. The suited agents were repetitive automatons who probably had never had an original thought in their lives. And Colonel Monroe. Well, he was just about as cold a man as she'd ever seen. He merely played at caring what happened to her, when deep inside, she was sure he was calculating the odds of her cooperation and how his role in this might further his own personal agenda.

The whole thing just made her want to cry, but tears didn't help. In fact, the three-minute tear-fest she'd allowed herself had only managed to make her nose run and her head pound.

She went to the door, surprised to find that it was unlocked. On the other side was a pair of guards wearing the same sort of vaguely military gear as David's. They each had big ol' freakin' guns at their sides and a look in their eyes that said they weren't strangers to using them.

"Can I get some aspirin or something?" she asked the blond guard.

"I'll check," he said as she shut her door, and she heard a lock turn on the outside.

So much for not being locked in.

A couple of minutes later, David returned with a bottle of water, two white pills and a briefcase.

Noelle's belly fluttered at the sight of him. He filled the doorway, his angular face shadowed with stubble. Even though she could see the signs of fatigue etched under his arctic blue eyes, he held himself as if he had all the strength in the world, as if he could just keep going until it was convenient to stop. His expression was relaxed, giving her some hope that things weren't quite as bad as she'd thought. She kept wishing that he'd touch her again like he had in the motel. A simple hug, or even an arm around her shoulders would have done a world of good toward helping her believe that she was going to make it through this.

But she was pretty sure that hugging was not on the agenda for a secretive military man like David. For all she knew, he'd be the one assigned to kill her if that was what they decided to do.

What a time to develop a crush. Sheesh.

David handed her the water and the pills, watching as she washed them down.

"I hope that wasn't cyanide," she said with a touch of humor. "Although that would certainly get rid of my headache."

"Not poison. I pulled them out of my own supply just to be sure, though."

He wasn't joking.

Noelle's stomach filled with acid. She flopped down into one of the hard wooden chairs and just focused on breathing.

It was beginning to sink in that her days were truly numbered. She just hoped they were at least in the double digits.

David shed the windbreaker he was wearing and draped it over her shoulders. The warmth from his body sank into her skin and helped to soothe her nerves.

Until she looked up at him. He now wore only a black T-shirt under that black multipocketed vest. His arms were bare from his biceps down, and in the ugly fluorescent lighting, she could see a fine network of scars over his hands and arms. They weren't from anything drastic, nothing life-threatening. Just a testament to the way he lived his life.

David No-Last-Name was a dangerous man.

But, he was also the only man in this house for whom she held even a sliver of trust.

"What are they going to do with me?" she asked.

David turned the chair across the table around and straddled it. "I won't lie to you. It doesn't look good. They want this code broken, and, failing that, they don't want someone else to break it first."

"They're really going to kill me, aren't they? That wasn't just a bluff to get me to cooperate."

David's steady blue gaze slid away and silence stretched out between them with icy fingers.

She knew the truth then. She was a dead woman.

"How long?" she managed to whisper.

David's eyes flickered toward a corner of the room. It was a signal.

It didn't take Noelle long to see the small black hole that undoubtedly housed a tiny camera lens.

"I don't know what their plans are for you," he said evenly, holding up two and then four fingers on a hand that was hidden from the camera by his body. "But if I were you, I'd start thinking twice about your position."

Twenty-four. Days? Hours? Was that all the time she had left?

The room started to fade away, receding as her fate loomed large before her.

This time tomorrow, she could be dead.

It was almost worse knowing when it was going to happen. At least when she wasn't sure, she could pretend that things were going to work out okay.

"I don't want to die, but I will if I have to. I won't let you use my work as a weapon."

David's jaw clenched and a vein in his temple throbbed. "Not everything we do is about killing, Noelle. We keep this country safe. We protect people."

"But you do kill." It wasn't really a question.

"When it's necessary."

"And who gets to decide when it's necessary?"

He scrubbed a wide hand over his head and pulled in a deep breath as if to calm himself. "There are a lot of bad people out there. It's not exactly something we broadcast on the nightly news if we can help it. We like for people to be able to sleep at night, not worry about whether or not they're going to wind up dead in ways they can't even imagine."

"You keep saying 'we.' Are you one of the people who get to choose between life and death for another human?"

David exploded into angry motion, flinging the chair away. "Yeah, I'm one of those people. I've held men in my rifle sights and decided whether or not to pull the trigger. I've set explosives on a building knowing that as soon as I pushed the button everyone inside was going to be blown to hell. I've even killed with my bare hands, breaking men's necks or choking the life right out of their bodies."

He leaned forward, his hands flat on the table, his eyes frigid blue with anger. "And I'm not sorry because I know what those men did. I know what they would have been capable of doing had they lived."

Noelle leaned back in her chair, needing to put some distance between her and his anger. But even in the face of such rage, she still thrust her chin up, refusing to back down on what was important. "You can't know what is in a person's heart. And if you can't know that, you can't judge them. It's wrong."

His nostrils flared as he studied her face. She wanted to get up and move across the room, but she held her ground under his scrutiny.

Slowly, he leaned down and picked up the briefcase he'd brought with him. His voice was no longer loud, but it was just as cold. "No, Noelle, you're the one who's wrong. I do know what was in their hearts." And with that, he pulled a stack of glossy eight-by-ten photos from a folder and flung them out over the table.

It was a collage from a nightmare in shades of blood and dead flesh. There were severed limbs, fingers, ears, tongues. Half of a penis. The faces of the victims were so badly beaten and mutilated they were nearly unrecognizable as human. There were men, women and even a couple of children that couldn't have even lived into their teens. Two dead babies.

Noelle fought the urge to vomit. She'd seen her share of horror films, but nothing could have prepared her for the real thing. Even with the added detachment of photos, she could almost smell the stench of blood and fear emanating from the pictures.

Her body started to shake and sweat as her mind

struggled to assimilate what he'd shown her. This wasn't real. It couldn't be. No one was that horrible.

"This," he said in a quiet, aching voice, pointing at the photos. "This is what was in their hearts."

Noelle didn't want to look, but she couldn't stop herself. Her stomach clenched painfully, but she forced herself to face the images of death and violence and evil with as much courage as she could. These were real photos. Real people. Real children.

Noelle's eyes filled with tears, but she blinked them away, looking up at David. Anguish burned in his blue eyes, which were also wet with unshed tears. His jaw was clenched and his lips were pulled into a snarl of self-loathing.

"And this one." His voice was nearly a whisper now, quiet with the tightness of grief. With a shaking hand, he pulled out a set of photos showing what had once been a beautiful young blonde woman. She was bound to a metal chair by thick leather cuffs around both wrists and ankles. She was naked and bruised over much of her tanned skin. There was a pool of blood under her chair that looked too large to have ever fit inside her slim body. Her thighs were stained with more blood and every one of her fingers had been severed and were lying neatly in rows on a table at her side. "This woman was my wife. My Mary." He swallowed audibly before he could continue. "The Swarm did this to her. They raped her and tortured her and beat her for the crime of being married to me. Nothing more. She was supposed to be safe at home while I was out on a training op. I wouldn't have even known she'd been taken if I hadn't received her wedding ring—still attached to her severed finger—in the mail."

It was the quiet grief in his voice that made Noelle look

up. He'd loved Mary. She could see it plainly, shining in his eyes, along with anguish, regret and self-hatred. He'd loved this woman and they had mutilated her.

Suddenly, all the people in the photos became real, not just images on paper. They had parents and siblings and friends who loved them. They'd laughed and cried and loved in return. They were people. Alive.

Turned into photos too grotesque to imagine.

David looked up from the photos and stared right into her eyes. There was so much pain there inside him that she couldn't look away. She felt that if she averted her gaze, even for a second, David would crumple under the weight of his guilt. She could tell that he felt like he should have saved his wife from this gruesome fate. Noelle was sure that he'd done everything he could to save the woman he loved, and it still hadn't been enough.

"This is what we're fighting, Noelle. This is why we need your help. Without you, the Swarm will find those weapons and they won't hesitate to use them. People will die, and only you can stop that from happening." His voice fell to a mere whispering thread of sound. "Please, don't let that happen. Don't let someone else's wife be tortured and killed like my Mary."

Noelle's body shook in rebellion against David's plea. How could he ask this of her? How could he ask her to throw away all her morals and do what she'd sworn she'd never do? What if her work was used to kill?

A tiny, new voice inside her answered, *What if it* wasn't *used to kill those monsters?*

Noelle forced herself to look at the photos again. David was right. Whoever had done this deserved to die. They needed to die before they could kill again. No matter how ugly or horrible the task was, someone needed to do it. The Swarm wasn't a group of people. It was a group of demons. Pure evil.

Someone had to stop them, but Noelle wasn't sure if she was strong enough to be that person.

The glossy eyes of the dead stared at her, pleading with her to help. Mary's lifeless, brown eyes begged Noelle to save her husband from his own prison of grief and self-loathing.

Noelle bolted from the table and bent over the small metal trash can, vomiting. She tried to breathe, tried to push away the images floating in her head, the ones that lay on the surface of the table only five feet away.

It didn't help. She couldn't stop her stomach from heaving.

And then David was there. He put a hand on her head and wrapped his arm around her stomach to help keep her muscles from cramping. He said nothing, but just the touch of another human, alive and warm, was enough to allow Noelle to regain control.

Slowly, she was able to breathe again and she leaned back against his chest, panting.

He stroked the cold, sweat-damp hair back from her forehead, just waiting for her to calm down.

Noelle didn't dare turn around and risk seeing those pictures again. She didn't think her sanity would hold out if she did. "I didn't know," she said.

She felt David nod behind her. He was close, holding her tight, comforting her. "I know. I'm sorry you had to see what makes good men kill."

"Did you, uh, kill the men who did . . . that to your wife?"

He went stiff, every muscle in his chest going taut, but didn't pull away. "I thought so, but I was wrong. There was at least one left. Maybe more."

"They rebuilt the Swarm," she guessed.

"Yeah," he said, his voice tight with hatred.

Noelle had no idea how difficult it must have been for David to lose his wife to such horrifying violence. There was nothing natural about his loss. He could find no comfort in the fact that it had been her time to go, as had been the case for Noelle's grandmother. His wife's life had been cut out from under her, spilled onto a cold cement floor. Stolen.

Noelle wondered what sort of strength it had to take for David to go on after something like that.

"I thought I'd made it impossible for them ever to do anything like that to a woman again. I thought I'd avenged her death and protected countless others from the same fate. I was wrong," he said. "The Swarm is still out there and able to strike again. I can't let that happen. I need your help."

Noelle understood what he meant, but it was a painful understanding. Men like David did horrible things so that normal people didn't even need to know about the kind of evil they fought. It was an honorable, messy, thankless job.

One she could help make easier. One he couldn't do without her help.

Noelle wasn't convinced that violence would prevent violence, but maybe knowledge could. Knowledge only she could provide.

Noelle steeled herself for what she was about to do, unwilling to turn away from David's plea for help. His wife's plea. She didn't want to deal with the guilt of causing the death of another, no matter how distanced she was from the act. But now she knew that something had to be done to stop the Swarm. Maybe David was right. Maybe the only way to stop them was to kill them.

As much as she despised the idea of providing the military with knowledge that could be used offensively, she had to be strong like David and do something she hated because it was necessary. Noelle only prayed that what she was about to do wouldn't murder her own soul.

She pulled away from him and leaned her back against the wall for support. She needed to look into his face and make sure that he was telling her the truth. "If I help, can you give me your word that you'll do everything in your power to see my work destroyed before it can be used against anyone but the Swarm?"

David nodded. "I'll do anything to find the rest of the men who killed my wife. That includes destroying government property."

"And can you promise they will let me go if I give them what they want?"

"No, but I can promise to keep tabs on you, and if they don't let you go, I'll break you out of wherever they're holding you." He gave her a feral smile. "Even if it kills me."

Noelle pinned him with a fierce stare. "I won't let you die for me, David. I'm not worth the price of another human life."

He shrugged as if his life was worth no more than the casual gesture. "You're a lot more valuable than you think."

"So are you," she told him.

Something in his expression shifted, softened. "Does that mean you want to help me?"

Helping David recover from the loss of his wife was one of the things she wished most to accomplish, even more than cracking that intriguing code. Noelle didn't know Mary, but helping David seemed like a fitting tribute to the woman who had loved him. She wasn't sure how she would do it, but she was going to do everything in her power to prove to David that Mary's death wasn't his fault. "Yeah. It does."

CHAPTER EIGHT

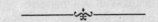

David desperately needed some caffeine, but his hands were shaking so badly that he didn't trust himself not to spill the scalding hot coffee onto his lap. He stared at the steaming mug on the table, willing himself to relax.

Monroe placed a fatherly hand on David's shoulder. "You did the right thing by showing her those photos, son."

It sure as hell didn't feel right. Just looking at them was enough to make him wish he'd died alongside Mary. The weight of his guilt bore down against his heart, crushing the strength right out of him. If it weren't for his need for revenge and his promise to see Noelle safely through this mess, he didn't think he'd have the will to keep breathing.

As much as he wanted to see the Swarm wiped out, he hated the thought of pulling Noelle into the middle of this dangerous mess. What if he wasn't strong enough to keep her safe?

"How long until we move her, sir? It's scary as hell to have her sitting around in a place as open as this."

Monroe leaned back in the office chair that had been brought in as part of his mobile office. One of the bedrooms in the old house had been converted into a work space, containing a computer, printer/fax machine, communications equipment and a closed-circuit TV screen that monitored the room where Noelle was being held. Nothing matched as it was all cast-off furniture from renovated offices, but it functioned, and that was all that mattered.

"I'm waiting on details regarding her transfer now," said Monroe. "There are three facilities fighting over her. I'm waiting for the pissing contest to run out of ammunition."

David pulled in a deep breath, trying to convince his body that he was relaxed rather than ready to strangle someone. "I want to be assigned to her protection team."

Monroe nodded his steel gray head. "You can escort her to her final destination, but after that, we're going to need you in the field, Captain."

David hated leaving Noelle alone.

No, not alone, he corrected himself. She'd be guarded 24/7 deep in the bowels of some impenetrable compound. She'd be safe.

Safer than she would be with him around. He couldn't let himself get involved. He couldn't forget what happened the last time he cared about a woman.

David cursed and slugged back the hot coffee fast enough it didn't have time to spill. The black liquid burned all the way down, making him feel more alert already.

"I don't like it," David admitted, though he wasn't specific about exactly which part he didn't like. Let the colonel figure it out.

"She'll be fine. And when it's all over, we can even let you come for a visit, if you like."

He did like, and that was the problem. "I just want to get this over with."

Monroe gave a whatever-you-want shrug but said nothing about David's choice. "I'll call in and see if there's any news on where she's moving. Why don't you go sit with her and bring her something to eat? It looks like you both could use a decent meal."

David glanced at the screen, which showed Noelle curled into a ball on the chair with her legs tucked up under her. She was covered completely by his jacket but still shaking visibly.

After she'd been sick, they let her clean herself up while someone got rid of the trash can and the photos.

He thought her color had been better when he left the room and that she might actually sleep a little, but it was obvious now that she was a long way from sleeping anytime soon.

David knew the feeling and felt that selfish need to comfort her again, as if he could make himself feel better by making her feel better.

Too little, too late.

"Okay, sure," said David, and went to the farmhouse kitchen in search of some food.

The lock on the door grated, making Noelle jump. She was beginning to dread that door opening. Every time it did, things got worse.

David came in, carrying a cupboard shelf like a tray. "You hungry?" he asked, his eyes roaming over her, covering every inch as if looking for something. She had no idea why he did that every time he came around, but she was a long way from being used to his scrutiny.

"I really just want to get out of here. If I never see this room again, it will be too soon."

"I can arrange that. Come on."

He spoke quietly to the guards outside the door and led her to a smaller room that must have been a child's bedroom at one point, judging by the faded Mickey Mouse wallpaper. The floors were bare wood and there was a smaller table set up in here—the old-fashioned drop-leaf style just big enough for two. Even though it was still a prison of sorts, it was much better than the last room, with its stagnant air and recent, but horrible, memories.

David set down the shelf, revealing several sandwiches, a couple of cans of Coke and a bowl of canned chicken noodle soup.

He ignored her statement and popped the top on a Coke. "This should help settle your stomach if it's still bothering you."

Noelle took the drink and sipped. Her stomach did settle some, but she thought it was more due to David being here than the soda. As unnerving as this whole mess was, he was a constant for her. Something in his steady strength and unwavering honesty gave her a slim thread of comfort, which was more than she found from anyone else. "When can I leave?"

David bit into a sandwich and chewed. "Soon. You'll be taken somewhere safe where you can work."

"Where?"

"I don't know yet, but we'll find out soon."

"Soon? Soon as in minutes, hours, days?"

His blue eyes slid to the soup. "You should eat something. There's no telling how long it may be until you get another hot meal."

"I don't want food. What I want is to get out of here right now. Barring that, I'd like some more aspirin since I puked up the last ones."

"I can do the aspirin, at least—if you promise to eat something so they don't make you sick again. The rest is out of my hands." He sounded truly sorry about that last part, which didn't do anything to make Noelle feel better about what was going to happen next.

Noelle took a sip of the soup just to get him moving toward those pills. Her headache was really getting bad.

"You took off your vest," he said, his tone casual, as if he hadn't just told her she was going to die a few minutes ago.

"It was bothering me."

"I'll get you a smaller one. I want you wearing it at all times. Just in case." He pinned her with a laser stare that would have made her cower if her circumstances had been different. She'd faced death today—both hers and that of countless others—she could certainly face his glower.

He left and came back shortly with aspirin and a smaller vest. Again, he watched her swallow the pills as if he was making sure she didn't hide them in her cheek or something.

What kind of a life did he have not even to trust someone to take medicine that she'd asked for in the first place? She wasn't sure she wanted to know.

Noelle made quick work of donning the vest. This one fit her just right, and she had to take off all but the innermost T-shirt she wore to get the straps fastened.

David watched her the whole time, chewing and swallowing mechanically as he did. He'd already plowed through two sandwiches and was starting on the third. From the looks of it, she doubted he'd tasted any of them.

The hard edges of the vest bit into her skin, but she welcomed the protection that the vest brought, limited though it was.

"Come finish your soup," he said when she was done dressing. "I promise it will make you feel better."

Noelle wasn't sure a bit of chicken broth and noodles was going to do much toward making her feel better, but it could hardly make things worse.

From outside the door came a loud boom, followed by rattling walls and the frantic shouting of orders. David was on his feet with his gun drawn before Noelle's heart had time to pump adrenaline through her system.

His face turned into something feral, predatory. She thought she'd just imagined that he'd looked like that the night she'd been attacked, but now she knew she'd been wrong.

This was the other side of David—the warrior. The killer.

He put the gun in her hands, clicking the safety off. "Stay here. If anyone you haven't seen today comes through that door, point and pull the trigger."

"I can't," she started to say, but David was already out the door with his second weapon in his hand.

The gun burned her fingers with the weight of cold violence. She'd never even held a weapon in her hands before all this happened, but she knew about how the safety switch worked and that there'd be one heck of a kick if she pulled the trigger.

She also knew that yesterday, there would have been no situation in which she would have considered using such a weapon. But a lot had happened since yesterday.

Noelle turned the small table on its side, spilling

soup and Coke everywhere. She slid behind the barrier, propping the heavy gun up on the edge.

If the Swarm was here, she wasn't going to let them take her alive.

David ordered the guards to stand at Noelle's door and went to find the colonel. He found Monroe at a window, a sniper's rifle in his capable hands.

"You're alive!" shouted Monroe, as David neared, keeping his head down.

"Yeah. What'd you expect?"

"I expected to find you'd been blown to hell by that RPG that just blasted a hole in the back wall of the house. It went right into the interrogation room. Someone knew where we were holding Noelle."

Shit. That wasn't good news. If it hadn't been for her request for a relocation and his uncommon softness toward her comfort, they'd both be dead right now.

"Is it the Swarm?" asked David as he moved in to take the colonel's place.

"We don't know, but that's where my money is. Get the girl out of here. Now!" Monroe had to shout to be heard over the last volley of gunfire.

The Swarm, or whoever was out there, had obviously found someone on the inside who would leak information about Noelle's whereabouts, or they wouldn't be here. Her location was top secret. "I'm not taking her to any of the official facilities. It's not safe."

"I trust your judgment. Just go! Take my Bronco, it's bulletproofed." Monroe slid keys and a satellite phone off his belt and pushed them across the floor to David, then he took the envelope containing the sample of text, crumpled it to make it more aerodynamic and threw that at David as well. "I'll contact you later."

"Don't," said David. "I'll contact you."

"Now's not the time to argue, son."

"An attack on this site means that one of your team has been compromised."

"Damn. You're right." Monroe's face was grim and pissed. Someone's head was going to roll for this. "Where are you going to take her?"

Already his mind was flying, trying to decide where to take her. Any official location he took her to would be an obvious target. Even if the secure facilities were safe, getting there wouldn't be. If he was running the Swarm, he'd have teams stationed on all routes leading into those locations. That way, they could get to Noelle before she was locked away safe and sound.

He had to get her someplace defensible. Chances were they wouldn't get out of here without a tail. He needed it to be remote so that when the bullets started flying, no innocents would get hurt.

He knew just where to go.

"I'll figure something out."

"You've got a plan, don't you?"

"Always."

"Fine. Just make sure it's a good one. We need her alive, Wolfe."

"Yes, sir," said David.

"I'll order the men to cover your exit. You've got ninety seconds to get moving."

David nodded and ran in a low crouch back toward

Noelle. He detoured by Monroe's office to grab her laptop, still in its case, knowing that she was going to need it.

No more than thirty seconds had passed when David announced his presence to Noelle with a shout so she wouldn't accidentally shoot him. As he swung the door open, his weapon was pointed at the ceiling and he kept to one side of the doorway to reduce the size of target he made.

Noelle was barricaded behind the table with the business end of the borrowed weapon pointed right at his head. Smart girl.

David couldn't help but grin at the fierce expression she wore, which made her look like some sort of warrior maiden. She might be a peaceful brainiac, but she wasn't a coward.

"We're getting out of here," he stated as he pulled her to her feet by one hand, keeping an eye on the doorway.

She stumbled against him, all warm and soft and frightened. Had things been different, he might have just pulled her into his arms and held her for about half a year. But things weren't different and the gunfire wasn't slowing down. He had only thirty-eight seconds left before Monroe would order his men to lay down cover fire.

David tucked her against his body making sure her head was low against his chest. That way he could shield her by positioning his body between her and the enemy. He took the weapon from her hands and pushed her down into a low crouch as they worked their way toward the rear exit of the old house. By his mental count, they had seven seconds left. David used that time to give Noelle a one-armed hug of comfort.

"Don't let them take me alive," she whispered against his neck.

David knew what she was saying. She'd rather die than be taken by the Swarm. She was braver than he'd thought she would be, considering that she had no training or experience in combat. He respected her for that. There wasn't time for him to explain that he'd die before he let her get hurt and that it was likely that every other man here would do the same. She was valuable and every man here knew it.

But rather than try to explain that to her, he just gave her another squeeze and said, "I'm not going to let them take you at all. Come on."

A loud volley of cover fire began and David urged Noelle forward with his body.

David still had keys to the Buick, so he tossed them to another agent on his way out, guessing that there would be at least one or two more vehicles leaving at the same time as a diversion.

He pushed Noelle in through the driver's door of the Bronco and had the vehicle careening down the gravel drive in seconds.

Behind him, the intensity of gunfire increased, and two other decoy vehicles were right on his bumper.

"Stay down," he ordered, and drove north as if Satan himself were on their trail.

CHAPTER NINE

They'd been driving for hours when David finally pulled off the highway. Noelle had no idea where they were and the added cloak of night made her feel vulnerable and edgy.

"Are we close?" she asked him. They were the first words either one of them had spoken in hours. David had been concentrating on driving, checking the rearview mirror often for bad guys, and Noelle had been content to be quiet and let him do his job.

David's eyes flicked back to the mirror for the millionth time. "A few more miles."

"Are we being followed?"

His big hands tightened around the steering wheel and his jaw muscles bunched in frustration. "Probably."

Noelle turned around in her seat and peered into the darkness stretching out behind them. There were a few houses along this stretch of pitted road. Most of them were set way back, hidden by thick stands of trees. This far out, night was somehow thicker and more ominous without the cheerful glow of streetlights to break up the gloom.

Of course, that ominous feeling could have been due to the fact that David seemed certain they were being followed no matter how empty the road behind them looked to Noelle.

"I don't see anyone," she told him.

"Neither do I, but my gut tells me they're out there, and I'll trust it over my eyes any day."

Noelle settled back in her seat so she could watch him without looking like she was. The faint glow from the dashboard lights highlighted the masculine angularity of his features and deepened the weary circles under his eyes. Even though he looked tired, nothing in his motions gave away even a hint of fatigue. Every movement was smooth, confident, controlled.

Noelle stifled a yawn and checked the clock. It was after midnight and she felt wrung out. And she'd slept last night—at least a little. As far as she knew, David hadn't.

"You want me to take over driving for a while?" she asked.

His eyes slid sideways and settled on her for a moment. Even though his glance was brief, she had the disconcerting feeling that she'd been measured, weighed and inventoried by the time he looked away. "No, thanks. You should try to get some sleep if you can. We'll be there within the hour."

"Be where?"

"Another safe house."

Noelle rolled her eyes. "Great. Do you think this safe house will actually be safe?"

"For a while."

"How long is a while? Days? Hours?"

"Get some sleep and let me worry about that part."

"Easier said than done," she muttered.

"I'm sorry I can't give you any guarantees. I wish to hell I could."

Noelle sighed and leaned her head back against the seat. "I don't mean to sound ungrateful for your help, it's just that this whole thing sucks some serious ass."

A small grin lifted one side of his mouth. "I'll second that."

"I mean, there I am, living my nice, quiet little life, perfectly content to be doing so, then suddenly, everything gets blown to hell. I didn't do anything to deserve this, unless you count being stupid enough to pick up a hobby in cryptology."

"Maybe you should consider collecting stamps in the future."

"Here's to hoping that I'll get the chance."

He turned his head and gave her his full attention for just a second. His glacier blue eyes flared with determination. "You will, Noelle. I'm going to get you through this alive."

His focus went back to the road, leaving Noelle feeling jarred. She didn't know David very well, but one thing was for certain—he meant every word he said.

After a long, quiet moment, she laid her hand on his shoulder. He flinched so slightly that she wasn't even sure it happened. Heat from his body sank into her chilled fingers and it was all she could do not to tighten her grip and feel the steely strength of his muscles beneath her palm. "Thanks," she whispered.

His focus remained on the rutted road. "For what?"

"Just for being here."

He shrugged the shoulder she was still touching, reminding her to move her hand away. "It's my job."

"Then thanks for showing up at work today."

The truck slowed and he turned onto a road that was

little more than a gravel trail. Brush scraped the sides of the Bronco, squealing like nails on a chalkboard.

David turned off the headlights and slowed down to keep the wheels on the road as it was plunged into darkness.

Noelle tensed, but remained silent, letting him navigate the big vehicle. In the distance, she could see a thick clump of trees and inside them, the perpendicular lines of a man-made structure.

David stopped the truck right outside the back door, close enough that there was just room to open the driver's door without hitting the house.

"I'm going inside to check things out," he said, unfastening his seat belt and pulling out one of his guns. With expert movements, he checked the weapon, clicked the safety off and surveyed the surrounding area. "Get behind the wheel, and if you see anyone besides me, drive away as fast as you can." He pulled a cell phone out of his jacket pocket along with a crumpled envelope. "Speed dial one and talk to Colonel Monroe and only Monroe. He'll tell you where to go."

Noelle took the phone and envelope, clutching them in shaking hands. "I'm not going to drive off and leave you here just because I see someone. What if it's just some kid here to make out with his girlfriend?"

"It won't be. And don't argue with me. If you see anyone, assume they're here to kill you."

The thought made her stomach clench painfully and she tried to shove it aside. "And what about you?"

"I can take care of myself."

"I won't leave you here to die."

He reached out and cupped her chin in his hand, forcing her to look at him. His fingers were warm and as unyielding as his eyes. "This is not about me, Noelle. You're the one they're after. If you don't stay alive long enough to crack that code, a lot of innocent people are going to die. I can't let that happen. So, you're going to do exactly what I just said and stop arguing before you get us both killed. Do you understand?"

Noelle gave a tiny nod, but it was apparently enough to satisfy David.

"Lock the doors behind me," he said as his fingers slid away from her face, releasing her.

David's focus shifted abruptly to his surroundings. He slid out of the car and disappeared around the corner of the house and Noelle scrambled into his seat, adjusting it so she could reach the pedals if she needed them.

She prayed that she wouldn't because she truly wasn't sure if she was strong enough to leave David here to die while she ran away. Without his presence, she felt exposed. Vulnerable. Her hands gripped the steering wheel until her knuckles ached.

Minutes slithered by slowly, forcing her to concentrate on remembering to breathe. Her body was shaking and breaking out into a cold sweat as she stared wide-eyed into the darkness.

Where the hell was he? Why was this taking so long?

Noelle strained to hear over the sound of the idling engine. She even cracked open the window, but heard only the wind singing through the nearly bare trees.

After what felt like half of forever, David reappeared inside the house, opening the back door for her.

Relief swamped Noelle, and she smiled at him even as her body urged her to crumple under the strain. Or run into his arms and hug him.

He motioned for her to come inside, and Noelle gladly turned off the engine, pocketed the keys and hurried back to David's side, where she felt at least some small measure of safety.

David shut and locked the door behind her, casting them into blackness. Noelle instinctively reached out toward him, collided with the hard, warm flesh of his arm, and wrapped her hands around it. She didn't care that it wasn't proper for her to be groping at him. All she cared about was knowing he was still right there with her.

"Easy," he said in a low, quiet voice. "I'm not going anywhere."

"Then you won't mind if I just hold on, will you?"

He gave an amused grunt. "I'm going to give you a flashlight, but you need to make sure you keep the beam away from the windows, okay? There are blinds on the windows, but if your beam hits them, it will show through to the outside."

"Got it."

He peeled one of her hands away from his arm and guided her fingers around the slim body of a penlight. His fingers showed her where the switch was, and when it was safely pointed toward the floor, he slid the switch on. A faint stream of light pooled on the vinyl floor, seeming bright in the relative darkness.

David pulled his hands away from hers and took a step backward. "I've got some work to do to make sure this place stays safe. I want you to get some sleep if you can. Use the couch in the next room."

"I don't think that's gonna happen. I'd rather help you."

He studied her briefly, frowning at what he saw.

"Fine. If you want to help, find us something to eat. I'm starving."

"Is there any food here?" she asked.

David nodded. "No perishables, but there should be plenty of canned goods in the cabinets and bottled drinks in the fridge. If we're lucky, there might even be some coffee stashed in the freezer."

"I'm on it."

David left the room—which Noelle now realized was the kitchen—to do God knew what. At least he hadn't left her to just sit here with nothing to think about but whether or not he'd come back.

Noelle covered the light with her fingers so that only a faint glow seeped through and carefully checked the cabinets for supplies. She found a drinking glass and set it upside down on the counter and placed her flashlight on top of it so it acted as a sort of lantern, giving her just enough light to work by. She found some canned stew, which she heated in the microwave and pulled a couple of sodas out of the fridge. Neither appliance had the usual light inside when the door was opened, making Noelle wonder just who owned this place. It was obviously set up for secrecy.

She put everything on the table but didn't dare call out for David. Instead, she took her flashlight and headed in search of him.

The house was small enough that it didn't take long to find him. He was in the basement in a windowless room filled with enough weapons and ammunition to outfit a small army. A single dim lightbulb swung over his head.

"What is this place?" she asked, watching him pack several boxes of ammunition into a canvas duffel bag.

"It's one of our safe houses."

"Our? As in . . . ?"

"As in not CIA. Military."

"Oh. A bit paranoid, eh?"

He shot her a quick grin. "That's one way to put it. I prefer the term 'prepared,' but call it whatever you like as long as it means I don't run out of bullets."

Noelle eyed the shelves lining one wall. There were boxes of food, gallons of water, gasoline, medical supplies, communication equipment, batteries . . . "This place looks like it was made as a bomb shelter."

"It was."

"Why don't we just hole up down here until I crack the code then?"

"I would if I thought it was safe."

"But you don't?"

"No. Someone on the inside knows about you. That's why we were attacked today. I don't want to take the chance that that same someone will know about this place and come after you. Anyone who knows the code and has his handprint on file can get in here."

Noelle felt the blood drain from her face. "You mean one of your guys is working for the Swarm?"

A snarl twisted his mouth, but his voice was steady. "Looks like."

"So how long can we stay here? Should I start working on the code?"

He grabbed a box full of medical supplies off the shelf and shoved it into the bulging bag. "I'm going to stock the Bronco with anything we might need, then get some food and a quick nap if I'm lucky. After you've eaten and had some sleep, we'll talk about the code. Until then, I need to focus on keeping you alive and that means taking advantage of these supplies."

He started filling another canvas bag, this time with food and water and a second medical kit.

"Do we really need all that stuff?"

"We might. Chances are we'll have to disappear for a while. You don't mind camping do you?"

Noelle thought about spiders and all the creepy-crawly things that lived in the dirt. "If that's what we have to do to stay alive, then I'll do it, but it's not my idea of fun. Besides, if you want that code broken, I'm going to need my laptop."

He nodded once. "Right. We'll need power." He pulled a couple of large batteries off the shelf and something that looked like an adapter she could use to plug her laptop into a cigarette lighter. Those went into yet another bag.

Noelle prayed that he'd find her a nice, safe hotel to live in for a few days rather than a spot of cold ground that was inhabited by bugs.

"I heated up some stew."

"Sounds great," he replied. "I'll pack this stuff into the back of the Bronco and be there in a couple of minutes."

Noelle grabbed one of the duffels he'd packed and hauled it over her shoulder. The thing weighed nearly as much as she did, but she managed to haul it up the stairs. David followed closely behind her with a duffel over each shoulder. Noelle set hers down by the back door and gawked as he picked it up and added it to his burden.

Even in the limited light, she could see the way his muscles tightened and rippled under the strain. He wasn't very bulky, but it was clear that every ounce of muscle he had was entirely functional. He was probably carrying over two hundred pounds and didn't seem to be hampered.

She was glad he was on her side. She was also glad that out of all the men at the safe house who could have escorted her here, it was David who'd taken the job. As far as she was concerned, he'd proven himself capable of protecting her twice now, and there wasn't another man alive that she would have trusted more than David to keep her safe from the Swarm.

"You still have the keys?" he asked.

Noelle dug them out of her jeans and handed them over. His fingers brushed hers for a brief second, but the contact sent a jolt of purely feminine need through her system. Damn, that adrenaline and hormone mix was potent.

She jerked away, cupping her hand as if it had been burned. Now was not the time to be thinking about anything but staying alive. It certainly wasn't the time to be wondering if David was as aware of their being alone in a very isolated, very dark house together as she was. Or if he was having the same distracting, utterly inappropriate thoughts that she was.

David watched her with those eyes that missed nothing. "You okay?"

Noelle swallowed her embarrassment. She'd been around enough men in her life that a simple touch should not have affected her, but her nerves were shot and her brain was on overload. Her more primitive instincts had been summoned by the threat to her life and they were screaming at her to get as close to David as possible. He would keep her safe.

"Yeah. Just tired."

He gave her a look that said he knew she was lying but let it drop anyway. "Back away from the door. I don't want you to be a clear target when I open it."

Noelle hesitated for only a second before she complied. "Do you think someone's out there?"

"Not yet, but I don't want to take any chances."

Before she could argue that it wasn't safe for him to go out there, either, he was gone and returned a few seconds later.

Noelle breathed out a sigh of relief as he locked the door and went to the kitchen sink to wash his hands.

She busied herself by finding a stash of coffee in the freezer and started a fresh pot. They were both likely to need the caffeine sooner or later.

They sat down to eat with Noelle's makeshift lantern between them. It was as intimate as any candlelit dinner, but not nearly as relaxing.

Silence filled the room, with the occasional gurgling hiss from the coffeepot. Noelle watched David eat his stew mechanically, stopping only to take long drinks of soda.

Noelle ate as much as the tension in her stomach would allow, wishing for something they could talk about to break the silence.

He glanced at her, then at her bowl. "Not hungry?"

"It's not that great," she hedged.

"Tastes fine to me, but then I've never been much of a cook. I haven't had a decent home-cooked meal since . . ."

He trailed off, but Noelle knew that he meant since his wife died. She wanted to ask him about her, but she could see from the strain in his expression that her death still hurt him badly. She couldn't stand that look of pain and guilt in his eyes and she'd have given anything to see it wiped away.

"What was she like?" asked Noelle in a nearly reverent tone. Any woman who could win a man like David had to be something special.

David's jaw tensed as if he wasn't going to respond, but after a few minutes, he closed his eyes and said, "Mary was wonderful." He was silent for a while longer, but Noelle let him take his time, deciding whether or not to share his memories with her. "She was a secretary at one of the local elementary schools. The kids loved her. She was always bringing home crayon drawings the kids had made for her. Our refrigerator was covered with colorful, clumsy, beautiful pictures." A wistful smile curved one side of his mouth. "She never threw a single one away. There were boxes and boxes full of the things. After she died . . . I couldn't bring myself to throw them away, either."

Noelle's heart ached for him—for what he'd lost, what he'd never had the chance to have. Tears burned her eyes, but she held them off, instinctively knowing that if she cried, David would stop telling her about Mary.

"She loved to swim and spent most summers by the pool when school was out. Eventually, she started giving swimming lessons to beginners. She called them ducklings." His smile warmed and his eyes held a faraway look. "She loved teaching kids more than anything. She was going back to school to get her degree so she could get a job teaching. In another year, she would have graduated."

His smile faded and sadness overtook his expression. His focus came back to the present and he stared down at his stew. "She would have made one hell of a teacher. She never would have given up on a single student, no matter how frustrating it got."

"She sounds like she was easy to love," said Noelle.

"She was. It still hurts that I can't be with her. I'd have done anything to trade places with her."

Looking into his face, witnessing his grief and the love he still held for his late wife, Noelle felt herself falling for him—slipping over the edge, just a little, in love with him. She tried to push the feeling away, knowing it would only cause her pain, but she couldn't. That sliver of love for David was part of her now.

Noelle had to clear her throat before she could speak around the lump of emotion that formed. "I'm sure Mary wouldn't have wanted you to die in her place."

"No, but at least my death wouldn't have ended her life like her death did mine. She was too full of life to let my death get her down for long. She was gorgeous. Men flocked to her. It wouldn't have taken her long to find someone else to love. Someone else who would have loved her in return."

"And what about you? Don't you want that? A wife and family to love again?"

He looked right into her eyes, a burning blue light glowing inside him. "I want that more than anything, but I don't believe in second chances. I fucked up. Mary died. I won't let it happen again with another woman."

"You can't take responsibility for something terrorists did."

"She was my wife. It was my job to keep her safe. If I hadn't been so busy out playing hero, I never would have gotten involved with the Swarm to begin with. Special Forces is for single men, not men with families. That was my mistake."

"So, you didn't deserve to have both a career and a family?"

His mouth twisted in a sneer of self-loathing. "Apparently not."

"You're being too hard on yourself."

"Mary is dead. I can't possibly be hard enough on myself to make up for that." He let out a harsh breath. "Listen, I don't want to talk about it anymore, okay?"

Noelle nodded. The fact that he'd said anything at all about Mary was a surprise. Somewhere in there, he must trust her at least a little if he was willing to share something that close to his heart.

"What about other family?" she asked in an effort to change the subject. "Do you have sisters and brothers?"

David clutched onto the change in topic like a lifeline. "One sister and a nephew. He's five now," said David with a tender lilt to his voice.

"What's his name?"

He blushed, which was such a strange thing to see on a hard man's face. "David. She named him after me."

Noelle smiled, picturing a miniature David with bright blue eyes and deep brown hair.

Something inside Noelle twisted and went tight with longing, but she didn't dare focus on it. Instead, she shoved it away and cleared her throat.

"You must be proud," she said.

"Yeah, he's a great kid, though I wish I could see him more often. It's been a while."

"Why?"

His expression closed down, became guarded. "I have to be careful not to get near the people I love. I worry that there are still men out there who would like to see me dead. Or worse yet, tortured by watching my family die one at a time. They're only safe if I stay away."

Noelle shivered against the sudden chill of violence his words evoked. "That seems like a horrible way to live—isolated from those you love. Isn't there anything you can do?"

He gave her a level look filled with icy calm. "I could go hunt them down and kill them first."

Noelle hated the concept of killing, but even more, she hated the idea, that someone would kill David first. They'd been thrown together under extreme circumstances, and even though she sensed the thinly concealed violence inside him, he'd been nothing but kind and gentle with her. She was beginning to care for him and it scared her.

"Do you know who these men are? Could you find them even if you wanted to?"

"When I took this job, I gave Monroe a list of names of men I wanted to find. He's going to . . . help me."

Noelle didn't even want to know what Monroe was going to do to help. She was better off not knowing. "And after that, will you be able to see your nephew again? Will your life go back to something resembling normal?"

"We'll have to see," he said, but Noelle knew he was hiding the truth.

"You do want it to go back to normal, don't you? Or do you just expect to die so it won't matter anymore?"

He ignored her question, his tone shutting down any chance of more personal conversation. "I've turned on the perimeter alarms, so if you hear a siren coming from the basement, get to the back door so I can get you out of here." He passed the car keys back to her, sliding them across the table so there was no chance their hands would touch.

Noelle didn't know if he'd done it on purpose, but she had a feeling that there was little David did that wasn't carefully planned.

CHAPTER TEN

There hours had passed and the Swarm hadn't shown up yet.

David was beginning to worry that they were waiting for him to pull Noelle out of her safe hiding place so they could get a clean shot at her. Whether they still wanted to capture her alive or kill her to prevent her from breaking the code for the U.S., he couldn't be sure, but neither was going to happen as long as he drew breath.

David glanced across the small living room to where she lay curled up in an overstuffed recliner. Her breathing was even, but he didn't think she was asleep. She needed her rest, but after all the adrenaline pumping through her system, he doubted she'd sleep unless he drugged her. And that wasn't an option. He needed her coherent enough to run away if it came to that.

David prayed it wouldn't. He didn't like the idea of her out there on her own.

The short combat nap he'd taken had helped clear his head, but it hadn't done a thing to ease the burning grit in his eyes. Only a few hours of real sleep would help that and he wasn't going to be getting that anytime soon. Not if the Swarm held back out of his reach.

Quietly, David went into the kitchen and dialed Monroe.

"Is the girl safe?" were the first words out of the colonel's mouth.

"Yes, sir."

"Where are you?"

"Location 1734. It looks just like location 1388. You remember that place?" David forced himself to sound casual, hoping Monroe would pick up on the clue and remember what had happened at location 1388 right before David had left Delta Force. He knew the chances of this call being intercepted were high. In fact, he was counting on it. Monroe had never been to location 1388, but he'd read David's report—the one detailing how he, Grant and Caleb had stayed behind and laid a trap while the rest of their team moved on to safety. David and his two buddies hung back so that they could ambush the Swarm when the terrorists followed the trail of false information Monroe had laid. Every one of the Swarm who showed up had died that night. David planned a repeat performance, and it all hinged on the fact that every word he said to Monroe would eventually make it back to the men who were hunting Noelle. If he was lucky, every one of the bastards would come hunting them and end up walking right into his trap.

"Those places all look the same, don't they? Smell the same, too," said Monroe. "I'll make sure your location is reported to the proper authorities."

Proper authorities, meaning whomever Monroe suspected of being the mole. David's eyes closed in relief. Monroe understood. "Thank you, sir."

"One of the decoys leaving the safe house was followed, so I don't think you have to worry about anyone finding you. You should be safe there."

Like hell, thought David. "Good," he said. "She needs to get to work. You know where to find me if you need me."

"I can send some support your way if you like."

"No, sir. I don't want to take the chance that the Swarm could follow anyone here and find us. I'm not sure how sound the perimeter is, so I don't want to take the chance they could slip through undetected." It was all lies, but David was pretty sure Monroe would know that.

"Agreed. There should be plenty of provisions at your location to hold out for days."

"Weeks, more like. We'll dig in for an extended stay while she works."

"Check in when she's made some progress."

"Yes, sir."

David ended the call and turned around to Noelle. He'd felt her approach during the conversation but didn't look at her and take the chance of getting distracted by the fear that she tried to keep hidden from him.

"So, are we staying here for a while, then?" she asked.

"No."

"But you just said we were."

"I lied."

"Why?"

"Because we have to assume that every word I was saying was either being overheard or recorded to be listened to later by the Swarm."

That fear in her green eyes flared and she wrapped her arms around herself as if she was trying to get warm.

David squelched the urge to do the job for her. Touching her was too damn distracting. "We have to make them think we feel safe here—that our guard is down. That's when they'll move in."

"But we don't want them to move in! We want them to stay away."

"I can't kill them if they stay away."

"So don't kill them. Let's just go somewhere else. Someplace safe."

"And where is that?" he demanded. "There is no place we could go that the Swarm wouldn't follow. We can't outrun them with just the two of us. We have to sleep sometime and you have to work on that code or all of this effort is for nothing."

"I don't want them to find us."

"I know, but that's the way it's got to be."

"What if you get hurt?"

"I won't," he said, making sure his tone was more confident than he felt.

"You don't know that. What if you get killed?"

"I told you to run if anything happens to me."

"And go where?" she demanded.

"Monroe will tell you."

"And will the bad guys be listening then, too?"

David cursed and rubbed his gritty eyes. There was no way he could fool a woman as smart as Noelle. He needed coffee just to keep up. "Monroe will be more careful than that. He'll use a secure line."

"I can't do this without you, David." She looked so vulnerable and defeated that he had to clench his teeth against the urge to take her into his arms. Comforting her would have gone a long way toward making him feel better but an even longer way toward him doing something that would end them up in bed together. As much as she appealed to him, he knew they'd both regret it if he lost his head like that.

"You can do this," he assured her. "You don't have a choice—not if you want to stay alive."

"And what if I want you to stay alive, too? I don't trust anyone else. Maybe I shouldn't trust you, either, but I do. You've gotten me out of harm's way twice, and I'm counting on you to do it again. With you by my side."

"Gee, you're not too demanding or anything, are you?" he asked with a hint of humor. He couldn't remember the last time he'd cracked a joke and his sense of humor felt rusty.

"I'm serious. I don't want you making any plans that involve me leaving you behind, got it?"

"You're not in a position to be making demands."

"Sure I am. I'm the one who can crack the code, remember? And I say that if things go bad, we run away together."

David surged across the floor with long strides until he had her backed up against a wall. He wanted to make sure he had her full attention and didn't hesitate to use his larger body to intimidate her into listening if that's what it took. The fact that he loved the way her body felt pressed against his was only an added benefit. Or an added torment, depending on how he looked at it.

He took her shoulders in his hands and pinned them to the wall. She had to tilt her head back to look him in the eye, which she did without even the smallest hint of submission.

"You'll run if I tell you to. This is not a game and as much as I'd like to, I can't guarantee that I'll be able to come with you. My job is to keep you alive. Period. That's what I'm going to do and no one, not even you, is going to get in the way of that. Got it?"

Noelle swallowed and licked her lips. David's gaze zeroed in on her mouth like a laser target. He realized his mistake then. He shouldn't have gotten so close. He could smell her scent, feel her warmth. Standing this close, it was easy to forget she was a job and not just a woman who pulled at his senses.

She licked her lips again and David jerked his eyes away before he gave in to the urge to taste her.

"I don't like to be bullied," she told him, though her voice sounded breathless rather than annoyed.

"I'm not interested in what you like or don't like." It was a total lie. He was interested in what she liked— whether or not she preferred her men to take things gentle and slow or hot and hard. Given the chance, he'd give it to her however she wanted it, but he wasn't going to be given the chance and he needed to get his brain out of his pants or he was going to get her killed.

"Well, it's good to know you care," she said, sounding hurt and irritated all at the same time.

"I do care. Too damn much. If things were different—"

A siren wailed from the basement, indicating the perimeter had been breached. The Swarm was here.

Adrenaline flooded David's body and he pushed away all thoughts but protecting Noelle. She'd gone stiff with fear and stared at him with wide, trusting eyes.

"You've still got the keys?" he asked.

She nodded.

"Good. When I tell you, I want you to run for the

Bronco and haul ass out of here. Head north and call Monroe as soon as you can."

David slid the satellite phone into her front pocket rather than trusting her shaking hands not to drop it. He pulled out his weapon and flicked off the safety. "I'll give you covering fire and call you on that phone as soon as I'm safely out of here, okay?"

She hesitated for a moment, but finally nodded. David took her by the hand and led her to the back door, pushing her body to where she'd be safest.

"Everything you need is in the car," he said. "Weapons, ammo, maps, fuel. The tank is full. Don't stop unless you have to or Monroe tells you to. You'll be fine as long as you keep moving."

It was still dark inside the house, so he cracked open the back door. The perimeter was set about a quarter mile away from the house, so they didn't have much time before the Swarm got there.

"Go," he ordered, giving her a little push to get her moving.

"Come with me. Please," she begged.

"I can't. I'll catch up with you soon. Now go!"

Noelle obeyed, moving with stiff, fearful steps. She unlocked the truck, slid inside and with one last look at David, started the engine and drove away.

David closed the door and prepared for battle.

Noelle kept the lights off as she steered the Bronco down the gravel driveway. In the rearview mirror, she could see dark shapes moving in the trees. Toward David.

There were too many of them. He'd never be able to fight them all off, no matter how good he was. It took only one lucky shot to kill a man.

Behind her, gunshots blasted away the silence.

Noelle hit the brakes and skidded to a halt. She couldn't do this. She couldn't leave him behind to die.

With a harsh wrenching of the steering wheel, Noelle spun the Bronco around and sped back toward David.

Half a dozen armed men pointed weapons at the back door of the house. They were hard to see in the dark, but Noelle had spent the past several hours in near darkness and her eyes were well adjusted. As she watched, they fired at David's location and he must have been firing back because one of them crumpled to the ground.

The others moved in carefully, taking turns firing so that David had to stay hidden or risk getting hit.

No way was Noelle going to let them sneak up on him like that. David had done so much for her and she wasn't about to repay him by running away and leaving him to die, no matter how much he claimed that was what he wanted. To hell with the ciphertext. His life was just as important as hers.

Dark shapes closed in on the house, creeping slowly, staying low to the ground. It was easy to forget they were men and see them as the monsters they were—monsters who wanted her and David both dead.

The rational part of her mind told her that killing was wrong, but the emotional part of her screamed for her to help David no matter what it took. If she didn't do something, he wasn't going to make it out of that house alive.

Before she could overthink the situation, Noelle gunned the Bronco's engine, and veered off the gravel, heading straight toward the closest enemy. He had his back to her, and with the headlights out and guns barking all around, he didn't notice her coming. The Bronco hit the man head-on with a sickening thud, tossing his body into the weeds like a rag doll.

Two other men turned and fired at the bulletproof Bronco. One of the headlights shattered and a spiderweb of cracks appeared in the side window, but it stayed in place.

The speeding vehicle was enough of a diversion that David managed to take out another three men in the time it took for the Swarm to figure out what was going on.

One by one, David took out the enemy until dead bodies littered the moonlit landscape.

Noelle clenched her teeth against the need to vomit. She'd never done anything violent in her life, and she was afraid that if she stopped to think about what she'd just done—about what she'd just seen—she'd completely lose it. She promised herself that later, she'd let herself be as hysterical as she wanted, but right now was not the time.

David still needed her.

The remaining gunman saw what had happened to his buddies and sprinted for the trees. Before he was able to slip behind cover, his body jerked and blood sprayed out like a geyser from the back of his head. He fell, twitched once, and didn't move again.

Noelle drove the car right up to the back door of the house and flung the driver's door open wide for David. He came out, not looking at her, but at their surroundings, searching the area for more bad guys.

"You drive," he said, and his tone was so flat and empty that she knew he was pissed at her for coming back.

She didn't care. She'd made the right choice and he could be as mad at her as he liked so long as he got in the damn car.

As soon as he got in, she turned the Bronco around and headed back down the lane.

"Stop here," he ordered.

Noelle did and watched as David got out and went to the man she'd run over.

Noelle swallowed hard, pretending that this was all just a bad dream. She never really killed anyone and in a few seconds, she'd wake up, wash her face and clear away all the blood and death from her dreams.

David approached the downed man carefully, keeping his gun aimed at his head. When he was close enough, he kicked the man's weapon away and bent down for a moment. She didn't know if he was checking for a pulse or maybe pulling off his mask to get a look at his face, but when he stood back up, he fired three rounds into the man's skull.

Noelle jerked three times, letting out a series of frightened yelps.

She couldn't fool herself any longer. This was more than just a dream. These men were all dead and she'd helped them get that way. She'd killed.

Frantically, she clawed open the door and vomited onto the ground.

By the time she was done, David was already back in the car and handing her a bottle of water. She took it with shaking hands.

Noelle rinsed the taste of acid from her mouth and trampled down every single thought that passed through her head. She could not deal with any of this right now without getting sick again, and they needed to get out of here. So, rather than dwelling on the horror surrounding her, she focused on driving. Just driving.

Owen's nose twitched against the stench of burning coffee. He turned the burner off and doused the pot under a stream of running water.

All around the little house were signs that his prey had been here. Empty bowls sat in the sink, a rumpled blanket was still on the couch. The back door of the house had been left wide open, making it easy for him to get inside without even using the code his contact had given him.

In the basement, he found the recordings of what had happened here less than an hour earlier, captured by the security cameras installed around the property. He watched, amused by the brave little display put on by Dr. Blanche. She was a more formidable woman than he could have hoped for. Lovely.

But it wasn't the woman who had surprised him the most. That honor belonged to Captain David Wolfe, who after two long years had suddenly reappeared out of nowhere. That's why he'd seemed so familiar earlier. They'd known each other for a long time. Even shared a woman once. That kind of connection could not be easily forgotten.

At the memory, the skin on the man's face stretched in a smile, making the scars on his cheek pull tight. If there was one man on the face of the planet worthy of his undivided attention, it was Captain Wolfe, and here he was, protecting Dr. Blanche.

Two birds with one stone.

God was truly smiling on Owen.

David spent as much time watching Noelle as he did watching their back trail. She'd shut down completely, following his directions automatically without saying a word. If she'd been crying and hysterical, he would have felt better, but her silence worried him. It was a sign she was close to breaking.

He still couldn't believe she'd come back for him. Couldn't believe she'd run over a man to protect him. He knew how she felt about violence, but yet she'd had the courage to put that ideal aside and risk her own life to save him. Of course, that courage could have gotten her killed and he couldn't let that happen again. Her life was too important.

And he'd nearly let her throw it away. For him.

Maybe Monroe was wrong and David wasn't the right man for the job. Maybe his two years away had made him slow, soft. Maybe his grief over Mary's death had made him weak. What if his best wasn't good enough and the Swarm killed Noelle, or worse yet, abducted her? He'd never be able to survive under the weight of that guilt. Never.

For the space of ten seconds, David thought about calling it quits. Let someone else protect Noelle—someone who was better than he. Stronger. Faster. Smarter. There were a dozen men like that in Delta.

But if he quit, he'd never be sure that the Swarm was taken out. There would still be a chance that they were out there, hurting people. Killing innocents. David couldn't walk away from that. He owed Mary's memory more than cowardice, and that's exactly what it would be if he walked away from Noelle. He wasn't afraid of dying, but he was terrified of failing. This op was his only chance to take out the group that had killed his Mary, and he could not pass it by.

Which meant he had to take care of Noelle. Keep her safe and make sure she never again risked her life for his.

David told her to pull into a deserted rest stop, which she did without question. When the Bronco came to a halt, she just sat there, waiting for the next set of directions.

He reached over and slid the gearshift into park, then debated what to do next.

He wanted to scream at her for disobeying his orders. He wanted to thank her for saving him. But most of all, he just wanted to hold her. The urge was too strong to resist any longer, so he stopped trying.

David unfastened her seat belt and pulled her unresisting body into his lap. His wide hands stroked up and down her arms, trying to calm her.

She sat still, a frozen lead statue in his lap, not moving or talking. She'd been traumatized and he was pretty sure he knew why.

She'd been willing to die to prevent her work from being used as a weapon, but tonight, she'd experienced firsthand what it was like to be forced to do violence. He doubted that anything in that brilliant mind of hers was equipped to handle it.

"Noelle, you didn't kill him," David said in a quiet voice.

Noelle jumped, her whole body going rigid. "Yes. I did."

"No. He was just stunned. Bruised, maybe a couple of broken bones, but he would have lived."

"I meant to kill him, which is worse than if I'd done it by accident. The sick part is that if I had to do it all again, I'd do the exact same thing. I'd kill that bastard before he could kill you. So much for all those years of listening to my parents tell me how important it was that my work never be used to harm others."

He cupped her chin and turned her head so that she was looking at him. He needed her to see the truth, so he waited until she was looking into his eyes. "You didn't kill him. I did. His death is my responsibility. His blood is on my hands."

"You wouldn't have had to kill any of them if it weren't for me."

"This isn't your fault. The Swarm were the ones who decided to start killing people in order to break that code. That decision had nothing to do with you. You just got caught in the middle."

Noelle leaned against David's body, tucking her head under his chin. She felt so right there, curled up against him. It took all his willpower to remember that she was only in his lap because she needed comfort—and only comfort.

"Is it over now?" she asked. "They're all dead, aren't they?"

He was quiet for a long time and could feel the subtle increase in her tension that told him she realized the truth. It wasn't over yet.

"I don't think there are any more men following us," he said. "But we have to be careful. The Swarm wants that code broken and they won't stop until it is."

"I don't think I can take any more of this." Her voice broke on a sob, but she held back her tears. Part of him wished she would let go and release all that guilt and fear. She'd cry, fall asleep exhausted and wake up feeling better.

David really wanted her to feel better.

"You're upset. You have a right to be, but you can't let that get in the way of moving forward. You still have a job to do and so do I."

"So, what now? Another safe house?"

"No. I have a better idea."

"You know a place where the Swarm can't find us?"

He shook his head, making his chin graze over her hair. The stubble on his chin caught her curls, tying them together. "No matter where we go, they'll find us eventually, but I know a place they aren't likely to look."

"Why not?"

"Because it doesn't exist."

CHAPTER ELEVEN

—◦❖◦—

Noelle only wished it didn't exist. She eyed the cabin as David pulled the Bronco up near the weathered front door. Rustic would have been a kind euphemism for this place. As it was, the cabin was more . . . primitive than she would have hoped for.

"What is this place?" she asked, hoping that the sound of good-Lord-please-don't-make-me-sleep-here didn't come through in her voice.

They'd been on the road for hours and David's mouth was bracketed by weary lines, but he still managed a small grin. "It's a hunting cabin owned by a friend of mine. He won't mind if we use it."

Noelle stared at the one-room cabin and detached outhouse with mistrust. She was sure there had to be things living in there. Things with more legs than she had, which didn't make good roommates.

David had been watching her and stifled a chuckle at the look on her face. She noticed his amusement but said nothing. The poor man had been going for hours and his weariness was beginning to show on his face. He needed to rest, and if this was where he could do that, she'd accept it. And sleep in the car.

"I'll clean it up a bit," he promised. "Once I get the generator going you'll see that it's not so bad."

Noelle pulled in a breath for courage and stepped up onto the porch. "I'd rather be here than dead. I'll give it that."

David grunted his agreement.

"I don't mean to sound ungrateful or anything," said Noelle. "But why this place?"

David started to unload the Bronco. "This is Caleb's secret hunting cabin, and I'm sure he won't mind if I use it."

"Who's Caleb?"

David's expression went blank as he shut down against her question. "A friend of mine. We went through basic training together."

Noelle wanted to pull the man back out from under the mask. She'd been given a glimpse of the real man when he'd told her about his wife's death. That man was loving and passionate and buried under a mountain of grief and pain and guilt. She wanted to do something to give him back his spirit, though she had no idea how to go about doing something like that. "Are you still friends?"

"Yeah, but I haven't seen him for two years." His tone was curt, his words clipped.

"Then how do you know he won't mind if we barge in here?"

He stared at her with a cold blue gaze for a moment before some of that ice melted. One corner of his well-defined mouth lifted in a wry grin. "Because if there's one thing Caleb can't stand, it's turning his back on a woman in trouble. The man has a soft spot a mile wide when it comes to the fairer sex. It's gotten him into some tight spots, but he can't seem to help himself. It's a sickness."

"So because I'm a woman in need of a place to hide, he wouldn't care that we're taking over his cabin without his knowledge?"

"Hell, Caleb would hand over the deed to the property if he thought you needed it. That's just his way."

Noelle smiled in response to the amusement in David's tone. "Sounds like a great guy."

"He is. I miss him."

There was so much aching emotion stuffed into those little words that it made Noelle's heart clench in protest against the pain she heard in his voice. "Where is he?"

David shook his dark head. "I have no idea. He and Grant, another buddy of ours, were inseparable for years. When I left the service, they went on working together without me. I hope they're still alive. Both of them are good men."

Noelle longed to reach out and touch him, but she didn't dare. His body seemed to be coiled too tightly, like the slightest pressure would make him explode. "Maybe when all of this is over, you can see them again."

David shrugged, the motion saying he didn't care, but the look of longing in his eyes gave the truth away. "Maybe."

Noelle hated seeing that pain of loss on his face, so she tried to change the subject back to that which had made him smile. "So, other than the fact that Caleb is a sucker for a woman in trouble, I can't see that there's a lot to rec- ommend this place."

"Ah, but that's the beauty of it. Caleb built this place with his own two hands and a little help from Grant and me. There was never any record of building permits or any traces that this cabin even exists. No address, no phone, no utilities. It's the perfect hiding place, if you don't mind roughing it a bit."

"I suppose I won't mind, then. I mean, being safe is more important than having a hot shower, right?"

David nodded slowly. "Or an indoor toilet."

Noelle cringed. No toilet was definitely much worse than no hot shower. Still, she wasn't stupid enough to turn down a place that provided safety, even if it wasn't going to be fun living here.

With David.

She was going to be alone with him here. No one knew where they were. It should have scared her, but instead the thought gave her a little thrill. "I promise I won't complain as long as you promise to remove any creepy-crawly things. I can deal with being hunted and having no hot water, but I refuse to share space with spiders."

"Deal," he said with a crooked grin as he hefted several bags of supplies toward the cabin. Muscles along his spine bunched with strength and Noelle couldn't help but stare. Every feminine part she had was acutely aware of David. She knew he was still in love with his wife, but that didn't stop her from wanting to know what it would feel like to be held by him. To be kissed and have her naked skin touched by those long, strong fingers.

Just the thought was enough to make her hands sweat and her heart speed. On an intellectual level, it was an intriguing physical reaction, but she wasn't really paying attention to that part. For the first time in her life, she was feeling the instinctive tug of a man who would certainly be a formidable lover.

He was watching her with narrowed eyes and she prayed he couldn't read her thoughts as they crossed her face. She felt like a teenager with her first crush, insecure and worried that the feelings would not be reciprocated. It was best if she kept her feelings hidden and saved herself the inevitable pain of rejection.

"You should probably stay out here until I convince the eight-legged natives to relocate," he suggested.

"Good idea," she said with a suppressed shiver. She told herself it was the thought of spiders that had her shivering and not David's scrutinizing gaze.

"As soon as I get the generator going, you can fire up your laptop and get to work on the code. That envelope should still be in your pocket with the satellite phone."

Noelle dug in her pocket and pulled out the phone and the envelope. She set the phone on the Bronco's hood and carefully opened the envelope.

"Maybe that will get your mind off having to use an outhouse," said David.

Noelle smoothed the wrinkled paper flat over her thigh. It was the ciphertext Monroe had shown her.

Noelle studied the page, and felt her heart give a kick of excitement. "I didn't think I was ever going to get another chance to see this."

"Guess you were wrong. I hope it's worth that shine of excitement I see in your face. I'd hate to let you down."

"I doubt I'll be disappointed. There's something truly magnificent here. I just don't know what it is yet." She took the page and wandered over to the weathered wooden stairs leading up to the porch. "I tend to zone out when I work. Ten minutes from now, I won't even remember what state we're in, much less our living conditions."

Already she could feel the lure of the puzzle at her brain, and she welcomed the distraction wholeheartedly. "This script is beautiful."

She hadn't moved in two hours.

David had managed to get the generator running, cleaned up the cabin so that it was livable, carried in all the supplies and thrown together a dinner of salad and turkey sandwiches.

The surrounding forest got dark fast when the sun started to set and by the way Noelle was squinting as she sat on the porch, the lack of light was starting to prove a problem for her.

"Why don't you come inside now," he said in a quiet voice so he wouldn't startle her.

She blinked and looked at him like she hadn't even remembered he was here. She wasn't joking about zoning out when she worked.

She took off her glasses to rub her eyes and massaged the back of her neck with one hand. "What time is it?"

"Dinnertime. Come eat."

"In a minute," she said as her gaze was drawn back to the page and whatever meaning she saw in what was gobbledygook to the rest of humanity.

David pulled the page from her hand, being careful not to tear it. "Oh, no you don't. It's time to eat. You can have this back after dinner."

She sighed but rose stiffly to her feet and followed him inside, stretching with a sinuous arch of her back.

David averted his eyes, refusing to stare. The innocent

motion curved her body into an intriguing arc that reminded him of a woman's sexual release and left his mouth dry with lust.

As she entered the cabin for the first time, her dark green eyes roamed the single room, though because of the deep shadows inside, he couldn't see her expression clearly enough to tell if she was disgusted or merely curious.

"It's not nearly as bad as I imagined," she said.

David felt some of his tension leave him as she made that statement. Until now, he hadn't realized just how worried he was that she wouldn't find this place bearable. Knowing that she did, he put thoughts of relocating out of his head for now. Sooner or later, they'd have to leave and he had a stock of alternate plans for when that time came, but for now, this was his best option for her protection.

He set a small kerosene lantern on the table. It was a tiny surface, no more than eighteen inches on each side, with three unpadded wooden stools for seating. The table was scarred from heavy use, and David could remember playing cards on it with his buddies before the cabin had even been finished. They'd sat outside, completely comfortable in the rustic surroundings with just each other for company. Man, he missed those guys.

The entire cabin was only twelve feet by fifteen feet, with a kitchen at one end and an open area at the other for sleeping and everything else. The place was heated with an old potbellied stove that was also used for cooking. Caleb had dug a water well on the property, and the gas generator ran a pump that brought water to the surface, filling a pressurized tank so there was at least a little water available through the kitchen faucet even if the generator was turned off. There was no lighting beyond what one small window in the door could offer during the day. At night, they'd have to use candles or lanterns.

The stock of firewood would last for a couple days, but David was going to have to cut more soon. If he knew Caleb, there was probably another pile of wood nearby that was already chopped and aging. David would make sure to replace whatever they used.

Noelle washed her hands at the deep kitchen sink, using a bar of soap they'd brought along with them. She hissed as she turned off the water and searched for a towel. "Man that's cold."

David nodded, handing her a new towel. All the towels he'd found in the drawers had been the recent home of little mouse families and he doubted that Noelle would enjoy using them. They'd worked great for starting the fire that now blazed inside the old black stove, though.

"It's well water, which is runoff from melted snow higher up in the mountains. Even in the summer it'll turn your fingers blue."

"I don't suppose that means I'll be getting any hot baths anytime soon, either, huh?"

The look on her face was so forlorn that David had to struggle not to laugh. She was so cute wearing his jacket, her red curls a complete mess, her full mouth turned down in a little pout.

"We can heat water on the stove for washing, but unless you want to curl up in the sink for a bath, that's as good as it's going to get, I'm afraid."

Noelle sighed. "It still beats that damn safe house."

They sat down to eat. Or at least David ate. Noelle stared at her plate as if it held the meaning of life.

"You're working, aren't you?" he asked.

Noelle jumped and looked at him with wide eyes like she'd just noticed he was there.

For some reason, it bothered him that she could forget his presence so easily. 'Cause Lord knew he couldn't forget hers. Every time he walked past her sitting on those steps, he couldn't help but stare. The sun had filtered down through the few leaves left on the trees, burnishing her hair into a blaze of deep copper. What he wouldn't have given to run his fingers through those curls, letting his hands get tangled against her scalp until he had a good, firm hold on her head, so he could kiss her just like he wanted, deep and hard, without a chance of her getting away before he was done.

It would have taken him a full hour to get his fill of her mouth. Her lips were so pink and smooth. He could just imagine how they'd feel against his mouth or roaming over his throat, chest, abdomen. Lower.

David's fork bent under the force of his grip and he had to pull in a controlled breath before he could relax his hand enough to set it down.

She looked at him with concern shining in her gaze and reached out a slender hand toward his face. "You okay?"

David didn't move. He could barely breathe under the weight of his lust, which tightened his groin and made his stomach cramp with need.

God, it had been so long since he'd had sex. He hadn't even so much as touched himself since Mary died, either. It just didn't seem worth it to feel any sort of joy, even the fleeting pleasure of shallow self-fulfillment. When he'd disconnected from the world, he'd disconnected from his humanity as well. He survived. Nothing more.

Her hand brushed his cheek, resting on the dark stubble that he hadn't bothered to shave. Her fingers were cold from washing and he could feel the imprint of each soft pad of flesh at her fingertips.

David couldn't help but reach up and cover her hand. Before she'd come along, he'd been so long without contact that he feared her pulling away—feared that it might be another two years or more before someone else had the courage to touch him like she did. He was too rough, too harsh to deserve anything resembling kindness.

Because the table was so small, her head was close to his and he could smell the faint scent of her shampoo mingling with the woodsmoke that wafted through the cabin. He could see a light dusting of freckles across her nose, an imperfection that only served to enhance the beauty of her pale skin.

He wanted to reach across the table and pull her close for a kiss that would eventually lead them across the room to where the sleeping bags lay. He wanted to taste her, to show her with his mouth and tongue what he intended to do to the rest of her body. He wanted to consume her, possess her, take her until she had forgotten every lover she'd ever had. He wanted her to be his. Completely.

The need clawed at his insides, screaming at him to pounce on her. He would woo her with his hands and mouth until he had her pleading for more. Only then, when she was on the ragged edge of sanity, wanting him as much as he wanted her, would he fill her and quench the need inside him.

But he couldn't do any of that to her. They had no life together. No future. She was already a hunted woman. If the Swarm found out that she was David's woman. . . .

He couldn't even bear to consider what would happen to her. If he wasn't careful, Noelle could end up just like Mary. Without even trying, David could still see Mary vivid in his memories, her lifeless, mangled body tied to that chair, sitting in a pool of her own blood.

"I'm fine," he snapped and pulled away in an uncharacteristically jerky motion. He went to tend the fire in an effort to put some distance between them. His body ached with painful arousal, but he welcomed the pain. It was something he could focus on, something he knew how to handle.

Noelle just stared at David's back as he added wood to the stove. He'd stripped down to just his T-shirt and jeans, and she could see under the dark fabric how every muscle shifted in perfect union as he moved. His wide shoulders blocked out the light from the fire, but she could feel the heat against her face.

Or maybe that was just her embarrassment warming her skin.

He had been about to kiss her. She was sure of it. Noelle wasn't the Queen of Dating, but she knew that look. He'd wanted her, and she'd wanted him in return. Man, had she wanted him to kiss her.

Her heart was still pounding with excitement, her skin tingling where his hand had covered hers. Under all those layers of clothes, her nipples had tightened and her stomach had filled with butterflies made out of Pop Rocks.

She'd never felt that way with Stanley. Not even close.

Her relationship with Stanley had been a way for her to

lose her virginity at the ripe old age of twenty-two. She'd cared about him. She never would have slept with him if she hadn't. She had even loved hanging around with him at first. But then their academic careers went separate ways, and so did they. It wasn't ugly or spiteful. It wasn't anything. It just happened, tepid and uneventful. That was kinda the theme of their whole relationship.

Nothing about the way David looked at her was tepid. She'd seen the heat in his eyes, melting that arctic blue into a scalding-hot sea. She wouldn't have minded drowning for a while, just to see what it was like.

But before she'd found the courage to let go of her inhibitions, he'd frozen over again, leaving her feeling cold and bereft.

Noelle had no idea what she'd done to put David off, but it was obvious that something had happened. Something had crossed his mind that had turned him from steaming hunk into frozen man-sicle.

And then she remembered his late wife.

How could she have been so insensitive? The poor man was still grieving for Mary, and showing Noelle those horrible pictures of his wife's death followed by a nice conversation about what a wonderful woman she'd been could not have made the grieving process any easier. David had disinterred memories that she was sure he would have preferred to leave buried if not forgotten.

He was just crouched there on the floor, motionless, staring into the fire. Noelle ached to go to him and offer comfort, friendship, but she couldn't imagine him wanting anything from her. She wasn't his wife, she wasn't even his friend. She was nothing more to him than a job. When the job was over, she'd probably never see him again.

The fact that that eventuality bothered her so much was not something that Noelle cared to dwell upon.

She looked at David's tense back, wishing she knew how to comfort him. As it was, all she could offer him was the privacy of her silence so he could focus on himself rather than her. She wasn't willing to give up trying to pull him out of his self-imposed mental isolation, but she knew that she could only push so far. Whatever she'd said or done had obviously broken open old wounds, and she was willing, if not happy, to let him lick them in peace.

"You should try to get some rest," she said. "You look like you could use it."

His ribs expanded with a deep sigh and he scrubbed a hand over his shadowed jaw. "Yeah. I'm up to about sixty hours of sleep dep now. I think it's finally safe enough to crash for a while." His tone was still sharp but heavy with weariness.

He pulled a matte black gun from the small of his back, checked it with quick, sure motions and placed it on the table beside Noelle's plate.

"Keep this near you at all times," he told her.

She gave him a resigned nod and pushed the gun and David both from her mind with an effort of will. She was here to do a job, and that was exactly what she was going to do.

CHAPTER TWELVE

David's internal clock told him it was just after 0200 when he woke from a much-needed nap. Only sheer exhaustion had allowed him to sleep uninterrupted for a whole four hours—more than he'd had at one time since finding out about Noelle and her need for protection against the Swarm. But rather than leaving him feeling refreshed, the sleep had left him achy, edgy and unsatisfied. Or maybe that was just the way he would have felt anyway, sleep or not.

Of course, the erotic dreams he'd had of Noelle hadn't done a lot of good toward easing his frustration. It was amazing that even though he'd never seen her nude, or even close to it, his mind still managed to fill in all the interesting little details of her naked body. In his dreams, she had the smoothest, pale skin and coral pink nipples that tightened eagerly against his tongue. Her thighs were slim, but strong, and when they wrapped around his hips, they pulled him close so that every aching inch of his erection was buried inside her sweet body. She'd moaned as he'd taken her, slow and deep, in a lazy rhythm that lured them both close to the edge of climax without pushing them over. David was in no hurry to end it, which is why he'd woken up before his body had found the physical release it so desperately needed.

David kept his eyes closed and focused on breathing, focused on putting a damper on his libido. He was a man, not a boy, and totally in control of his actions, if not his bodily responses. No matter how much he wanted to reach over and pull Noelle under him to finish what his dreams had started, he wouldn't. He couldn't use her that way, even though he thought he'd seen something approaching desire in her eyes over the dinner table.

She deserved better than him—more than what he could offer her. And she was vulnerable right now. Taking advantage of that would be unforgivable. He'd done enough unforgivable things in his life that he didn't need to add to the stack.

The cabin had cooled considerably, and even inside his sleeping bag, he was barely warm enough.

He'd positioned the sleeping bags as far apart as the walls would allow in the little space, putting the top of one toward the foot of the other. It was as lacking in intimacy as possible, given the circumstances, but it wasn't nearly lacking enough that David didn't think about how nice it would be just to zip the two bags together and slide inside with Noelle. Naked.

David gritted his teeth until the ache in his jaw pushed away his unwelcome thoughts.

He glanced over at Noelle's sleeping bag to see if she seemed warm enough.

Not only was she not there, sleeping, but her bag was untouched. She was still sitting where he'd left her at the tiny table. She had a pencil in her hand, and was scribbling furiously in a notebook he'd bought for her when they stopped at a megadiscount store for some spare clothing and cleaning supplies.

The light from the lantern cast a yellow glow over her features, setting her hair aflame with warm color. Even though her eyes were shadowed with fatigue and a frown of concentration shaped her brow, she was still beautiful in firelight.

He wondered what she'd look like stretched out naked beneath him with firelight flickering over her body.

Instantly, he was aroused again, thick and hard and ready to put into action his inappropriate thoughts.

David cursed silently, hating that he was at the mercy of his libido whenever he looked at Noelle. It was ridiculous that he couldn't control himself long enough to do his job. But even more, it was humiliating that he was beginning not to care about proprieties and protocol.

He focused on breathing, like he had for his marksmanship trials, until he was able to stand without scandalizing Noelle. Or tearing his jeans.

Not that she'd notice if he'd walked over there stark naked. The woman was nothing if not laser-focused on her work.

He walked quietly over to the potbellied stove, added more logs to the dying embers and put an ancient percolator on for coffee. He wouldn't be sleeping anymore tonight.

Noelle finally looked up and smiled at him. "Hi."

The sweet, inviting curve of her mouth was like a punch in the gut. It had been so long since he'd had a woman greet him in the morning with a soft smile and a friendly word. Such a simple thing and yet her open welcome was so . . . tempting. It made him think of late mornings after long nights spent making love. It made him think of breakfast in bed that never got eaten because other, more carnal hungers took over. It made him think of the simple pleasure of having a home and a woman who loved him to wake up to every morning.

It made him wonder if Noelle longed for those simple things as much as he did.

"Do you know what time it is?" he asked, his voice deep and rough with sleep and longing.

"Not really. Did I wake you?"

"No." She hadn't made a sound beyond that of pencil scratching over paper. If she had, he'd have woken, no matter how tired he'd been, probably with a weapon in his hand.

David eyed the plate of wilted lettuce and the majority of her sandwich sitting next to her. "You didn't eat."

"I will in a minute," she said, waving her pencil.

Frustration rose up like a tidal wave in David's chest. He was sure it was only partly due to her negligent care of herself. The rest was pure lust, as raw and gritty as it got.

David grabbed the pencil and the notebook, and the paper away from her, ignoring the irritated expression of impatience on her face. "Hey! I was using those!"

He slammed her papers down on the butcher block counter and shoved the plate of food back in front of her. "You're done working tonight. You're going to eat, then sleep, and when you wake up, I'll give your stuff back."

Her delicate chin thrust up in the air. "You can't tell me what to do."

"The hell I can't. I'm the one with the gun, remember?" He picked up the sandwich and placed it to her mouth. "Eat."

Noelle rolled her eyes and took a bite. "Fine," she said around a mouthful of dried-out bread. "But when I'm done eating, I'm going back to work. People's lives are at stake, I'll sleep later."

David crossed his arms over his chest and straightened to his full height, giving her his best do-it-or-I'll-make-you stare. "The last thing we need is for you to get delayed because you're too sick to finish the job. Don't be stupid about this." As it was, he wasn't sure he was going to live through resisting his lust for her so much as another day. Delays were entirely out of the question.

She scowled at him. Of course, the whole effect was ruined by the dark circles and drooping shoulders. Whether she admitted it or not, she was tired.

"Can I at least wash up first?" she demanded. "I haven't showered since Friday night." She paused, frowning. "What day is it anyway?"

Lord save him from distracted academics. "Monday, just barely."

Her eyes opened wide and she jumped from her stool. "Oh, no! You have to get me to a phone so I can call in to work. Joan will be worried sick if I'm not there."

"I'm sorry, but she's just going to have to worry, then. We won't be making any calls."

"But I have to." She clutched his arm, those slim fingers curling around his biceps.

David suppressed a shudder of sheer male victory. She'd touched him again and it felt even better this time than it had before. He was quickly becoming addicted.

His body's response was as irritating as it was predictable. He had to get over his jones for this girl and fast. "Listen, if you call Joan, you could be putting her in danger. I'm sure the Swarm had you under surveillance before the attack. It's likely that they know who your friends and family are and have put phone taps on anyone they think you might contact. It's even possible they could somehow trace the call back to us as well. And if not, then they might try to get the information out of Joan through . . . unpleasant means."

"But I wouldn't tell her where we are." Her voice was frantic, pleading.

David steeled himself against the urge to soothe her. She didn't need soothing. She needed the truth so she wouldn't do anything dangerous. "It wouldn't matter if she knew or not. They'd still hurt her. I know you don't want that."

Her hands went limp and fell away from him. His arm burned in fury at the loss of her touch. David clenched his teeth and held his ground.

She nodded, bowing her head, but not before David saw a single tear glitter behind her glasses.

It was his undoing. He ordered his dick to shut the hell up and pulled her into his arms. She was stiff and cold, but she didn't pull away. Finally, her arms snaked over his shoulders and she buried her face against his throat.

"I hate this," she whispered. Her warm breath flooded over his skin, making him shiver.

He was on the razor edge of offering comfort and taking more, but he held his balance. "I know. But it will all be over soon." He prayed it wasn't too much of a lie.

She looked up at him, her eyes bright with tears, her nose pink. "And then what? I know I can't go back to my old life. As you pointed out, this will only happen again the next time someone finds a bit of ciphertext like this one. All I know how to do is what I've learned in school, which is entirely unique, and any job I could get would be like a red flag, even if I changed my name and identity." She pulled in a resigned breath, which pressed her small breasts against David's ribs in a delightful, distracting caress. "I'll never again get to work in academics, will I?"

He wasn't going to start lying to her now, but he did try to soften the blow with a quiet, understanding tone. "If you want to continue doing the same work you have been doing, the only safe option you'll have is to work for the government, probably in a secure facility under their protection."

"I can't do that. After this one job, I'm never going to work for them again."

"The military isn't all that bad, Noelle."

Noelle shook her head, making the tangled curls sway over the back of David's hands. He had to grip her waist hard to keep from grabbing those curls and plundering her mouth, but her soft curves gave way to his fingers, making his resistance a new kind of hell. "It may be a necessary evil, but I have to stand by my conscience. I have a responsibility to ensure that no harm comes from the things I create, and I just don't trust the military to share that responsibility with me."

It stung that she shunned everything that David had spent his life doing. She wasn't the only one who shared the opinion that the military was evil, but public opinion had never really bothered David before. He'd done what *he* thought was right. End of story.

Even when it meant walking away from everything he'd worked for because he knew he was no longer going to be able to lead his team safely. His emotions made him a liability.

His voice was a little more curt than he intended. "That group you don't trust is going to a hell of a lot of trouble to keep you alive."

She pulled away and stared up at him. "Only because I have something they want. Monroe was willing to have me executed if I didn't cooperate. That isn't exactly a friendly organization."

"We're not designed to be friendly. We're designed to get the job done, no matter how unpleasant it may be."

"I'll do this one job, but after that, I'm done. If I did anything else, I wouldn't be able to sleep at night."

David grunted. "And I can't sleep at night knowing there was something more I could be doing to help protect the lives of innocents."

"As long as you get to choose whose lives get protected and whose don't."

David felt his lip lift in a near snarl. "I didn't choose for my wife to die. The Swarm did that. Don't stand there and act all sanctimonious when you don't know what the hell you're talking about."

A wave of guilt spread over her features. "I'm sorry, David. I can't imagine what it must be like for you to lose the woman you love."

David's eyes slid shut and he willed himself to hold his emotions under tight rein. He couldn't afford to lose it right now, no matter how much he grieved for his Mary. "I know you're not happy about this situation, but I need you to cooperate and get this code broken as fast as you can. Whether or not you agree with the military's strategies for dealing with the bad things out there, you're part of that strategy now."

"I know, and I will do the best I know how, just don't expect this one job to become the beginning of anything more. After this is done, I'm walking away. I won't ever work for you guys again."

"Don't make any decisions about that now. You'll have plenty of time later to decide what you want to do when there aren't people trying to kill you."

"That's just my point. As long as I'm still able to be an asset to any covert group—be they the U.S. government or otherwise—there will always be someone out to use me as a weapon. Or kill me. I'll never be free again."

She was right. David just wished she hadn't been smart enough to figure it out so soon.

"Listen," said David, forcing his voice to quiet to a soothing tone. "It's after two in the morning. Get some sleep and I promise things will look better when you're not so tired. Maybe not great, but better."

She turned away and went back to her work. Her movements were stiff with fatigue, but sharp with determination. "I'll sleep when this is over."

CHAPTER THIRTEEN

The next morning, a buzzing, flashing light brought Noelle out of her state of concentration. She'd been losing her ability to focus anyway, due to her increasingly massive fatigue. As good as she was at missing sleep and still functioning, she was really starting to feel the effects of this stressful situation. If she didn't take a break soon, she was going to start pounding her head against the drafty cabin wall.

Noelle rubbed her eyes and stood to see what was making all that noise. David's phone sat on top of his zipped duffel bag, blinking and vibrating impatiently.

Noelle didn't dare answer it, and a quick scan of the cabin told her he was nowhere around. She picked up the phone, hooked it on her waistband and went out in search of him.

She had no idea if the call was important or not, but she didn't want to take any chances that he'd need to talk to whoever was on the other end right away. She just hoped the phone had voice mail, because she wasn't going to answer it and take the chance the call would give away their location.

The air outside the cabin was nippy but smelled clean.

After being inside the cramped space for so long, it was nice to have the bright, open sky over her head rather than heavy wooden beams. Her coat kept out the worst of the cold, but she shoved her hands deep into her pockets to keep her fingers warm.

With a little rush of embarrassment, Noelle knocked on the door of the outhouse, hoping she wasn't interrupting anything important.

He didn't respond, a fact for which she was immensely grateful.

A light dusting of snow covered the ground and Noelle could see David's big boot prints etched plainly into the snow. She followed the path, which headed into the trees growing on the slope leading down the mountain. About fifty yards along, the footprints vanished along with the snow.

Noelle stood there, looking around for any sign as to which way he'd gone. She found none.

Rather than wander around in the trees and get lost, she cupped her hands around her mouth and shouted for him.

On the third shout, he appeared silently out of the trees, panic sharpening his features. He pushed her to the ground, his hand covering her mouth, his body pressing hers flat against the cold earth.

"We're not alone," he whispered against her ear. "I just hope they didn't hear you yelling."

Fear lanced through her and she went stiff beneath him. She tugged at his hand, which he moved so she could whisper. "The Swarm?"

David shook his head while staring at her mouth. He stared for a long time, her question apparently forgotten. Just when she was sure he was about to kiss her, he rolled off her and braced his weight on his elbows. His shoulders were hunched and his voice was clipped and harsh. "Hunters, but I'm not taking any chances. I've been watching them all morning."

Lying on the ground without David's warmth protecting her left her feeling cold and vulnerable. When she tried to sit up, David said, "Stay down. They're just down in the next valley."

She rolled to her belly and propped herself up on her elbows, mimicking David's position. "What are they doing?"

David pulled out a pair of binoculars and peered down into the valley. "Drinking beer, mostly. It doesn't look like they heard you."

"Isn't it a little early for beer?" asked Noelle.

David shrugged. "Guess not for them. They've been out here since daybreak."

"Why would the Swarm sit around drinking beer when our cabin is less than a mile away?"

"I don't think they would, but even if they are just hunters, if they stumble across the cabin, it's going to cause problems. Caleb's cabin isn't supposed to exist, at least not on public records. If these fools mention that we're staying up here to someone back in town, we'll have to leave."

"Can't we just go somewhere else?"

David shook his head. "This place is about as safe as it's going to get unless you want to keep moving around. I didn't think you'd be able to get as much work done that way."

Just the thought of trying to work in a moving car made her stomach queasy. "So what do we do?"

"I'll keep watching them and make sure they don't get any closer."

"And if they do?"

He gave her a sinister little smile. "I'll convince them this is a bad way to go."

"What are you going to do? Set out bear traps or something?"

"Or something. Right now, I need you to go back to the cabin, where you'll be safe. I'll handle things out here."

Noelle didn't really want to go back to the cabin alone. She knew she should be brave and tough and force herself to go back to work, but she was tired and worried. She was feeling particularly vulnerable with those men down in the valley below, though she didn't want to admit anything of the sort. David had enough to worry about without having the added worry of her feelings. She was a big girl and could take care of herself, at least under normal circumstances. Unfortunately, these were far from normal, and she really needed to be close to someone she trusted.

David.

"I'd rather stay. The work isn't going too well and I needed a break to clear my head."

"I'll take you for a walk later. Right now I really need you out of harm's way. Even if those men are just hunters, they're still drinking and carrying weapons. It's not a good combination." He gripped her shoulder, feeling her through her coat. "And you forgot to wear your vest." He said that last part with a paternal frown better suited to a naughty child than a full-grown woman.

Noelle didn't like it a bit and she fought off the need to get defensive with him. He was right. She never should have left without wearing her Kevlar vest. She'd have to get used to it if she wanted to live. "I was in a hurry," she said, remembering why she'd come out here to begin with. "The phone was ringing." She dug under her coat and pulled it from her belt.

David took the phone, his look grim. "Did they just call once?"

Noelle nodded. "I think so. I mean, I was working, but it did distract me."

"Hell of a phone," he muttered as he turned it off.

"Aren't you going to call and get a message or something?"

"No." He didn't elaborate.

"What if someone's trying to get in touch with us? What if it's urgent?"

"Look," he said in a frighteningly even tone. "Someone at that safe house leaked your location. That's what caused the attack. I'm not about to trust anyone until I know who that leak was."

Noelle couldn't suppress a little shiver of fear as it raced up her spine. "You don't have any backup?"

He looked away, but not before she could see the frustration lining his face. "I'll do fine without it. You should go."

Suddenly, it no longer mattered if he thought she was a coward. As long as he let her stay, he could think whatever he wanted. "Do you mind if I stay a while? I could, you know, be your backup."

His features softened and he looked like he was about to smile over her offer. "Just exactly how much do you know about covert surveillance?"

"I know that I can't do it from inside that cabin." Just

thinking about going back to the dingy little room again was enough to make it hard to breathe. The weight of her situation was bearing down upon her, wearing her thin. She wasn't making much progress with the code. She needed a break—to be out in the open for a little while, breathing fresh air.

He looked like he was about to refuse, but after searching her face, he gave in.

"Just stay low and quiet."

Noelle grinned, feeling momentarily free of her burdens. She scooted a little closer to David in an effort to stay warm. "I promise."

David glanced at Noelle, expecting her to be staring off into space, working on something only she could see. Instead, he found that she'd fallen asleep. She hadn't even been out here ten minutes.

So much for backup, David thought with an indulgent grin.

She'd curled up on her side in an effort to stay warm and David covered her with a thin survival blanket he pulled from his pack.

As it always was whenever he looked at her while she slept, David felt something shift in his chest—become more comfortable and somehow tighter at the same time. She looked so trusting and it tugged at every one of his protective instincts whenever he glanced her way. He was the only thing standing between her and death, and yet she trusted him enough that she just dozed off with armed men in the next valley.

It had been a long time since anyone had trusted him like that. He was humbled, willing to do anything to prove he was worthy of her trust. He couldn't fail her.

Noelle's red hair blended in perfectly among the fallen leaves, her gold-rimmed glasses glinting like the clusters of snowflakes still clinging to branches here and there. Her cheeks were flushed pink and her lips were parted, breathing silvery plumes of warmth into the air. Man, what he wouldn't give to be here with her for the sheer enjoyment of it. He'd never made love on a cold forest floor before. He'd had enough sleeping on frozen ground during his career for him ever to choose that over a nice, warm bed. But right now, David couldn't think of a better place to get naked with a woman than right here.

He'd keep her warm with his body and heat from the passion he'd light deep inside her. He'd love her so good she'd forget all about the cold air and scattered leaves.

He'd make it so good she'd forget she was a hunted woman.

David slipped her glasses from her nose to pocket them for safekeeping. His fingers grazed along her cheek and he closed his eyes against the smooth satin of her skin brushing against his knuckles. She murmured something low and incoherent and shifted toward his touch.

He pulled away and forced himself to focus on his surroundings. He could no longer lie on his stomach without pain as his erection grew in response to the feel of her skin. Not even the frozen ground was enough to keep his lust at bay.

Forcing his thoughts back to the men below, David peered through the binoculars. It appeared as though they were packing their gear to leave, now that the beer had run out.

David watched them leave the way they'd come. He'd scouted earlier and seen a couple beat-up trucks parked along the side of the only road leading up this side of the mountain.

He was glad they weren't camping out for the night. David didn't think he would be able to stand being out here in the cold all night while Noelle stayed alone in the cabin, unprotected. And he certainly couldn't let her stay with him without the benefit of a fire to keep her warm. Without one, she would freeze by morning.

Unless he kept her warm another way.

David spat a caustic curse into the frigid air. He could not keep thinking of her as a woman. He had to think of her as a job, an op, an assignment.

The assignment let out a sleepy sigh of contentment, which felt like a warm hand stroking his body.

Noelle shifted and David had to pull the blanket back up over her shoulders again. He hated waking her now that she'd finally gone to sleep.

David wasn't sure how much longer her body was going to be able to keep this pace before something had to give. She was relentless with herself in pursuit of the solution to the code Monroe had presented. David had seen men with less determination make it through Special Forces training.

If she wasn't careful, she'd push herself too hard and burn out. David was going to make sure that didn't happen. She'd proven that she trusted him and he was going to prove himself deserving of that trust. If he got her out of this mess unscathed, it would go a long way toward convincing himself that he wasn't a total fuck-up.

That would be really nice.

David tucked the blanket further under Noelle's shoulder and settled in for a few more cold hours of guard duty—as many hours as it took for her to regain her strength.

Owen leaned down and plucked the curly red hair from the twig that had snagged it from Noelle's head. He'd spent hours admiring that fiery hair, watching her lying here on the ground next to Captain Wolfe.

He had to give David credit. Even with the distraction of a lovely woman, he'd done a hell of a job keeping Noelle out of reach. It had taken Owen four stolen cars and three gallons of coffee to follow them here undetected. He'd never had to go to so much trouble before to stay hidden.

Owen smiled, causing the horrible burn scars on his cheek to pucker. He loved a challenge.

A less intelligent man than Owen might have already broken into their cozy little cabin while David slept, killed him and taken Noelle. But Owen was smarter than that. He knew the girl would work better while she was with someone she trusted. He was in this for the weapons the ciphertext would locate and the money they would bring on the black market. His boss, Mr. Lark, had been clear that securing the weapons would earn Owen a place of power in the newly restructured organization. If that meant waiting for the girl to finish her work before he abducted her, then that was what he'd do.

Besides, it was fun finding ways to evade David's security measures. The man had taken what the forest could offer and turned these things into deadly weapons meant to kill anyone who dared enter his domain. It had been a long time since Owen tested his skills against a worthy opponent, and the man guarding Noelle was as worthy as they came.

Too bad for him Owen was much better.

CHAPTER FOURTEEN

❖

Noelle cleaned up the mess from dinner, helping for the first time since they arrived at the cabin. So far, David had taken care of everything mundane—the cooking and cleaning—giving her time to work. It was a luxury that she wasn't used to, but wouldn't mind trying to get that way.

Man, he'd make a great husband. Too bad he was still married to a dead woman.

He'd gone out again for about the fifth time, hauling in another armload of wood. One wall of the cabin was completely covered by the results of his chopping efforts and by her quick calculation, there was enough wood there to last them for over a month.

She dried her hands and laid the dish towel out on the counter to dry. "You expecting an early snowstorm or something?" she asked him.

David dusted off his hands, but didn't quite meet her gaze. "No sense in not being prepared. Besides, I had the time. If we don't use the wood, Caleb will."

Noelle had to admit that the idea of being snowbound with him wasn't entirely unappealing. She'd gotten used to the rustic setting and except for missing hot showers and a real toilet, it wasn't a hardship to be here with him.

Part of her even enjoyed it. She was having the first real adventure of her adult life.

Then again, he had been doing all the work. If he'd asked her to hunt or fish with him, she would have had an entirely different story to tell.

The simple fact was, she enjoyed David's company. He was courteous and left her alone to work. He only badgered her when she forgot to eat, which probably wasn't a bad thing. It had been a long time since she'd had someone around who took care of her. It felt . . . comforting to know he was there.

And he was certainly no hardship to look at.

David fed the potbellied stove and Noelle just watched. She loved the way his body moved—the way his muscles slid powerfully under his skin. She repeatedly had to keep herself from reaching out and laying a hand on him to feel the intriguing movement. She told herself that she was an intellectual and wanted to research everything that interested her, but deep down she knew it was more than just interest that urged her to reach out for him. She sensed that he was starved for human contact, that he had isolated himself from the world.

And even if that feeling hadn't been there, David interested her as a man. Too much for her own good.

"If you don't quit staring at me like I'm one of your indecipherable notes, I'm gonna get nervous," he said.

Noelle jerked at the sound of his voice, her face heating in a blush. "I'm sorry. I just keep wondering what it must be like to be so strong. I was always kinda puny for my age."

He stepped forward, his long stride placing him only inches from her. "'Puny' isn't the right word."

Noelle lifted a red brow. "Oh? And just what word would you use, Mr. Muscles?"

His gaze heated as it swept over her body. She was getting used to his repeated surveying of her every time he stepped into the room, but this was different. Warmer. His lids were heavy and his fists were clenched at his sides. "Delicate," he said.

Noelle would have snorted at his ridiculous statement if it hadn't been for his serious expression. He sounded like he meant what he said. Even liked it. "Nice try soothing my ego, but it's really not necessary. I'm proud of myself—what I've done with my life."

"You should be. But you should also be proud of the fact that you're a beautiful woman."

This time, Noelle couldn't help but laugh. She was smart, loyal, dedicated, and stuck to her morals no matter how inconvenient they became, but she was not beautiful. Until she'd met David, she'd never even really cared that she wasn't.

But now, with him looking at her with those hot, blue eyes, his muscles taut, his luscious body only mere inches from hers, she wanted nothing more than to be a temptress. She wanted to drive him to his knees with her beauty. She wanted him to take her in his arms and show her just how beautiful he thought she was using only his tongue. "You're the one who is beautiful. All that strength makes me want to touch you just to see how it feels."

She was so swept away by the mental image that created that she didn't even realize she'd said those words aloud. Until she saw his expression change and become more guarded.

Fire bloomed in her cheeks and she wanted to crawl under a rock until she died of old age.

Her chin dipped and she pulled in a breath to help herself recover from humiliation.

David's fingers lifted her chin, forcing her to look into his eyes. They were nearly black, his cheeks slashed with color, his nostrils flared as if in anger. But it wasn't anger, it was something else. Something she'd never thought to see on his face.

Desire.

He bent down to kiss her, giving her no time to escape. His arm was an iron brace at the small of her back, holding her still. She couldn't pull away. She wasn't sure if she even wanted to.

David kissed her, hard and demanding. His tongue teased her lips, coaxing her to accept him into her mouth. He tasted like the coffee they'd shared after dinner. He smelled like the forest at sunset.

Noelle had kissed before, but never like this. Her experience was lukewarm compared to the fiery passion that now swept through her system.

Her hands slid up his arms, clutching his hard shoulders to steady herself. Her body sang with excitement, making her head spin and her knees weak.

She should have been marveling at the way her body reacted on an intellectual level. She should have been analyzing how hormones triggered her blood to pump faster, her eyes to dilate, her skin to heat to the point of meltdown. But all she could think about was how good his tongue felt sliding over her own, how her nipples had hardened to sensitive points that rubbed against the muscled wall of his chest. Her head was filled with his masculine scent, driving awareness of everything else out of her mind.

For the first time in her life, her brain was turned off and her body turned on.

It was as wonderful as it was frightening.

And then he broke the kiss and she was left alone, clutching at his shirt, panting as if she'd just run a mile uphill.

David looked down at her, his eyes fixed on her parted lips. She could feel how hot and swollen they were from his less-than-gentle kiss. She wondered if his felt the same way.

Noelle lifted a shaking finger to his mouth and just barely touched him, wanting to feel with her hand what her lips had already felt. David jerked at her touch, cursing low and vile.

"This was a mistake," he said.

The cold air filling the cabin swept away any remaining feelings of contentment and wonder Noelle might have had.

A mistake? The best thing she'd ever felt in her life was a mistake? She couldn't draw enough breath to speak, even if she had been courageous enough to refute his claim.

"We can't do this," he said, as if trying to convince himself. "It's wrong."

Noelle found the strength to let go of his shirt and stand on her own two feet. She put a good yard between them before she was able to speak. The distance left her feeling cold and bereft, but not as much as the harsh glint of shame in David's eyes.

She was completely aware of her own sex appeal, or lack thereof. She wasn't about to force a man to kiss her if he didn't want to. She had more self-respect than that.

Still, she couldn't stand the thought of staying in the small space with him for even one more minute. She had to get away and cool off and remember her priorities.

She grabbed her coat on the way out of the cabin. Before shutting the door, she said, "It felt pretty damn right to me."

David couldn't have followed her out of the cabin if he'd wanted. His dick was too hard, making his gut ache and his brain sputter in an effort to function in spite of a blood deficit.

What the hell was wrong with him? He knew better than to let something like that happen. He just hadn't been smart enough to care.

Even now, standing alone in the chilly cabin, his blood was pumping hot, his skin putting off wave after wave of frustrated heat. He'd been a fool to kiss her, but man, oh, man, it had felt good. She was right about that part.

She tasted like liquid fire and her body fitted so perfectly against his that it was hard to imagine she hadn't been made just for him. It was a ridiculous notion that an educated, brilliant woman like her would want anything to do with a Neanderthal like him. What could he possibly have to offer her but a few steamy hours of mind-blowing sex? His career was over. He wasn't a pauper, but he lived frugally on what he'd managed to save over the past dozen years or so. He wasn't a kind, gentle man who would sweep her off her feet into some romantic fantasy world. He was just a guy—a former soldier who hadn't even been able to keep his own wife safe.

He didn't deserve a second chance at happily ever after. Obviously, he hadn't even deserved the first one.

The image of Mary's body flooded his mind. Bloody, tortured and lifeless.

David slammed his fist into the neat stack of firewood, sending logs flying across the cabin. He hated it that every time he thought about Mary, he only saw her death. He couldn't even remember the good times they'd had together anymore. He knew they were there, in his memory, but he just couldn't see them. All he saw was her battered corpse, reminding him just what would happen if he let himself be selfish enough to bring another woman into his life.

Noelle had enough problems without his adding to them. He had to keep his distance. He had to be professional. No matter how much he wanted otherwise.

Not even if she tasted like liquid fire and fit perfectly against his body. Not even if she melted into his kiss like she'd been starving for it all her life. Not even if she begged.

Blood dripped from his split knuckles, a faint patter in the quiet night.

He had to do the right thing. He had to keep her safe— even from himself. No matter how much he wanted her.

David looked at the door, still swinging loose on its hinges. She'd forgotten her vest and the gun he'd insisted she take with her whenever she left the cabin. If she wasn't careful, she'd run into one of the protections he'd set up in a perimeter around the cabin. They were primitive, but lethal.

He spat out a searing oath and followed her outside. He didn't know how he was going to resist kissing her again when he found her out in the moonlit night, but he had to find a way.

CHAPTER FIFTEEN

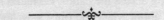

Noelle didn't hear his approach, but she sensed him just before she saw his large form slip out from between the trees not two feet away.

It was dark outside and Noelle hadn't gone far—just far enough that she couldn't see the cabin through the thick trees. Just far enough that she could feel like she was alone.

Being alone made it easier to accept David's rejection and remind herself of what was truly important in life. Her work.

She wasn't a fool. She hadn't forgotten what was at stake if she failed her task to discover the hidden meaning in the ciphertext.

"You forgot your vest," said David. His voice was barely more than a whisper of dark sound.

The wind shifted restlessly through the branches of the trees, scattering dry leaves. It smelled of frost and woodsmoke mixed with a hint of David.

She wondered if she'd ever forget the way he smelled. The way he tasted.

Noelle didn't take the vest from his hand. She felt safe out here, no matter how foolish it was for her to feel that way. The only threat she faced was David's ability to make her lose control.

He let out a frustrated sigh and slid the vest over her arms. His arms reached around her to fasten the straps, putting her once again in his embrace.

Noelle looked up at him, already feeling the way her body responded to his nearness like a drug. An addictive one.

Her heart sped and her nostrils flared to pull in his scent. His motions were jerky but gentle as he pulled the straps taut.

Shadows hid his eyes, but accentuated the tight line of his jaw. He'd shaved recently, she noticed, and she could smell the faint scent of soap on his skin.

Desire rioted through her belly, making her feel weak and breathless. She'd never felt this way about Stanley, nor anyone else for that matter. Her reaction to David was unique and utterly mystifying.

He pulled away, and the loss of his body heat was immediate. She shivered and wrapped her arms around her body to warm herself.

"We need to get back to the cabin," he said.

Noelle couldn't stand the thought of being closed up with him in such a small space. At least not unless he was going to finish what he started.

"I'll come back in a little while. I just need some air."

He nodded but didn't move. "I didn't mean to hurt you, Noelle. I swear. I just . . ."

Noelle tightened her grasp around her middle, trying to ease the empty ache that chilled her from the inside. "We don't have to talk about this. Just forget that kiss ever happened."

"I was a jackass and I'm sorry. I should never have let my feelings get in the way of the job."

The job. That's what was really important here—not her feelings, or David's. They had a job to do, and lives depended on their success. "It's okay," she said. The words were hollow because it sure didn't feel okay.

"No, it's not. It sucks ass, but that's the way it is. That's the way it has to be. Do you understand?"

Noelle understood perfectly. His wife had been murdered by the same men who were trying to kill her. Neither one of them had any business getting involved with each other. They both had jobs to do, and neither was getting any easier.

"Just give me some time alone to clear my head so I can focus on my work." She needed to think and she couldn't do that when he was standing so close.

After a long pause, David nodded. "Don't be long," he said as he slipped back into the shadows.

Noelle stared up at the clear night sky. She could do this. She was strong enough to resist him. And smart enough to know there was no other choice.

Owen slid deeper into his hidey-hole, grinning. They'd kissed. How sweet.

David was too distracted by Noelle and his obvious lust for her to notice Owen in his hiding place not two hundred feet from the cabin. From here he had a clear view of the tension tightening Noelle's slender arms around her body.

He could also see David keeping watch over her from

a few yards away, his face hardened with frustration and guilt. Poor baby.

In the dark, Owen doubted she could see David guarding her, and if he'd left her alone, Owen would have had a hard time resisting the urge to move in too soon.

Mr. Lark was breathing down his neck, anxious to get his hands on those weapons—or more importantly, the money they would bring on the black market. He'd already started preparing a list of well-funded customers for the auction, which put undue pressure on Owen to hurry. When he did earn that coveted place at Mr. Lark's right hand, he was going to have to teach the man that money wasn't everything. Power was much more important—more enjoyable—and although money could buy power, fear could buy even more.

The auction was just going to have to wait. Owen was enjoying himself too much to hurry, considering how his plans had just shifted with that kiss. Noelle was no longer just some high-powered brain. She was a woman that David cared enough about to kiss, which made her much more interesting. And useful.

CHAPTER SIXTEEN

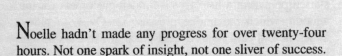

Noelle hadn't made any progress for over twenty-four hours. Not one spark of insight, not one sliver of success. The code was winning and people were going to die.

She had always worked well under pressure—there were few academics who didn't—but this level of pressure was more than she was able to handle. She was beginning to think that she'd failed.

The bowl of soup he'd put in front of her an hour ago had cooled, been reheated and cooled again. It smelled great, but her stomach roiled at the thought of eating. She knew it was stupid to starve herself like this. It was even counterproductive, but every time she did anything but focus on the problem, her head started filling with images from those horrible pictures David had shown her. It had gotten so bad that she was unable to sleep, or even close her eyes for very long.

She hadn't had more than a few short naps since they'd arrived at the cabin, and except for that nap in the woods, she had only slept a couple of times at the table, bent over her work in exhaustion. If this didn't stop soon, she was going to go insane. And welcome it.

"You should try to rest for a while," said David from

the cabin door. She had no idea how long he'd been standing there, watching her.

His body nearly filled the doorway, blocking out the bright rays of sunshine behind him. He'd shaved recently, and even though the stubble was gone, he looked no less dangerous. His hair had grown out some to reveal even more splinters of silver in the black hair at his temples, making her wonder if his body was just really fit for his age, or if his hair was going prematurely gray. Based on what she knew of his past, she guessed the latter.

As always when he left the cabin, he wore his Kevlar vest. Under it was a long-sleeved flannel shirt with the sleeves rolled up to reveal his thick forearms and all the beguiling muscles she couldn't help but notice. From the dark stain of sweat around his collar, she guessed he'd been chopping wood again.

He seemed to do that a lot, which made her wonder just how long he expected them to be here.

Other than chopping wood, he spent much of his time outside the cabin during the day, doing God only knew what. A couple of times, he'd brought back some fish and even a rabbit, which Noelle staunchly refused to eat. She wasn't a vegetarian, but Thumper was absolutely not on the menu.

"I wish I could sleep, but every time I close my eyes, all I see is the code scrolling through my head." And the faces of the dead. She didn't tell him that, though. What was the point? It would only make him feel guilty for having shown her the photos. He had plenty of self-imposed guilt without her help.

Noelle shut the screen of her laptop to conserve the battery. David had said there was plenty of fuel to run the generator for several weeks if they only used it to recharge her laptop and pump water. She hoped breaking this code wouldn't take nearly that long because she knew her body wouldn't hold up that long under the stress.

David closed the door, making the cabin seem smaller by his mere presence.

"It's going to get cold tonight," he said as he stripped out of his vest and hung it on a nail beside the door next to Noelle's vest and coat. "There's no cloud cover to hold the heat."

"Get cold? It's already cold." Noelle wore a jacket, and she sat snuggled inside her sleeping bag at the table to keep her legs and feet warm while she worked. And even that wasn't enough insulation. Going outside was even worse. Being strictly an indoor sort of girl had given her no experience for the joy of sitting on frozen wood while icy drafts blasted her butt.

For the first time in her life, Noelle wished she could pee standing up.

"It's going to get colder, but I'll be sure to keep the fire built up tonight, before it starts to get dark."

"It won't help," she said. She set her glasses on the table and thrust her hand into her hair in frustration, where her fingers immediately got caught in the thick tangle of curls. Had she remembered to brush her hair today? She didn't think so, but the days ran together when she didn't sleep, so maybe she had.

David's blue eyes slid over her body and searched her face. "What's wrong?"

She thought about not telling him, but knew that in the end, he'd figure it out anyway. Besides, talking about it couldn't make things any worse. "I've hit a wall. Hard."

"A wall?"

She felt shame burn high on her cheekbones. "I've run every decryption algorithm I've ever developed in every permutation possible. There's something else in this code that I sensed the first time I looked at it—some elusive quality that seems to shift every time I think I see the pattern. It's mathematical, I know that much, but there is something more. Something almost arcane in the way the symbols are strung together." She trailed off, shaking her head. "No matter how long I work, the solution keeps evading me."

"You should try to get some sleep."

Noelle rubbed her tired eyes. "I can't. This isn't just a matter of passing a course, or even completing my dissertation. People's lives are at stake. If I fail, people will die."

"That's a lot of pressure to be putting on yourself. You're not used to it. Relax. Give it time. As long as you're safe, that's what matters. You can take all the time you need."

She pushed out a frustrated sigh. "It's hard to relax when I keep banging my head against the same wall." She looked at him, hoping he wouldn't see the desperation that threatened to overwhelm her. "What if I can't do it?"

"You can do it." He sounded utterly confident. "What do you normally do when you hit a rough patch?

She shook her head, making her curls brush over her cheeks. "Usually I just go on to another project and give my brain time to work things out on its own. If I focus on the problem too hard, I just can't seem to find a solution. I have to let it be for a while. But . . ."

"But?"

She looked right into his eyes. "We don't have time for that. Do we?"

If he was disappointed by her inability to break the code, it didn't show in his expression. "We have all the time you need. I'll keep you safe."

Her shoulders sagged a little in relief. She suddenly felt fragile. Exhausted.

"Why don't you get a nap? You're probably just too tired to think."

"I need to distract myself for a while and let my brain work in peace."

"You don't need a distraction. What you need is sleep."

"I can't sleep, David. I've tried."

"I know. I've heard you shifting in your sleeping bag last night, trying to sleep."

She looked up at him, her cheeks warming with embarrassment. "I'm sorry I kept you awake."

David shrugged. "I'm a light sleeper."

"I'll try to be quieter," she promised.

"I don't care about that. I'm worried about you. You need to take a break."

"I can't. I need to—"

"Take a break," he insisted. "You look like you're about to fall over."

Noelle rubbed her eyes. They felt gritty and hot, while the rest of her was bone cold. It felt like it had been a long time since she'd truly been warm. She promised herself that if she ever got out of this mess, she'd take a weeklong shower so hot it would melt the ceramic tile.

David lifted her bodily off the stool by her arm and handed her her bulletproof vest. "Time for a walk. Maybe some exercise will get your synapses firing or at least help you sleep."

"At this point, I'm willing to try anything."

She saw his jaw clench for a brief moment as if biting down his frustration. Then it was gone and he offered her a faint smile as they walked out into the sunshine.

The air was cold, but clear. The wind had picked up over the past couple of days, bringing with it the clean scent of frost. She had no idea what time it was, other than daytime. In a way, it was kind of freeing not to worry about schedules or classes or meetings. If it weren't for the single, monstrous deadline looming over her, she would have been enjoying the freedom.

But she did have that deadline and so did nameless others who were unknowingly depending on her for their lives.

"No you don't," warned David with a sharp tone. "You're going to stop thinking about whatever it is you're thinking about right now. I've been watching you for days, and I know that look."

"What look?" she asked.

"That look that tells me you're not going to eat my cooking, no matter how many times I reheat it for you. The one that makes your eyes fill with fear and your skin go pale."

Noelle didn't realize she'd been so transparent. Or perhaps he was simply that observant. "I try not to think about it, I really do."

"You'll solve this puzzle. I know you will. You're just too close to it right now. Give yourself a break."

"I wish I could." She stopped, her legs suddenly no longer able to propel her forward. "You know what's at stake."

He nodded slowly, making the silver strands in his dark hair glitter in the sunlight. "You can't let yourself think about that. One step at a time. That's all you need to think about."

"Is that how you do it?"

He reached out and rescued a lock of hair that was trapped under the shoulder of her vest. "I'd be overwhelmed if I stopped and thought about helping you crack this code, then getting you out of here, then finding the mole on Monroe's team, then getting the information back to Monroe, then finding a safe hiding place for you while we used the info, then—"

Noelle covered his mouth with her hand, unable to hear any more. "I see your point. One step at a time."

He wrapped his hand around hers and pulled it from his mouth. His fingers were warm against her chilled skin, making her wish she had his internal furnace.

Rather than letting go, he held her hand in his, warming it. "The point is that you can only do what you can do right now. The rest has to wait its turn."

She looked into his blue eyes and wished she'd found him under different circumstances. He'd proven he was a caring man. He put others before himself—even to the extreme of risking his life for a living. And he was so fun to look at. His face was masculine, with sharp angles and deep ridges under his cheekbones. His mouth was soft and hot, and she could still remember the way it felt—firm and demanding against her lips.

Just the memory was enough to help warm her, starting with the blush spreading out from her cheeks.

A faint smile curved his lips as if he'd been reading her thoughts. "We're not going there, either," he said with mock sternness. "Come on. I want to show you something."

Since he had her hand captured, she had no choice but to follow along behind him. He kept his stride short so that she could keep up, her weary body pushing her forward. They headed through the trees, his movements sure and focused. A couple of times, he led her around a section of ground, pointing out that he'd set a trap here and there to ward off any unwanted visitors.

They were going straight uphill, and Noelle had to stop several times to catch her breath. "I really need to get more exercise," she panted, embarrassed that she couldn't keep up.

A strained look crossed his face, and he turned his back before she could figure out what she'd said to cause it.

They reached the top of a ridge, and David stopped. The wind whipped around them, tossing her hair into her face. Noelle shoved it inside the neck of her jacket with an irritated jerk of her hands. She'd forgotten to cut it for, oh, the past four years or so, and it was becoming a hassle.

"There," he said, motioning with his hand toward the horizon.

Noelle looked and her breath caught in her chest. The view was magnificent! From here, a series of spiky mountains stretched out as far as she could see. In the valley below, the trees had not all lost their leaves yet. A few held on to brilliant swatches of reds, oranges, and yellows, which blurred together into an image even Monet would have appreciated. A silver ribbon of river slid through the valley, looking calm and silent from this distance, even though she knew it had to be seething with frigid water, bubbling and churning as it ate away at the rocky banks.

From this view, everything looked different—softer and more continuous. Rather than individual trees and rocks, everything merged together into one giant whole. Pieces lost meaning, rendering the entire landscape into one single work of art. Individual, discrete objects making up one continuous whole.

From a great enough distance, discrete objects looked continuous.

Just like the ciphertext.

Time stopped for Noelle as the import of her thoughts rang loud and clear in her mind. That was it. She figured out the key to the puzzle. Thanks to David and his mountain view she'd found the answer. She could crack the code!

Noelle went pale, and David thought she was going to faint. He grabbed her and pulled her toward him, easing her down to the ground before she could fall.

The look of awe on her face as she surveyed the mountain view had been well worth the uphill hike, and he was sure that the fresh air would clear her head like nothing else could. With the exception, perhaps, of hot, wet sex.

But that look on her face now scared the hell out of him. He was sure something had gone terribly wrong. Maybe she was afraid of heights or something.

"Noelle? You in there?" He kept his voice low and calm, even though he wanted to scream and shake her into responding.

Finally, she pulled in a breath. Her eyes were wide and unfocused and a fine sheen of sweat had broken out over her forehead. David touched her skin and it felt cold and clammy. Quickly, he stripped off his coat and draped it over her to keep her warm. She didn't have enough damn insulation to be out here in the cold, sweating.

"Noelle?" He sounded more frantic this time, even though he tried his hardest not to.

He pushed her head down toward her knees to keep her from passing out and cursed himself for not forcing her to eat like he should have. What was he thinking, dragging her on an uphill hike when she hadn't had a decent meal or a good night's sleep in days?

"I've got it," she said, her words muffled by her awkward position.

"What?" He bent down to hear what she had to say.

Noelle pushed against his arm and he let her sit up. "I figured it out. The ciphertext. I figured out what I'd been missing about the code."

David wasn't sure she was completely coherent, but he wasn't about to question her here. He needed to get her back to the cabin, where he could get her warm.

"I need a pen, paper. Something!"

David patted his vest pockets for something she could use to write and found a forgotten ballpoint pen, but no paper. She snatched the pen and started scribbling across her hand.

David watched the strange symbols she scrawled, unable to make any sense out of it. It looked vaguely mathematical, but there were no numbers, only the Cyrillic script he'd seen on the paper Monroe had given them.

She ran out of room to write on her hand and started ripping off her clothes to get to her arm.

"Here, use mine," he offered, pushing up his sleeve and stretching out his bare forearm to her.

The tip of the pen tickled, but he didn't dare make a sound for fear that he might interrupt her train of thought and mess up whatever epiphany she was having.

Minutes flowed by in chilly silence, with only the howl of the wind and the rattle of dry leaves to tarnish it.

When she had nearly filled up one arm, David offered the other, breathing a sigh of relief as her scribbling began to slow.

She stopped, and the look of elation shining in her features made him want to lean down and kiss her, just to see what victory tasted like on her lips.

"We need to get back. Now. I can do this, David."

Her smile made her look younger, more vulnerable and totally desirable. If he could resist her when she looked at him like he'd just handed her the world, he could resist any woman.

Careful not to smudge her work, he pushed his sleeves down, buttoned his coat securely around her and took her hand as he led her back down the mountain.

Owen walked through the empty cabin Noelle was sharing with David to check on the girl's progress. He'd seen them hiking up the mountain, waited until they were far enough away he'd have a safe measure of time to snoop around, then proceeded to do just that.

He flipped through her notes, taking photographs of each page of indecipherable garbage. If something happened to the girl, then at least he'd have some notes to help the next brainiac pick up where she left off.

He had no idea how far along she was toward a solution,

but a quick inventory of their supplies told him that they only had a few more days of food left until someone would have to run into town for more.

Owen was a patient man. He could wait. Chances were good David thought she was safe up here with all those traps laid to protect her. When it was time to go into town, David might even leave her behind to work.

That was when Owen would make his move. Without David, it'd be a simple thing to swoop in and pick up the girl along with all of her work. Once he had her, his position in the Swarm would be solidified. He'd move up in the organization and earn his seat by Mr. Lark's side. They'd no longer look at him and see only his burn scars—they'd see the man behind the scars and come to appreciate his vision for the Swarm. With Owen behind the helm, the Swarm would no longer have to work in the shadows. They'd become a force to be reckoned with and feared.

Owen smiled as he slid his fingers over a pair of panties left to dry on the laundry line strung up in the cabin.

If Noelle was a good girl, he might even keep her alive long enough to play with her for a while. Just like he'd played with David's wife, Mary.

CHAPTER SEVENTEEN

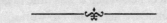

A couple of hours later, Noelle had finally reached a stopping point. She wasn't done yet, but she could see the solution glowing on the horizon, no longer completely out of reach. A few more hours of computations and she'd be able to start writing the program to execute code-breaking algorithms she'd created. Once the program was written and debugged, she would be able to put the ciphertext in and see what happened.

That was the true test of her new thought process.

She stretched, arching her back to relieve the tension in her muscles. She'd spent so many hours sitting on this hard, wooden stool, that she thought she might have a permanent round indentation in her backside. Her shoulders ached, and her fingers were nearly numb with cold, but she felt better than she had in days.

She knew she could do this, and the relief that she would succeed was like a drug racing through her system, making her feel alive.

And hungry.

Something savory was cooking on the potbellied stove, and the aroma of onions and spices filled the tiny cabin, making her mouth water. She couldn't remember the last time she felt so ravenous.

A quick survey of the cabin showed no sign of David. She thought she'd heard the door latch shut as he left, but that could have been a distant memory of two or three hours ago. Time didn't really flow normally when she was working, so she couldn't be sure.

Noelle washed her hands in a trickle of frigid water and splashed a bit on her face to clear away the grit from her tired eyes. She was weary but also elated by her success, giving her an edgy sort of energy that didn't quite translate smoothly into the motion of her limbs. Her head was completely awake, but her body was about to fall over. She'd really been abusing it over the past few days. It was time to make up for bad behavior.

Noelle peered longingly into the pot simmering on the stove. Bits of carrots and celery and what she hoped was chicken and not Thumper, floated lazily through steaming broth.

She had no idea where David was, but with food on the stove, she doubted he'd be far. The idea of sharing a meal with him was appealing enough that she was willing to brave the cold outside and see if she could find him.

Noelle slipped on the Kevlar vest and pulled her coat over it to keep out the cold. She'd learned her lesson about calling his name, so instead, she scanned the trees, looking for signs of which way he'd gone. There was no snow on the ground today, but she could still see the shallow impressions of his tracks in the dirt and places where what remained of the plant life had been crushed. She had no clue how to tell which tracks were fresh, so she headed off in the direction she'd found him last time.

The forest was lovely, if no longer green. Dry leaves crunched under her feet and twigs snapped. She'd heard stories about people who could move silently in the woods, but being here, she was beginning to doubt there was much truth in them. It would take a ghost to move quietly through all this dry, crunchy debris.

Owen made no sound as he moved toward Noelle. He was beginning to see why David was drawn to her. There was something alluring and fresh about her—a basic honesty in her appearance unmasked by the deceit of cosmetics. An honest woman was such a rare find that Owen had to fight the urge to take her now.

It wasn't time yet. Her work had to be finished before he could play with her.

Unless she got too close. Then he'd have no choice but to take her now.

Owen stilled, deciding to let fate choose. If she came to him, then he'd know she was meant to be his now.

The game of chance thrilled him and his body trembled in anticipation. She was so close—only a few yards away. His camouflage and the vast number of trees and brush concealed him from her sight, but he could see her clearly. Each fiery curl, a spattering of freckles. She'd lost weight since she'd been here, and the dark circles under her eyes were new, too.

David wasn't taking very good care of his new woman. Clearly the man didn't deserve her.

Noelle came closer, a pensive frown flattening her pink mouth. She stopped and looked around, then studied the ground. A couple of steps closer and she'd be within reach. Just two steps. Silently, Owen urged her closer, his mouth moving in the shape of her name.

The color drained from her face and her eyes widened with fear. He had no idea what had scared her, and he knew she hadn't seen him, but his wonder over what had frightened her fled in the face of her beauty. She was perfect—terrified and quivering with the force of it. There was nothing more beautiful to Owen than a terrified woman.

She made a little whimpering sound that made Owen's dick harden in answer. It was all he could do to keep himself from reaching out to her and curling his fingers through her hair until she screamed. He was sure she'd have a lovely screaming voice.

He felt his fists clench and closed his eyes to regain control over himself. He had to think of the job first. If he failed Mr. Lark, he would be executed as an example to the others. Owen understood that was how it had to be, but that understanding didn't comfort him. He had to quit drooling over the woman, put his need for revenge against David on hold, and do his damn job.

Owen's body cooperated, relaxing once again. When he opened his eyes, he saw Noelle stumbling off back toward the cabin. Fate had betrayed him. Noelle had betrayed him, and she'd have to be punished for it. Owen could hardly wait.

He stayed in place until it was safe to move from the cover of brush and half-fallen limbs. He went to the spot where Noelle had been and tried to figure out what had scared her. He studied the ground where she'd been looking.

No wonder the poor thing had been afraid. Pressed into the dirt were several footprints. Two from David's heavy tread, one of Noelle's dainty prints and a third set. Not Owen's. He was far too careful to leave behind such obvious proof of his presence here.

Which meant they had a visitor.

Owen smiled. Maybe fate hadn't betrayed him after all.

CHAPTER EIGHTEEN

———— ❧ ————

Are you sure it was here?" asked David, crouching to look at the ground where Noelle said she'd seen the footprints. He saw his own boot prints and several of Noelle's, but that was all.

"I'm sure," said Noelle, though her voice wavered with uncertainty.

Ever since she'd run back into the clearing with that panic-stricken look on her face, David's blood had been running hot. He didn't dare leave her alone in the cabin while he checked out her claims of new footprints. He was keeping her right by his side until he knew it was safe.

"I don't see anything," he told her.

Noelle bent down and pointed. "Right here," she said, pointing to a section of ground covered with dry leaves.

David carefully swept the leaves away—leaves that had been on this patch of ground a long time, protected from the wind by the thick roots of a tree—but there was nothing underneath, just unmarred ground. He studied the area, looking for any other signs of intruders, but found nothing. If someone had erased the footprints she thought she'd seen, they'd done a damn good job and hadn't left a single trace. David had worked with some of the best

Spec Ops forces out there and he'd never known anyone who was that good. Not even Grant.

Maybe she'd just seen the way his footprints stacked on top of one another, which formed a new pattern. A lot of people made that same mistake when they first started learning about tracking.

Noelle's voice was faint, hard to hear over the sound of the wind in the trees. "I'm not lying to you."

"I know you're not. I also know that you've been working like crazy, not sleeping enough or eating enough and stress can do odd things to people. It can make them see things that aren't there or misinterpret things that are."

She wrapped her arms around herself, looking vulnerable and afraid. "You think those footprints were some sort of hallucination?"

David saw nothing out of place, felt no sign of anything wrong other than his nagging worry for Noelle. He'd been meticulous in his patrol of the area and none of his security measures had been triggered. He knew she wouldn't lie to him, but no one could stand the kind of pressure she was under and not crack just a little.

David pulled her into his arms, needing to soothe her, needing to take away her fear. "I think that you saw something, but I don't think it was anything to worry about."

"I can't stand the thought that I might not be able to trust my own mind. My brain is all I have."

It was such a ludicrous statement that David had to fight the urge to spend the next hour listing all her attributes. She was courageous, honest, caring, so beautiful it made his chest ache. He wished he knew how to show her just how much she had to offer, but all he knew to do was ease her fear. "Your brain is fine. Just overworked."

"If I can't trust my own mind . . ." She clung to him with an almost palpable sense of desperation.

"You can trust me. I'll keep you safe." He had to. He couldn't even consider any other possibility. He had to do whatever it took to protect her, even if that meant admitting he couldn't do it alone.

David needed help. There was too much ground here to cover alone, and he knew of no better place to take her now that all of the safe houses were potentially compromised. And if she was right about those footprints, and there was someone out in the woods with enough skill to evade his detection, then they were in more trouble than he thought.

There were only two men on the face of the planet he trusted enough to help him protect Noelle. Caleb and Grant. He hated calling them in away from their duties, but he hated the thought of letting Noelle come to harm more. When David had left Delta, Caleb had made him memorize a phone number that he could call anytime, day or night. Though they never said it, David knew Caleb and Grant were both worried he would kill himself after what happened with Mary. They promised that if he called, they would come. No questions asked.

He wasn't sure if the number was still good after two years, but it was his best shot at keeping Noelle safe.

By the time they'd gotten back to the cabin, Noelle was pretty sure she was losing her mind. She'd seen those footprints. Or thought she had, but there was no disputing that they weren't there now.

David was right. She was under too much stress. Too bad there was nothing that could change that anytime soon to relieve it.

"Food will help," he told her, offering her a steaming bowl of the soup he'd made.

"At this point, I'll try anything." She cleared her work off the little table so they could sit and eat.

"Sleeping would be a good idea, too." His voice was low and gentle. Just like doctors talked to crazy people.

"Yeah. I'll try." But she didn't make any promises.

She finished off most of her meal under David's watchful gaze. She wasn't sure what he was looking for, but his constant attention was making her body heat and her mind wander off into the forbidden realm of what his mouth felt like against hers. Dusty sunlight from the single window glinted off silver splinters of hair at his temples, and the deep shadows made his face seem more angular, his jaw wider.

His expression was so solemn and she wished she knew how to make him smile—how to make him laugh.

He went to the stove to refill his bowl with more soup. "Want some more?" he asked her, catching her gaze with those lovely blue eyes of his.

More of him? Yes. She wanted to kiss him again—make sure that surging heat he'd lit within her wasn't just her imagination, too. "No, thanks. I'm going to make a trip outside, then try to get some sleep. I'll be back in a minute."

"That's a good idea. Don't forget your vest," he reminded her.

Noelle strapped herself inside the vest and pulled on her coat. The sky was clear and blue, but the wind was cold. She made quick use of the drafty facilities and was headed back inside to the relative warmth of the cabin when something made her stop. She wasn't sure if it was a noise she'd heard or the forest going quiet under the sound of wind through the branches, or if it was just her imagination, but Noelle turned around and searched the trees to figure out what had spooked her. Fear dampened her palms and she was sure she could hear the sound of her heart racing even through the heavy padding of her coat.

It was just her imagination again. That was all. Just like those footprints. She sure as hell wasn't going to run to David with claims of phantoms in the woods again.

The low branches of a nearby bush shifted suddenly as if someone had walked by them, making them snap back into place.

Noelle's body tightened with terror. That was *not* her imagination. Not this time.

She wanted to run, but her legs felt heavy, locked to the earth. "David!"

He burst out of the cabin with a big black gun in hand. He hadn't bothered pulling on his coat or his own Kevlar vest. "You okay?"

"I, uh, heard something. I think. Saw some branches move."

"Where?"

Noelle pointed to the spot, and David placed himself between those branches and her.

"Get inside and stay low," he ordered.

Noelle's legs were heavy, but at least this time they moved when she asked them to. David wasn't wearing his vest and she wasn't about to leave him out here without it. She ran back inside and grabbed it off the nail by the door.

When she swung the door open to bring it to him, his voice lashed out at her, cold and hard. "Don't you dare come out here."

"I won't stand a chance of surviving alone if you get yourself killed." Just the thought of him being hurt was enough to make her break out in a cold sweat. "Besides, it was probably just an animal."

"I'm not taking any chances."

"Neither am I," she said, taking the vest out to him. She was not going to cower in the cabin when there was anything she could do to help him stay safe.

His jaw was tight with anger, but he let her slip the vest over his wide shoulders while he kept the gun in his hands. "Show me exactly where you saw the movement."

Noelle pointed to the bushes just to the right of the Bronco. "Right there."

The bushes swayed again, and David shoved her behind him with one arm while he aimed his gun at the branches. "Get back inside," he ordered in a voice she was sure made grown men jump to obey.

Before Noelle could turn, a deer shot across the clearing, disappearing in the thick trees on the far side.

Noelle's heart hammered and she had a death grip on David's arm.

"Just a deer." Relief was clear in his tone. "To be on the safe side, I'm going to check it out and I want you back inside. I'll just be a minute."

Noelle hated to leave him alone, but she knew she was of no use to him now. This was his area of expertise, and all she could do to help was stay out of his way. She went back inside the cabin, hating the sturdy little building more by the second.

She found the gun that David had given her and set it carefully beside her, keeping her eyes fixed on the cabin door. Her hands were shaking too badly for her to trust herself not to shoot David when he came back. And he would come back. It was just a deer. She had to believe that.

Seconds ticked by slowly. Her pulse pounded painfully in her temples, and the ragged sound of her breathing seemed too loud in the empty cabin. Seconds turned into minutes, and although her breathing slowed, adrenaline still rushed painfully through her bloodstream, making her sweat. She stripped out of her coat but left the vest on.

David had his vest, too. At least she'd managed to protect him that much.

The heavy tread of boots sounded just outside, and Noelle placed her hand on the gun, just in case. She didn't dare dwell on how easily her mind had turned to violence as a solution. She was sure it made her a hypocrite, but she didn't care—nothing so trivial mattered when David was still out there alone.

"It's me," said David, right before he came through the door. "There was no one out there. Just that deer."

Noelle just drank in the sight of him, thankful he'd come back in one piece. He looked beautiful.

"You okay?" he asked her, his voice gentle.

Noelle nodded. "You?"

He spread his thick arms wide, putting himself on display. "Not a scratch."

"That's good."

"You look a little shaken," he said, his eyes surveying her with that cautious, worried look that made her think he was questioning her mental stability. He checked the safety on her gun and slid it out of her easy reach. Not a good sign.

"I really thought there was someone out there. Guess that's twice now I've let my imagination run away with me." She felt like some silly little girl who jumped at her own shadow.

"You did the right thing when you called me."

"But it was just a deer."

"It doesn't matter. It could have been someone who wanted to hurt you. Better safe than sorry."

"I feel like an idiot."

David's hand wrapped around the back of her neck and he pulled her face close to his until their foreheads touched. She could see the gray flecks in his blue eyes as he pinned her with a steady, truthful stare. "You are not an idiot. You and I are a team. We'll stick together and everything will be okay. Do you trust me?"

"Yes," she whispered and ran her tongue over her dry lips.

His eyes locked on to the movement and she saw his pupils expand, felt his shoulders shift with a sudden intake of breath. He was going to kiss her and she couldn't think of anything that she wanted more. If she was going to die in the next few days, she wanted to go with no regrets, and missing the opportunity to kiss David again would definitely be regret-worthy.

He took her face between his square, callused hands. Her stomach jumped and her heart skittered to life, pounding noisily against her ribs. She could feel the surge of adrenaline sliding through her veins, mixed with those hormones of hers that had her body growing warm and soft. She shivered as his heat sank into her skin and let her eyes fall shut so that she could simply feel.

The first brush of his lips was soft, almost tender—nothing like the desperate pressure of his mouth during their first kiss. He coaxed her lips apart and she welcomed him eagerly into her mouth, tasting her own excitement mirrored in him. His tongue swept over her bottom lip, teasing and playful, before stroking boldly over her teeth.

He lifted her to her feet and she could feel the steady strength of his arms around her. A low, needy sound rumbled in his chest and she could feel it vibrate the tips of her breasts, making her nipples grow hard and tight. His hands slid from her cheeks down her throat and over her shoulders, where they gripped and released her repeatedly as if undecided on what was the best course of action.

Noelle had no such trouble deciding. She let her hands wander over his shoulders, down his chest and around his waist to grip his back and feel the sleek strength of the muscles just below the line of his vest.

He felt so good under her fingers—strong and solid and so very warm. For the first time in days, she was no longer cold to the core or sweating in fear. The simple pleasure of just being warm made her head spin.

His hand slid lower, cupping her bottom in his wide palm. Streamers of pleasure shot through her torso and settled into happy little wriggling knots low in her belly.

She sighed into his mouth, giving away just how good his hand felt, placed so intimately.

That rough sound emanating from David deepened as he pulled her forward against him so she could plainly feel the hard ridge of his erection against her abdomen. In the tiny corner of her mind left for rational thought, she realized *that* was certainly nothing like her experience with Stanley.

A brief, faint whimper of feminine need filled the air of the cabin and David separated their bodies. His eyes were nearly black with lust and his chest bellowed with labored breathing. "We've got to stop," he panted.

Noelle knew the words he said, but it took several seconds for her to process them into something she could understand. "Why?" was all she could manage.

His gaze drifted down to her mouth and he licked his lips as if tasting her upon them again. "Because this is not supposed to happen."

"It's not?"

She felt his hands tense against her arms and couldn't suppress a shiver of delight.

His nostrils flared and he clenched his jaw. "I can't focus on my job when we're like this. All I can think about is the way you taste, the way you feel."

"And that's bad, right?" Her voice sounded far away—weak and breathless.

David cursed and closed his eyes. "It's good. So damn good it could get us both killed. I can't let myself get distracted right now."

The languid warmth of passion was beginning to fade in the face of reality. It took every ounce of willpower she possessed, but she managed to peel his hands from her arms and stand on her own. Her knees were shaking and her body felt like it had had all the blood drained out and replaced with sawdust. She was so weak she could barely stay upright, but she found the strength to nod. "Neither one of us has any room for distractions. I'm going to get back to work."

Owen found the visitor that night eating dinner outside a tiny tent. It was a kid who couldn't have been twenty yet. His short blond hair was left uncovered to catch the light of the moon, and the fool was actually stupid enough to light a fire.

Amateur.

Owen pressed the barrel of his weapon against the back of the young man's skull. The pouch of stew he'd been eating fell to the ground in a sloppy puddle, and the boy raised his hands slowly.

"Why are you here?" asked Owen.

"Take it easy, man. I'm just camping." His voice cracked like a teenager's on the brink of puberty.

"Lie to me again and you won't live long enough to regret it. What is your name?"

The young man stiffened and his hands started to shake. "Brian Lorenz."

"Why are you here, Brian Lorenz?"

"I was sent here."

Owen's trigger finger tensed. "Sent? By whom?"

"Mr. Lark sent me. Said I might find you here, or rather, you'd find me. He said I'd never see you coming, but if you did find me, I was supposed to tell you to hurry the hell up."

Now they were getting somewhere. Owen's boss was either testing him or testing the boy. Perhaps both. "Why did he send you? Or are you merely a messenger boy?"

Mr. Lark commonly sent fools like this boy on impossible missions. If they failed, there was one less fool in the world, and if they succeeded, they earned a coveted spot within the ranks of the Swarm. In the past year, only seven people had been offered an invitation, and dozens had died in an effort to earn one. Mr. Lark was selective and only allowed the most dedicated and skilled people into his organization. He believed that everyone should earn their place in the world and Owen's was by Mr. Lark's side, helping him steer the Swarm to fulfill its true potential. Owen was not going to let this fool boy mess things up.

"I'm here to earn my invitation into the group."

"The group?" asked Owen, forcing the question to sound mild.

Brian's voice dropped to a conspiratorial whisper. "The Swarm."

Owen slapped the back of Brian's head with his free hand, making Brian yelp in pain. "Never say that name again," ordered Owen.

Brian moved his arm like he was going to rub the spot but wisely stopped himself. "I got it, man. We're cool."

Cool. The child clearly had no concept of who Owen was within the organization—practically Mr. Lark's right hand. If Owen had the luxury of time and a soundproof room, he would have enjoyed showing Brian the specialized skills he brought to the Swarm. "What are your orders?"

"Same as yours. Kill the man. Bring the woman in alive along with all her work."

"And you think you're a better man for the job?"

Brian hesitated, and Owen encouraged him to answer the question by pressing the barrel of his pistol more firmly against the boy's skull.

"He said you might be competition."

"Competition? You think you're in a class to compete with me?"

"Guess we'll see." It was a challenge. The cocky boy was actually issuing him a challenge.

The easy thing to do would be just to pull the trigger and have the matter settled. One less fool in the world. But that would have been loud and messy and Owen didn't have the patience for cleaning up that kind of mess tonight.

Brian's presence was a problem, but maybe it was also a blessing in disguise. A gift from Mr. Lark for his years of faithful service.

Owen's mind began to churn with ideas of how he could put the boy to good use. His youth was a definite asset. Young bait was always best—it tugged at all those parental instincts he knew so many people had.

"Perhaps we should work together," Owen offered.

"Isn't that against the rules or something? I mean, if you help me, then I haven't really earned the invitation into the Sw- uh, group, have I?"

"I assure you that Mr. Lark doesn't care how the work gets done as long as it does."

"So it won't ruin my chances of getting in?"

Trusting idiot. It was a wonder the boy had lived this long. "No. In fact, Mr. Lark will see you as clever for getting me to partner up with you."

"You'd let him think it was my idea?" asked Brian far too eagerly.

"Why not? I've already earned my place."

"For real? You ain't shittin' me?"

Owen rolled his eyes, glad he was standing behind Brian so the kid couldn't see his disgust. If Brian was this gullible, Owen was doing the world a favor by getting rid of him.

Owen lowered his gun and stepped into the firelight letting the boy see his scars. Brian flinched. "Holy shit! That's harsh."

Owen's trigger finger twitched, but he kept himself in control. "You have no idea. Now put out that fire before David sees it and you get us both killed."

CHAPTER NINETEEN

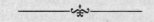

Noelle let out a sigh of relief as soon as she was sure David was asleep. She'd been unable to concentrate with him watching her across the room, even when he was pretending not to.

He was beautiful with the faint light painting shadows over his strong jaw and muscular shoulders. He looked confident and capable, even in sleep, and had a presence that could fill a lecture hall. In the tiny cabin, Noelle was feeling a bit overwhelmed. Especially after that kiss. She desperately needed to finish her work so they could get out of this place.

And go where?

Noelle let herself think about what she would do after—after she solved this puzzle, after she was safe and sound, after David had gone on his merry—or perhaps not so merry—way.

That thought made her breath freeze in her lungs. After having spent so much time with David, she realized that she didn't want him to leave. As large as his presence was, it was a comfort knowing he was around. She might not have felt safe from his pull on her, but she certainly felt safe from everyone else.

He'd already told her she couldn't go back to her normal life. When she did go back, would she still have to worry about someone breaking into her home at night? Would she have to worry about armed terrorists seeking her aid? Would she have to worry about all those things without David around to make it okay?

The thought was too much for her to deal with and still get her work done, so she boxed it up and shoved it into the deepest part of her brain—the one reserved for student loan payments and the death of the career she'd worked so hard to attain.

Noelle poured herself a cup of coffee that was thick with caffeine and blessedly hot. The food in her stomach kept the black stuff from burning a hole in her gut. She'd eaten what David had put in front of her, and she felt stronger for it. Of course, a full tummy made her sleepy, but that was something she could handle. Too many late-night cram sessions had ensured that skill was in her repertoire.

Usually, she didn't take many notes while she was working on a problem. Then again, usually, she had plenty of time to let the solution come to her, and she wasn't under quite so much pressure. Since her mind had begun to rebel at keeping in all the thoughts necessary to solve such a complex code, she'd begun taking copious notes in order to remember every thought that passed through her head.

She'd nearly filled a notebook with scribbles, and every time one of her ideas didn't pan out, she went back to those notes for a new possible solution. Unfortunately, the notes she needed to recall now were the ones she'd scrawled over David's arms earlier that day.

With a silent scream of frustration, Noelle slid out of her warm cocoon and padded in triple-socked feet to where David slept.

Light from the lantern was low but seemed bright in the dim corners on this side of the cabin. She could clearly see the angular line of his cheek and jaw, shadowed by a new growth of whiskers. His dark hair shone with splinters of silver, concentrated at the temples. He was lying on his side on top of his sleeping bag, his pistol in easy reach. The position made his wide shoulders seem even larger when compared to the narrow span of his hips. Even while in the deep relaxation of sleep, he looked powerful. Dangerous.

Noelle stifled a small shiver of female longing. If only he hadn't stopped kissing her, she might have known what it was like to experience a man like that up close and personal.

Very personal.

Being careful not to move him more than necessary, Noelle unbuttoned his sleeve and moved his arm into her lap, where she could read her notes in the faint lanternlight. She had to work to get the flannel over the muscular girth of his forearm. It wasn't an easy task, struggling with the deadweight of his arm, but she managed to get him into a position where she could lean over her lap and read the notes she'd made.

She was surprised that she hadn't woken him up. Maybe he was more tired than he'd let on.

She ran one finger lightly over her writing, recalling now what her train of thought had been when inspiration had struck. She was right, this wasn't a code—at least not exactly, it was more of a system that could be used to create a ciphertext that could then be decrypted. Both the text and the key to unraveling it were hidden within that single page. The text on the paper was a series of simultaneous equations strung together, but where one stopped and the next began, she couldn't be sure. Without that, there was no hope of figuring out the solution.

Noelle bit her lip, deep in concentration. If this theory was right—and instincts told her it was—she was zeroing in on her goal.

All she had to do now was keep her mind on her work and off David's well-muscled, sleeping body.

David watched Noelle through a tiny slit of his eyelids. He prayed that if she thought he was asleep, she'd finish touching him and go away before he got stupid and started kissing her again. If he started, he didn't think he'd be able to stop this time.

He knew how to feign sleep and he did so now with every ounce of skill he possessed. It was easy to keep his breathing deep and even. His heartbeat was another matter entirely. It was all he could do to lie still as she caressed his skin with a single, slender finger, sliding it lovingly over the sensitive underside of his arm as she followed the scrawling line of her notes.

All kinds of stray thoughts passed through his mind about just how it would feel for her to touch him so gently in other, more sensitive places. He would, of course, return the favor in kind. He was a gentleman, after all.

No, no, no. He was not going to think about touching her. He wasn't going to think about what her slim body would look like naked, laid out before him like some sort of delicious dessert—a mixture of strawberry pink and sweet, creamy white. He was not going to think about how her skin would feel under his questing fingers, all warm curves and soft planes. He was not going to think about whether or not she'd shiver as he touched her or moan softly in the back of her throat. Maybe both.

The fire surging through David's veins increased its pace as his unwelcome thoughts made his heart pound harder. It hadn't been difficult at all to go without a woman for two years. Why was it now suddenly so impossible to even pull in a breath without wanting to have hard, hot sex with Noelle?

Her bottom lip was between her teeth and he wanted to kiss that look of concentration from her face so bad that it made his guts ache just resisting the urge.

The lanternlight burnished her curls to a fiery copper and bathed her skin with golden highlights. She was beautiful by firelight. The flaws of fatigue and strain were washed away by the gentle glow, leaving behind only her natural beauty. This is what she must look like when there weren't people out to kill her. When she didn't have the lives of countless others in her hands.

She frowned in thought and reached for his other arm, which was pinned under his head as a pillow. She must have realized that she couldn't free his arm without moving his head, because she hesitated, then gently stroked the side of his face.

"David? Can you roll over?"

Her cool fingers caressed his cheek from temple to jaw, over and over. He pretended to sleep just so he could enjoy being petted, even though there was not one part of him that was not completely and widely awake.

Her fingers strayed to his hair, where she played with the short strands as if enjoying the texture. "David?" she whispered.

Noelle bent down and he could smell the subtle scent of her skin and feel the warmth of her body near his. His eyes were closed completely again, and he had only the warning of one warm breath against his neck before he realized what she was doing.

Her lips met his skin just below his ear in a soft kiss. It was one of his own personal erogenous zones, and the feel of her mouth pushed his lust past the point of being bearable. His jeans became painfully tight, restraining his raging erection. He was a man, not a saint, and Noelle had just found his limit.

He grabbed her body and dragged her up to his mouth, swallowing her startled gasp in the midst of a demanding kiss. She opened her mouth to him, eager and melting within seconds.

He no longer cared that he was breaking rules or taking risks. He'd done everything he knew to do to resist her and none of it had worked.

He wrenched his mouth away from her and with a powerful thrust of his hips, pinned her beneath him on the sleeping bag. He could feel the feral expression on his face, but there was nothing he could do to help it.

His voice was low and rough, nearly alien even to his own ears. "Tell me you won't regret this later," he demanded.

Her mouth was parted and wet in invitation, making it nearly impossible for him to hold on to his one remaining rational thought—her agreement. Her eyes were deep, forest green with the triumphant gleam of a woman who was about to get what she so desperately wanted. He could feel her trembling slightly beneath him, though whether from anticipation or fear, he wasn't sure.

She lifted her chin and looked him directly in the eye, licking her lips. "No regrets," she promised in a breathy voice, and he knew she was telling the truth. It was enough.

David let go of his restraint and kissed her soft mouth with every ounce of pent-up sexual frustration and longing he'd kept inside for over two years. She accepted his ferocity and sighed into his mouth, her needy hands seeking over his back and shoulders.

His tongue thrust into her mouth, tasting her acceptance. His hands found their way under layers of clothing to cup the soft curve of her breast in his hand. Her nipple tightened and he could feel it stabbing eagerly through the thin fabric of her bra, demanding the touch of skin on skin.

He had to feel her naked body against his, with nothing between them but lanternlight. She had on so many damn clothes that it was going to take him a year just to get her out of them. His fingers weren't cooperating; they were shaking with need and a hint of nervousness.

David hadn't been nervous with a woman since he was fifteen. Hell, he wasn't even sure it was possible to be so nervous anymore, but apparently, Noelle made a lot of things possible.

She arched and wriggled beneath him, her slender fingers working at the buttons of his flannel shirt as her mouth pressed hot, wet kisses along his neck. "You taste so good," she mumbled against his skin.

David's jaw clenched against the urge just to slide off their jeans and take her hard and fast. He was sure he'd last maybe ten seconds once he got inside her.

He forced himself to focus and only years of military training allowed his brain any room to function. He pulled her sweatshirt over her head, sending her glasses skittering across the wooden floor. The second shirt came off with less effort and he swept the remaining T-shirt over her head before her lips had found his skin again.

He lifted her chin for a kiss, coaxing her to open for him. She didn't hesitate; her mouth was eager and her tongue danced boldly with his. The little whimpering sounds coming from her throat were driving him wild, forcing rational thought right out of his head.

Somehow, he'd remembered how to get a woman's bra off one-handed. His other hand couldn't wait to feel the smooth skin of her breast against his palm. Her nipples were tight, begging for attention, and he couldn't resist tasting her. He flicked his tongue over the rosy tip, and Noelle hissed in response.

"More," she begged, her voice low and breathless in the confines of the small cabin.

David drew her nipple into his mouth, feasting on her sensitive flesh. She arched beneath him, fisting her hands in his shirt.

At this rate, he was going to lose it before he even got her pants off if he didn't slow down. Every little response she made was like throwing lighter fluid on his fiery lust.

His fingers unfastened her jeans and slid them, her leggings and panties all off in one sweeping motion. Other than the thin shoulder strap of her bra, which was still hanging loosely over one arm, she was completely naked.

David didn't dare look at her all bare and laid out before him. He knew he didn't have the strength for that just yet. He needed to be inside her, deep and hard.

He made quick work of the buttons that remained by sending them flying across the room as he ripped off his shirt and undershirt.

Noelle's green eyes darkened as she looked at his naked chest and she let out a feminine sigh of approval. Slim fingers parted the dark hair, searching for the warmth of skin beneath. Her short nails bit into his skin as if testing the texture of the muscle beneath.

His gold wedding band, which he wore on a chain around his neck dangled over her, giving David a moment's pause. He couldn't think about that now. Not now. Before the thoughts of Mary could invade, he focused on Noelle.

Her mouth was wet and swollen, and there was a deep blush that spread out over her chest, reaching down toward her breasts. David couldn't keep himself from taking her mouth again in a deep, possessive kiss. His tongue thrust inside her mouth in an unmistakable rhythm. In response, her hips pressed against him, eager and restless.

David's hand moved down her torso, over her pale stomach, and his fingers parted the damp, red curls between her thighs. She was slick and hot against his fingers, her back arching and her legs parting to coax his contact to become more intimate.

David obliged. He slid one long finger slowly inside her. She was tight. Hot. Wet.

She moaned into his mouth and her fingernails sank into his shoulders. Her body wiggled anxiously beneath him, but he pressed his weight down against her to hold her still.

Sweat slid along his temple as he tried to kick his brain into functioning. He didn't want to mess this up. He wanted it to be good for her. So good she'd want more.

Because God knew that once wasn't going to be anywhere near enough to sate him—not with a woman he wanted as much as he wanted Noelle.

Her muscles clenched around his finger, squeezing him tight. Instantly, his mind shut down and instincts took over completely. Somewhere in the back of his mind, he heard himself make a deep, growling noise that sounded completely unfamiliar. He shoved his jeans down just enough to free himself, pressed Noelle's thighs wide apart and slid his erection inside her in one long, slow thrust.

Noelle let out a high-pitched sound that could have been either pleasure or pain. He had no clue and couldn't make his mouth form the words to ask. He was lost in the hot grip of her body where she fit him like she'd been custom-made just for him.

He held his body still, buried so deep he could feel her pulse beating in double time with his own. Already he was on the razor edge of orgasm and he knew that if he moved now, he'd be lost.

Beneath him, he felt Noelle's slender body relax somewhat. Her breathing was fast and he could feel each breath warm and soft against his shoulder.

He struggled to regain some sort of control over his lust, but it was a losing battle. Noelle drew her knees up in invitation, letting David slide fractionally deeper. David hissed, but Noelle made a sweet sound of pleasure and shifted her hips in an effort to make him move against her.

David needed no further coaxing. He simply let go of his self-control and allowed himself to feel. Every slippery inch of movement drove him closer to the brink until he was mindless with the need to come. Her body gripped him lovingly, accepting his urgent thrusts with soft, yielding heat. He wanted her to come with him, but he couldn't wait. Need was riding him hard, lashing him, making him mindless.

His hands caught her hips, angling them so he could plunge deep one final time. Pleasure so intense it was painful swept through his body like a lightning storm as he came hard, buried to the hilt inside Noelle.

For long moments, all he could do was breathe as jolts of pleasure shot through his limbs. He knew he was crushing Noelle, but he couldn't make his body work to support itself. Soft, loving hands caressed his back while her body cushioned his.

Finally, conscious thought returned, and with it came guilt. "I'm sorry, Noelle." His voice was rough and dry, and he swallowed in an effort to bring moisture to his mouth.

He wanted to explain to her that it had been years since he'd had sex and that he wasn't usually so quick on the draw. He wanted to promise her that he'd make it up to her. With interest.

But all he could do was recover from the single most powerful orgasm of his life.

He was still semihard inside her and he didn't want to leave. Not yet.

He propped himself up on his elbows and stared down

at her. She was beautiful—her eyes were still dark with desire, her pale skin was rosy, her nipples were tight buds against his chest and her mouth . . .

He couldn't quit staring at her mouth, which was swollen and cherry red.

Incredibly, he felt himself grow hard again. Noelle felt it, too. She shivered and let out a moan of need.

"Don't worry," he whispered. "I won't stop this time until you beg me to."

CHAPTER TWENTY

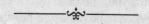

Noelle was ready to beg, but not for David to stop loving her. Her whole body quivered with need, hovering on the edge of something wonderful.

She could feel David inside her, so hot and thick she thought she'd die from the sensation of being stretched and filled. His chest hair tickled her body, making her nipples stand up eagerly for more. Wave after wave of his heat washed over her skin, accompanied by the musky scent of man.

David's face was no longer so grim since he'd come. She could see a lessening in the monumental tension she always sensed inside him. A faint grin played at the corners of his mouth.

Yellow lanternlight cast a golden glow to his tanned skin and highlighted the angular edge of his jaw, the softer curve of his mouth. A gold ring dangled from a chain around his neck. It was a plain wedding band, without diamonds or ornamentation, but no less beautiful for its simplicity. No less meaningful.

Noelle suffered a little spear of guilt. His wife was dead. She wasn't exactly the *other woman*, but she felt like she was betraying something holy and pure by being with a man who still loved his wife enough to wear his wedding ring.

She reached up to touch it with one finger, but David grabbed her hand before she could and pinned it against the sleeping bag by her head. "I don't want to think about that right now. Just you," he said.

Noelle nodded and shoved aside her feelings of guilt for the time being. There were so many sensations rioting through her body that it took little effort to be swept away by them.

He was such a beautiful man. She had no idea why he'd be willing to share himself with her like this.

But she was so thankful he was.

David's hand slid beneath her hips to squeeze her bottom and angle her body up toward his slow, steady thrusts. With each shift of his body, nerve endings tingled and sparked. Deep inside her, pleasure was building upon itself, following a geometric progression that left her gasping in awe of its power.

Noelle was no temptress and even though she wanted to do something to add to his pleasure, she couldn't think straight enough to figure out what that might be. She was too busy feeling the way his wide hand slid down her side, stroking and enflaming every cell as it passed.

David stared into her eyes and slid deep, holding that position while giving his hips an expert rotation. Sizzles of feeling shot out from her belly, making her gasp in wonder.

David chuckled in the darkness and moved so that he was kneeling between her widely spread thighs, still inside her. He grabbed her thighs and pushed them toward her chest as he bent down to take one hard nipple into his mouth.

Noelle hissed and arched her back in response. His body moved over hers in a series of powerful strokes, and she knew that if he kept it up, she was going to fly apart at the sheer intensity of her pleasure.

David sensed it, too. She could feel it in the way his long fingers clenched against her legs, the way his breathing sped as it puffed out over her chest. His suckling became stronger, and to her delight, the light scraping of his teeth against her sensitive flesh nearly sent her over the edge.

Part of Noelle was afraid. She'd never had an orgasm and hadn't really believed that they existed for women—until now. Now, with her climax barreling at her at lightning speed, she knew she'd been wrong.

She wanted to take the time to study what was happening to her, to break it down into little, interesting pieces so that she could examine the process more thoroughly. But David had other ideas. He didn't give her time to think or examine. He increased his pace, slid a hand down between them to stroke the knot of nerve endings shielded by her damp curls.

"I'm going to make you come now," he whispered against her breast.

Noelle couldn't have found the mental capacity to speak even if she had the breath. Her whole body was tightly coiled, held captive by the feeling of his erection thrusting into her, his mouth on her nipple and his finger working magic between her thighs. She wasn't sure how much tighter she could be wound, but David moved with confidence. He knew exactly what he was doing.

And then so did Noelle. She came in a burst of pleasure that seared her nerves and raced through her blood like lightning. She couldn't control the waves of pure sensation coursing over her limbs, pooling in her belly. She didn't want to. It was the most amazing thing she'd ever experienced in her life.

Her voice filled the cabin with keening cries of joy that echoed in the still, cool air.

Slowly, the world returned to Noelle. She lifted David's head and kissed him in an expression of wonder and gratitude.

David grinned. "I'm glad you liked it, but we're not done yet."

Not done? An anxious flutter landed low in her stomach, jumbling her overstimulated nerves. "I'm not sure if I can take any more."

His smile darkened with sensuality, and he moved his hips forward, reminding her of his presence still thick and heavy inside her. "Let's find out, shall we?"

A long, sweaty time later, they found out just exactly how much more she was able to take. And give.

Noelle was still asleep hours later when David woke and pulled himself away from her warmth. She drew in a stuttered breath, then snuggled down into the cozy sleeping bag.

David grinned. After trying to coax her into getting a decent amount of sleep for days, it seemed funny that he'd finally found the right tactic to use. Wear her out with sex.

Just the memory of her sweet, feminine body writhing against him was enough to get him hard again. Even after four times, he was ready to go for a fifth. He hadn't been like this since he left high school. Several times in one day, sure. Several times in a few hours? Not so much.

Maybe it was the years of self-imposed celibacy that had him running hot. Or maybe it was the way Noelle reacted to his touch, the way she sounded when he slid inside her eager body, the way she smelled after her skin was hot with lust and sweat, the way her eyes went wide with shock when she came for him.

Oh yeah. It was definitely that part that made his jeans fit horribly.

But rather than get back in the sack with Noelle and give in to his unquenchable libido, he turned his back and forced his mind to focus on business. He had to go check the perimeter and make sure it was still secure. Every time he walked a circuit of the cabin, his gut nagged him with worry. He was sure he hadn't missed anything, but it wouldn't take too much skill to circumvent the primitive security measures he'd put in place.

It was the best he could do with limited resources, but it wasn't good enough for Noelle.

Then again, neither was he.

That thought was enough to kill any remaining warmth he carried from the previous hours in bed with Noelle. He prayed to God she'd meant it when she'd said no regrets.

David hiked the property, focusing solely on the land, looking for any signs of trespass. None of his traps had been sprung, none of the vegetation had shifted out of place. There were no tracks other than his own and that of a couple of deer.

That nagging worry was eased, but not cured. He'd keep a close eye out while Noelle worked. She seemed to be making progress, and as long as he didn't distract her too much, they'd be out of here soon.

Somehow that thought wasn't as appealing as it had been just yesterday. Sex with Noelle had changed everything. He was no longer dragging his feet as he made his way back to the cabin. Instead, he found himself hurrying to get there. He wanted to see her again. Hell, he even wanted just to talk to her.

After last night, they had some serious talking to do. He hadn't worn a condom. He didn't have any with him. He didn't even think about them these days since his life didn't include sex. He sure hadn't thought about them last night as he came inside her, deep as he could go. Repeatedly. It was exactly what he would have done if he'd been trying to get a woman pregnant.

Not just any woman. Noelle.

An odd, fluttering excitement filled his belly. He should have been scared shitless just thinking about a baby. He should have been panicked, dripping cold sweat and shaking like he'd just puked his guts out.

Instead, he thought about whether or not she'd still be naked when he got back and whether or not he could wake her up with only his tongue. He imagined how easy it would be to push himself into her while she was still slick from the last time he'd come inside her. His jeans stretched and his balls ached for release.

What the hell was wrong with him? He didn't have any right acting like a caveman. Hell, he hadn't even talked to Noelle about sex, much less kids.

Kids? As in plural?

Now he was completely nuts. All that time in isolation had sent him over the edge. That was the only possible explanation he could find for why after one night with Noelle, he was already thinking about making a family.

Family had no place in his world. Especially not now. He couldn't even safely spend time with his sister or her son without worrying about who was watching him and whether or not he'd put the people he loved at risk just by being in the same room with them. Even to consider the notion of settling down in a house in the suburbs to fill every room with kids was complete madness.

He was a walking target. This was his last mission and he fully intended to go out in a heroic blaze of glory, taking every one of the Swarm with him. Not only did he not care if it killed him, part of him hoped it would.

But if that was the case, then why was he thinking about babies?

It had to be some sort of biological imperative—like a woman's biological clock, but for a man. He didn't really expect to live to see Christmas, so his caveman side was making him want to leave behind a little slice of his genes for future generations. That had to be it. It was the only thing that made any sense at all.

When he walked into the cabin, Noelle was just pulling a heavy sweatshirt on over her head. Other than her shoes, she was completely clothed.

Disappointment slowed his steps as he shut the door behind him. Man, he'd really been hoping she'd still be naked.

Noelle gave him a hesitant smile. "Have you seen my glasses?"

David picked them up from where they'd been thrown the night before, cleaned the dust off with his shirt and held them out to her.

His hand was shaking.

He cursed silently and clenched his jaw against the urge to kiss her.

"Thanks," she said, her smile faltering.

No doubt he looked about as friendly as a riled grizzly bear. He tried to find a smile, or at least still his features into a mask of neutrality, but he couldn't.

She licked her lips in a nervous gesture and her green eyes slid toward her shoes. "I, uh, suppose I should get to work."

David cleared his throat so he could talk. "Let's eat first, okay?"

She gave him a small nod and started toward the kitchen area. David grabbed her arm and stopped her. He couldn't let this awkward morning-after stuff continue.

"Noelle," he said, trying to sound casual. He was going to tell her how, although it had been the best sex of his life, he couldn't let it happen again. It was too danger-ous for either of them to become emotionally attached. They had to stay focused and professional and keep their distance. Emotions ran high during crisis situations, and this certainly qualified. It was natural for them to come together in an effort to release some of the tension that had them both pulled tight enough to shatter. But instead, he said, "Are you on birth control?"

Noelle blinked in confusion, then her eyes went wide. "Yes, I mean, no. I mean, yes I take the pill, but they were in my purse and that didn't come with us and so I haven't . . ."

She sank to the floor, boneless, no stool required. "Oh, God."

David sat down beside her and pulled her into his lap.

Her whole body was shaking. He didn't say anything. He just held her until she could work through her thoughts. Fortunately, it didn't take too long.

She looked up at him, her face was a pretty shade of embarrassed pink. "I'm sorry. I didn't even think about it last night."

David couldn't blame her there. Neither one of them had been doing all that much thinking. "Me either."

"What do I do?" she asked him.

How about get married? his mentally ill mind asked silently. He really wished he deserved another chance at happily ever after. It would have been nice to try to make things work with Noelle. "Not much *we* can do now, I don't guess. I mean, no sense closing the barn door once the horses are gone, ya know?"

She gave a slow nod. "I'm not sure I like being compared to a barn, but I get your point. Anyway, I think it is too late in the month for me to get . . . you know."

"Pregnant?" She couldn't even say the word. That didn't sit well with David, considering he'd been all goofy over the mere thought of it this morning.

"Yes. Pregnant." If she hadn't been staring right at him when she said it, he wouldn't have seen the way her eyes dilated. Of course, it could have been his imagination, or a change in the lighting filtering in from outside. But he didn't think so. She hadn't pulled away from him, and that was a good sign.

He stroked a hand over her mussed curls, trying to comfort her. "We'll figure everything out, okay?"

"Um, okay." Her voice shook so hard he could barely make out the words.

Not a good sign at all.

Noelle couldn't concentrate worth a damn. The symbols kept running together as her thoughts strayed to other things. David. Sex. A baby.

Her head landed on the scarred table with a thump. What in the world was she going to do if she ended up pregnant? It wasn't that she didn't like kids, because she did. She'd even thought about having one or two of her own, in that sort of vague, one-of-these-days kind of way. But one of these days turned up to be today, possibly, and she couldn't stop thinking about it. Her life was already so complicated. When this was all over, she was going to have to go into hiding to avoid being hunted down again, she was sure of that. It was one thing to turn her own life upside down, but to drag a kid along with her?

And that was if she even survived.

At least that thought reminded her she had bigger worries than an unplanned pregnancy. If she didn't successfully complete her task, she wouldn't be around long enough to even find out if she was pregnant.

David's wide, warm hands settled on her shoulders. "Want to take a walk and clear your head?"

"How can you be so calm? You just found out this morning that a fling you had last night might end up haunting you for the rest of your life."

She felt him tense behind her. "Fling? Haunt me? Is that how you see what happened between us?"

Noelle groaned in frustration and turned around to stare up at him. "Honestly, I don't know what to think. I mean, I hardly know you. Sure, you seem like a nice guy and you're sexy as sin, but a child is a big deal."

He crouched down so he was at eye level with her. "It is a big deal, but you're not alone. I was there, too, remember? I knew what I was doing."

"No you didn't. If you'd known I could get pregnant, you would never have touched me."

His blue eyes warmed with desire. "Wanna bet? I'd take you again right now if I had even a hint that you wouldn't try to slap me."

He wasn't joking. Something inside her went liquid and hot in response to the completely sincere look on his face.

Baby or not, the idea of getting naked with him again was a potent force, urging her to forget everything else around them and just give in. It would be so easy to just give in. Too easy.

"I'd never slap you," she whispered.

His nostrils flared and his eyes darkened to midnight blue. He slid one blunt finger over her mouth, his eyes focused intently on his touch. "Don't tempt me, Noelle. I'm about two minutes away from meltdown and we still don't have any condoms, so unless you're willing to risk it, you'd best not test my self-control."

Her lungs seemed to malfunction and her skin was too hot and tight on her frame. Her body ached to feel the callused slide of his hand over her skin, his mouth at her breasts. And lower.

She shivered remembering the way his tongue felt so hot and wet and excruciatingly gentle between her thighs. Man, oh, man. If she lived to be a hundred, she'd never forget the way it felt to fly apart with his fingers buried inside her and his tongue dancing circles over her clitoris. And that was nothing compared to the sheer power of coming around his erection while he thrust deep and hard, giving her no way to escape the force of her orgasm.

She'd never known sex could be like that.

She doubted that it would be like that with anyone besides David.

Her body screamed at her to give in. Yeah, she might get pregnant, but would that really be so bad? She was smart. She'd find a way to make things work for both herself and a baby. She had no illusions that David would be in the picture, but that didn't scare her. She would learn to be a good single mother. Lots of women did.

What really scared her was knowing that every time she opened herself up to him physically, she was getting that much closer to falling for him. She wasn't a fool. Sex and love were too closely linked for her to ignore the correlation. She knew that women fell in love with men who were wrong for them all the time.

And David was definitely wrong for her.

He was career military. She was opposed to violence of any kind. The two had no place together. Add to that the fact that he still had the death of his wife haunting him, and he was about as wrong for her as a man could get, no matter how right he felt in bed.

If she fell for him, she'd end up hurt. Her life was already such a mess that she just couldn't risk doing anything that would make it worse. Falling in love with a man she couldn't have would definitely make things much worse. Sex would just make him more appealing to her than he already was.

That, she couldn't handle.

"I'm sorry. I can't," she whispered.

"You mean you won't. You already proved beyond a doubt that you can last night. Quite well in fact."

"I don't regret what we did last night. I just don't think that's it's smart for us to be getting . . . distracted right now."

He jerked away, his movements harsh and angry. "You're right, of course. You don't have to explain," he said through clenched teeth. "I'll be outside."

The cabin shook with the force of the door slamming behind him. Cold air swirled through the room, chilling Noelle both inside and out. She hated to see him go like that, but she didn't blame him for wanting to put some distance between them. It was the only way she was going to be able to resist him.

Noelle swallowed and urged her breathing to return to normal. She was itchy and agitated inside. Her body felt twitchy and unstable and she knew this had to be what sexual frustration felt like. She wished now more than ever that her normal, laser-focused tunnel vision would kick in, and the world—including her frustrated body—would fall away. But it didn't happen. Her focus was held captive by thoughts of David. Thoughts of what they'd done last night.

Maybe she shouldn't have refused him. Lord knew she yearned for some companionship right now—someone she could turn to during this stressful time. Someone who would hold her and tell her it was going to be okay. She didn't even care how big a lie it was.

David was only human, no matter how formidable a human he seemed to be. What if he yearned for the same thing?

Their situation was dangerous. Men had tried to abduct her, or kill her. Noelle could tell by David's steely determination that no matter how bad things got, he'd protect her, even if it cost him his life.

In fact, sometimes, when she looked at him, she wondered whether or not part of him didn't have a death wish. He grieved for his wife; the fact that he still held on to his wedding ring and the way he spoke about her proved that.

Maybe that was why he was fearless in the face of danger. A man who didn't mind dying would have little to fear.

But that didn't mean he didn't want companionship while he was still alive. No one wanted to die alone. Was David any different?

Something deep in her gut told her that she'd better be careful. She was falling for David. Hard.

Noelle told that something to shut the hell up and get back to work.

CHAPTER TWENTY-ONE

Someone had breached the perimeter David had set in the forest.

David crouched low and went still, seeking out signs of where the intruder might have gone. They were good, he'd give them that. The only way he'd known they'd come this way was because they had disturbed some limbs that David had twisted together across one of the paths toward the cabin. The intruder had seen the security measure too late and tried to put the vines back the way they'd been before, but David could see the subtle differences. One of the leaves had been torn and lay on the ground, bruised where the heavy tread of a combat boot had crushed it.

David forced the rising fear down and put his senses on full alert. He had to get back to the cabin and get Noelle out of here. Fast.

As Noelle opened the door to go out and use the drafty outhouse, she saw movement in the trees in two places. Something was wrong with this picture and her instincts were screaming at her to hurry up and figure it out. She

froze in place, her work-fogged brain struggling to make
sense of what she'd seen. Her breathing sped and her heart
started fluttering in fear. Movements in two places. Only
one David.

Panic flooded her system, making her feel heavy and
sluggish, as time slowed, and her overworked mind started
spinning in place, trying to figure out what to do.

"It's just deer," Noelle whispered to herself, but her
instincts were going off, screaming at her to run.

Through a thin patch in the woods, Noelle caught a
glimpse of a shape moving through the trees. A human
shape. It slid slowly over the rough ground with cautious,
stealthy steps.

Oh, God. The Swarm had found her.

Shaking with terror, Noelle backed up into the cabin
and grabbed the gun that was always sitting on the table
for her to use in case of emergency. As much as she
loathed the cold, lethal weight of the weapon, this certainly qualified as an emergency and she was relieved to
feel the chill of it pressing into her palm.

She was not going to let the Swarm take her without a
fight.

The uncomfortable bite of the bulletproof vest that
David insisted she wear when she left the cabin was a
welcome friend right now. She silently thanked David for
his constant nagging and overprotective streak.

As she stepped out of the cabin, her hands trembled so
violently that she was sure she'd never hit a target smaller
than the moon. But the threat the weapon innately held
was better than nothing.

Her only chance of getting out of this safely was
to get to David. If they cornered her in the cabin, she'd

be trapped. There wasn't even a back door to use as an escape route.

The thought of being cornered by the Swarm threatened to drive her to her knees, but she pulled in a deep breath and forced herself to focus.

The front porch of the cabin held no cover from bullets, but the pile of chopped wood a few yards to the side of the cabin had potential. A few more yards beyond that was the bulletproof Bronco. If she could make it that far, she was sure she could escape into the woods.

But first she had to make it that far.

Her mind started running through calculations to determine just how much wood had to be between her and a bullet to stop it from hitting her, but without knowing the density of the wood or the mass and muzzle velocity of the bullet, she had no clue. A lot, she guessed.

A gust of wind whipped through the trees, stirring them all into motion. She heard the pounding of heavy feet getting closer. She didn't have any more time to wait. She had to get out of here.

With speed she didn't know she had, Noelle sprinted for the pile of logs and crouched behind it, praying it would protect her. Her lungs burned from the short sprint and she was sure she was going to throw up from fear. She managed to keep holding the gun, but her palm was so sweaty the thing kept sliding around in her grip.

If running this little bit of distance left her panting and dizzy, there was no way she was going to be able to outrun the men in the woods. She wouldn't get a hundred feet before they caught up with her.

She had to think of something else or she was a goner.

Her tired brain sparked and stuttered, and she clutched

the weapon in her hand so tight it made her knuckles ache.

The gun. That was it. It wasn't just a weapon used to kill, it could also call for help. She pointed it into the air and squeezed the trigger. The backfire stung her hand and jarred her wrist, and the boom was louder than she expected, even though she'd anticipated it. She just hoped it had been loud enough for David to hear, wherever he was. If he heard the shot, he'd come to help her. She was sure of it. All she had to do was survive long enough for him to get here.

In an effort to buy some time, she peeked through a hole in the pile of logs and yelled, "Stop moving, or I'll shoot!"

The movement in the brush stopped.

Noelle let out a small, shuddering breath. At least they were listening. "Throw out your weapons," she shouted.

A few tense seconds passed, then she heard the thump of steel hitting frozen ground. She peeked and could see the black outline of two handguns in the dirt a few feet beyond the tree line.

This was too easy. If they'd been members of the Swarm, they wouldn't have given up so easily—not against one poorly armed, out-of-breath woman. Maybe the men were just hunters out for a few hours of fun stalking deer. Did men shoot deer with pistols? She'd always thought they used rifles or maybe shotguns.

Noelle cursed herself for her lack of knowledge on the subject. She really couldn't be sure of anything.

"Come out slowly with your hands on your head," she ordered, proud her voice wavered only a little.

One man came out from under the cover of some brush.

Just as she'd asked, his hands were on his head, and he moved so slowly that it looked like a slow-motion scene in an action movie.

He wore brown camouflage that blended perfectly with the autumn forest surroundings. His face was smeared with paint, obscuring his features. Other than the fact that he was a tall, lean man, she couldn't see anything specific about him—not even hair color. He moved with that same sort of predatory grace she'd seen in David and beneath his camouflage, she could see the outline of a Kevlar vest.

This was no local hunter. He was the real thing.

Noelle stood from behind the log pile, her gun quivering as she pointed it toward him. She didn't want to shoot anyone, but she would if she had to. "Get on the ground. Facedown. Tell your buddy to come out."

The man started moving as if to lie down, but said nothing. He was moving too slowly, though, almost like he was trying to stall for time.

A sick feeling twisted Noelle's stomach. His easy surrender was a trick.

Noelle moved to flee, but it was too late. Before she could even turn, she was lifted off her feet and the gun was wrenched away from her sweaty grasp. She tried to scream, but a hard hand covered her mouth even as the air was crushed from her lungs by a thick arm under her breasts, trapping her hands at her sides.

Panic seared her nerve endings, giving her strength. She thrashed and kicked, landing a couple of solid blows to the man's legs that brought forth grunts of pain from her captor. She shook her head trying to dislodge his hand enough to bite it, but his grip was too firm.

Beneath the thick band of his arm, she twisted her hand and dug her fingernails into his hard thigh, but it did no good. No matter what she tried, he held her tight, unable to get away.

"Hold still," he commanded in a low, gravelly voice. "I won't hurt you."

Noelle felt the man holding her go completely still a second before she heard David, his voice an icy cold thread of sound. "That's right. You won't hurt her, at least not while I've got this gun to your head."

"Easy," said the man holding Noelle. "I'm letting her go, David. Don't shoot. It's Caleb."

The second his grip eased, Noelle scrambled away, trembling with fear and adrenaline. Her legs were barely able to hold her up and her head spun from lack of air. She was breathing too hard, too fast.

"Caleb?" asked David as he jerked the big man around to look at him.

"Yeah, and Grant, too," Caleb said, motioning with his head toward the second man. "Your woman has him kissing dirt."

Grant pulled his lean body off the ground and brushed the dust off his legs. "I only played along so Caleb could have time to get over there and disarm her. I was afraid she'd do something stupid and shoot one of us."

David looked Noelle over from top to bottom and back again. "You okay?"

She nodded, her breathing starting to slow. Relief made Noelle's head spin and she sat down on the chopping stump to regain her sense of balance. "You know these guys?"

"Yeah. You sure you're okay?" He lifted a hand as if to

stroke her mussed hair but stopped himself short and let his hand drop.

"I'll be fine. They just scared me." Though "just scared" was a pretty generous way to put it. She wasn't sure whether she wanted to hug them for being good guys or punch them out for scaring ten years off her life.

"Sorry about that, ma'am," said the big guy, Caleb. "I didn't hurt you, did I?"

Her fingers were a little sore from clawing at him, but she didn't see the need to mention it. "No."

Caleb's dark eyes went to her sore fingers as if he knew she was lying.

"Did I hurt you?" she asked.

"Just enough to make me regret picking you up. My shins will never be the same. You're tougher than you look."

"And smart," added Grant, giving her a charming smile. "That gunshot was a good way to call David."

"No kidding. I don't think I've ever run faster in my life," said David.

Noelle felt like a fool. She wasn't sure how she was supposed to have known these were David's friends, but she still felt silly to have mistaken them for terrorists. "Sorry I thought you were the bad guys. Guess I've been a little jumpy lately."

"You didn't do anything wrong, Noelle," said David. "I thought about telling you they might be coming, but I wasn't sure my message would get through."

"It got through fine," said Caleb.

David pulled Caleb to him in a hard hug. "Thank God."

Caleb was a few inches taller than David and had at least fifty pounds of muscle on him. David was built, but he could pass for normal in street clothes. Caleb, however, wouldn't have been able to do anything to disguise his muscular bulk.

Grant, on the other hand was leaner than both men, with a build that reminded Noelle of long-distance runners. His movements were fluid and easy as if each one had been carefully choreographed and planned weeks in advance. He had gold eyes that glittered with humor.

Grant leapt over the pile of logs as if it were no more an obstacle than a rumpled rug. So much for her thoughts of being safe behind the log pile.

Grant hugged David, smacking him on the back hard enough to raise dust. "You sound surprised that we'd get the message."

"We told you when you left the Army that all you had to do was call, and we'd come," said Caleb. "You called. We came."

"I wasn't sure the number was still good. A lot can happen in two years," said David.

"Not so much that we wouldn't be here for you," said Grant. "How many times did you save our asses? We couldn't leave a debt like that hanging."

David eyed Grant, his mouth twitching with a grin. "And if Monroe asks if I've seen you?"

Caleb's face was a stony mask of neutrality, showing none of the humor David and Grant shared. "It'd be awfully hard for you to see us, considering we're stationed in an unnamed desert thousands of miles from here."

David nodded in understanding. "As much as I'm relieved to have you here, I don't want either of you screwing up your careers because of me."

Grant smiled, smooth and friendly. Even under all that

paint he was a fine-looking man. "Hell, Captain. We're not here for you. We came on account of the lady here. You know how I can't keep my hands off the redheads." His smile turned warm as he looked at Noelle. Oh, yeah. This guy was a serious womanizer.

David tensed and Caleb laid a restraining hand on his shoulder. "Easy, David. Grant doesn't know she's your woman."

Noelle blushed and wondered if some sort of macho battle was about to break out over her, the gawky nerd with messy hair and baggy clothes. How surreal.

Grant held up his hands in surrender and took a meaningful step away from Noelle. "I think I just found one redhead I can steer clear of. I guess that just proves there's always a first time for everything."

David's eyes searched Noelle's body, hovering at her face. "You sure you're okay?" he asked.

Noelle's pulse had slowed, but she was still quaking inside. The adrenaline crash after this scare wasn't going to be fun. Already she was starting to feel cold and weak. And she really had to pee.

Caleb gave her a sheepish look. "Sorry if I hurt you. I tried to be careful, but I couldn't take the chance you'd put a bullet hole in my buddy."

"I'm fine."

"You're cold," said David, reaching out a comforting hand before he let it fall to his side without touching her. Again.

She offered him a feeble smile. She still wasn't done shaking inside and hated it that she wasn't made of sterner stuff. "I'll go put on some hot coffee. Anyone interested?"

Caleb and Grant nodded, but David just stared, his blue gaze hot and unwavering. "Go warm up. We'll be in in a minute."

It was a dismissal, and she knew it. Even so, she was glad to obey just to be back inside where it was warm, where David didn't look at her like he was about to kiss her.

If he kissed her, emotions without names would boil up inside her, just like they had last night. She was already on edge, struggling to keep control over her fear and worry and lust. There was no room for anything more right now. Anything more and she'd break.

David had to use every ounce of self-control just to keep himself from taking her in his arms and stripping her naked to make sure she was all right. She was shaking and pale, and he just wanted to hold her until all the bad stuff went away. The things that had raced through his head when he heard that gunshot and saw her thrashing and fighting to get free of Caleb still made his blood run cold. He'd never been more afraid in his life.

Not even when he'd been about to descend into the Swarm's camp and recover Mary's body.

He wasn't sure what was happening to him, but whatever it was, it wasn't good for his thinly held control.

"She's cute. Kinda pixielike," said Grant, strategically standing well out of striking distance from David.

David scowled at Grant. "She's a hell of a lot more than just cute, and you stay the hell away from her. Got it?"

Grant grinned. "Oh, yeah. I got it loud and clear, sir."

David looked at Caleb, who was slowly studying the tree line. Even months under the desert's hot sun hadn't managed to lighten Caleb's coal black hair. His skin was even more tanned than David remembered, and that wasn't the only thing that had changed. The man inside seemed to be more of an emotionless soldier than David remembered. It was habit for any fighting man to keep watch, but Caleb was more than just cautious. He was suspicious and watchful as if he expected an ambush at any moment.

David was so relieved to have him at his back it nearly drove him to his knees.

"How did you know about Noelle?" he asked Caleb.

Hard, black eyes met David's. "You mean how did I know she was your woman?"

David nodded.

Caleb shrugged one massive shoulder. "She had your scent and the smell of sex all over her. No way she'd smell like that if you'd just accidentally brushed up against her."

David felt himself harden at the words. He'd done a lot more than just brush up against her, all right. He was dying to do it again. Too bad Noelle didn't feel the same way.

Neither man mentioned Caleb's uncommon olfactory sense. They'd gotten used to his uncanny abilities years ago.

"Good choice in women, by the way," said Grant as he pulled a camouflage cloth off his head, revealing his sun-bleached hair. "She's no wilting flower to stand back and let herself get killed. It was smart to fire that gun to get you to come running, and, frankly, I'm surprised she didn't try to shoot me. I mean, she wouldn't have hit shit with her hand shaking like that, but I wouldn't have been shocked if she'd tried."

"I should have been here," said David, hating himself for not being close enough to save her the fear of encountering two strangers with weapons. What if it hadn't been his buddies?

His gut clenched into a knot at the thought, and he ruthlessly pushed it away. Thoughts like that would freeze him up and make him useless to her.

"Yeah, and we're supposed to be back in that desert hunting sand rats," said Grant. "You can't be everywhere at once. Get over it."

Easier said than done, thought David. "How did you two get here so fast?"

"A few days ago we got word that you'd rejoined Delta. We'd been trying to find you, but until your call came through, we had no idea where to look."

"Why were you looking for me?" asked David.

"We've been monitoring communications throughout the Middle East. Your name came up," said Caleb.

"Needless to say," continued Grant, "we started listening a little harder. Word's out that you're back in the game and there are a lot of bad-ass men out looking for you. The Swarm is back up and running, and as you're the man who nearly destroyed them before, they want you dead as a message to anyone else who might try to do the same."

"You gonna fill us in on the woman?" asked Caleb. "All we know is you came back to Delta for one last mission. Is she it?"

David nodded. "She has to stay alive, no matter what."

"That goes without saying," said Caleb evenly. "She's a woman."

"No, it's bigger than just the fact that she's a woman.

A few weeks ago, some of our guys took down a group of men they suspected of selling weapons. They weren't just any group, they were the Swarm."

"So how does she fit in?" asked Grant.

"She's smart. Really smart. Monroe tracked me down and pulled me back in to protect her. She's the only surviving person who has any chance at all of cracking this old code. It contains the location of a cache of stolen warheads. Needless to say, the Swarm wants it for themselves, which means they also want her."

"Oh, God," whispered Grant, his golden eyes going wide with fear.

Caleb's face darkened with anger, his nostrils flaring.

David looked from one horrified buddy to the other, trying to figure out what the hell was going on. "You gonna share why you're both so freaked out?"

Caleb swallowed hard before he spoke. "We also intercepted a communication talking about how some U.S. scientist is selling off plans for the production of unmanned aerial weapons deployment vehicles. The new ones designed to be undetectable by radar, with enough range to reach anywhere within a couple of hundred miles inland. We weren't too worried because there'd been no chatter about bioweapons, which was our biggest concern."

"But if they get their hands on those nukes . . ." concluded David, feeling his stomach sink to his boots.

"Then they'll have everything they need to wipe out any major U.S. coastal city of their choice," finished Caleb.

David's buddies both looked at him as if hoping he'd tell them they were wrong. He wished to God he could. "We can't let that happen."

"How close is she to breaking the code?" asked Grant.

"I don't know. Close, I think, but I don't want her knowing about this. She's already under too much pressure."

Both men nodded in agreement.

"What can we do to help?" asked Grant.

David took a deep breath before he was able to speak. Things were quickly becoming more complicated than he liked. "Did you bring any gear? Perimeter alarms, communications equipment?"

"No. We just barely managed to get here at all. We figured they wouldn't look for us for a while, considering our op, but missing equipment . . . that'd be spotted right away."

David spat out a violent curse. "This place isn't secure."

"No, it's not," said Caleb. "I built it to be private, not necessarily defensible. I can usually take care of myself no matter where I am."

"I don't mean to insult your cabin, man. I just don't know where else to take her."

"A safe house?" suggested Grant.

David grunted. "Not so safe. The last two we were at were attacked. Someone on the inside leaked her location the first time. The second time I did it myself so I could take them out."

The buddies shared a look that promised violence if they found the person responsible for leaking classified information.

"So, how do you want to play this, Captain?" asked Grant, his gold eyes glinting with eagerness.

David shook his head. "We stay here until she's finished cracking the damn code. Once we know what it says, we may know what to do next. Until then, I'm open to suggestions."

Caleb's black eyes narrowed in thought as he scanned the tree line. "There are only a couple of ways up this mountain and only one road that comes all the way up here. Grant and I can keep watch there while you stick by her side."

"I don't know if that's such a good idea," said David. "I'm not sure she really wants me around."

"I'll stay with her," volunteered Grant, waggling his blond brows.

David gave him an order that would have been anatomically impossible to obey.

Grant just smiled.

Caleb shook his head like a father over bickering boys. "I'll stay with her if you want, and you know I'd never touch another man's woman, but I think if you ask her, she'll want you instead."

"A man can dream," said David.

"You two go get that coffee," said Caleb. "I'll go get our gear."

"Want some help?" offered Grant.

"No. I know you're dying to talk to David about something, so now's your chance to gossip like an old lady."

Grant blinked in surprise but said nothing as Caleb jogged off with long, powerful strides.

"What's he talking about?" asked David.

Grant rubbed the back of his neck as if it ached. "I thought I was being subtle. All I did was say how nice it would be to find you and get to talk to a man on the outside who understood what it was like to be part of Delta. I didn't think Caleb would figure out I wanted to talk to you alone."

"About what?"

Grant pressed his lips together in a thin line. "I'm thinking about getting out. Leaving the military."

David tried not to show his surprise. Grant loved his job—or at least he had for as long as David had known him, which had been since basic training. "Why?"

Grant's golden eyes closed. "It's starting to get to me." He swallowed and David could see his friend straining to hold back some unnamed emotion. "Last month, we took out a camp of hostiles that were involved in gathering some serious firepower. It wasn't anything new, except these were . . . kids. God, some of them couldn't have even been teenagers yet."

David was glad he had no idea what killing a child felt like. At least that was one sin he'd never committed.

"That doesn't make them any less deadly," said David.

Grant nodded, but didn't open his eyes. "I know. We lost a good man that night in the firefight. Like me, Evans hesitated when he saw they were just kids. It cost him his life."

"And you're worried the same thing might happen to you."

Grant looked at him then, a frantic, painful gaze that begged for help. "Or one of the other men. If anything happened to Caleb because of me . . ."

David tried to shut down his reaction to the thought of either of his friends getting killed, but it was too late. That worry had already taken root and started to grow, piling right on top of his already respectable pile of worries. "He can take care of himself," said David, trying to convince himself that was all there was to it.

Grant gave a humorless grunt. "And everyone around

him, apparently. But we're partners. We cover each other's backs. Now that you're gone, I hate to leave him."

David felt a stab of guilt once again for leaving his friends behind. He should have been a stronger man— should have been strong enough to put his grief aside and keep fighting. "What does he say?"

Grant's mouth lifted in a grin. "He says I need to get married and give him some kids to play with. His brothers aren't doing their procreative duty fast enough to suit him."

"Is that what you want?"

Grant was quiet for a while, staring out at the surrounding forest. "Yeah. It's what I've wanted for a long time. We visited Caleb's brother, Saul, last year. He's having some trouble with the ranch back home. Saul could use a hand and I have two good ones."

"So what's holding you back?"

"Caleb. He's . . . scaring me lately. Something happened a few months ago. An op went bad and he blames himself. He's taking chances he shouldn't." Grant pinned David with a hard stare. "You know what I mean."

David felt his gut give a sickening twist. Caleb's guilt was making him take risks he shouldn't. Making him not care whether or not he lived through an op. When guilt got too big to bear, oblivion looked like a good solution. David knew all too well. "Yeah, I know."

"So you see why I can't just leave. No one else knows Caleb like we do. He needs me to keep him steady so he doesn't do anything stupid."

"Does he want out, too?" Getting out of Delta was what saved David's life and those of his buddies. He'd gotten careless in a job where that flaw could easily have been fatal.

Grant shook his head. "Not a chance."

David sighed. He didn't like this at all. Grant and Caleb were his closest friends, and even though he hadn't been able to keep in touch with them for a long time, it was like no time had passed at all. Being with them again was as natural as breathing. He had to figure out some way to keep them both safe.

"What about reassignment to something safer? Intel? Training? Would Caleb go for that?"

"I don't know. He might if it comes as less of a suggestion than an order."

"You want me to talk to Monroe?" asked David.

Grant heaved out a weary sigh. "He'd kill me if he knew I'd put you up to it. He'd kill you for doing it."

"He'll kill himself if we don't."

"I've been thinking about asking him to come with me to his family's ranch. You know, an extended leave without actually making a commitment."

"What good is that going to do?"

"It would give him a taste of life on the outside for a while. He has a great family—four brothers and a baby sister. They're all hardheaded, but they welcome him home with so much love it's hard to believe he'd be able to leave them again, especially since he's needed there. Who knows, he might even catch himself a woman and change his mind about going back."

David thought of Noelle. He hadn't known her for very long, but already, he wondered just how much he'd willingly give up if he thought he had even a slim chance of keeping her. "It could work."

"I have to try something, Captain. I can't let him keep risking his life like this. He's saved me a hundred times over. The least I can do is try to save him this once."

"I'll talk to Monroe about an extended leave, assuming you both aren't kicked out completely for coming to help me." Part of him hoped they were. At least then his friends would be safe. Maybe not happy, but safe.

Grant gave a sheepish grin. "Caleb would do damn near anything for you. The fact that there was a woman in trouble only sweetened the deal."

"He's a good man."

"One of the best," agreed Grant. "Which is why I have to keep his ass out of trouble. I could never stand to face his family if I let him get himself killed."

David knew that facing Caleb's family would be the least of Grant's problems if Caleb died. He'd have to learn to live with the guilt of knowing he couldn't bring Caleb back. That was a hell of a lot worse—something David knew from experience. "God willing, you won't have to. One way or another, we'll protect Caleb, even if it means getting him kicked out."

Owen frowned at the arrival of David's men. He liked a challenge, but the odds were quickly being stacked against him. That simply wouldn't do.

He wasn't foolish enough to risk losing the girl, which meant he was going to have to call for backup, and not some snot-nosed punk like Brian. Real backup—men he'd trained himself—men who knew the price of failure.

Owen slid silently back out of sight. The big guy they

called Caleb kept looking his way, and even though Owen knew he couldn't be seen, those black eyes of Caleb's were still disconcerting. He was going to have to do something about that man before things got out of hand. He was far too dangerous to leave alive.

Caleb walked away, going in the opposite direction from Owen, but it was still time for Owen to gather his men. He had some planning to do and not much time left to do it before Mr. Lark sent someone else. Someone competent this time.

The time for patience was over. It was time to take the girl.

CHAPTER TWENTY-TWO

Noelle was still embarrassed by having mistaken David's friends for the bad guys, so while they ate dinner, she sat off to the side, trying to be invisible. David and his buddies talked about strategies and perimeter defense and a bunch of other things that made her eyes glaze over. She tuned them out and let her mind focus on her work until they all fell silent and looked expectantly at her as if someone had just asked her a question and was waiting for a response.

"What?" she asked.

"Do you want any more to eat?" asked David, but something in his tone led her to believe that wasn't his original question.

"No, thanks."

Caleb looked from David to Noelle and spoke in a low, even voice. "Grant and I will clean up. Why don't you two go for a walk?"

Noelle went soft at the thought of being alone with David again, and when he stood and reached his hand out toward her, she found she wasn't able to refuse. She wanted to touch him too much.

Silently, he helped her strap herself inside her vest and

coat and led the way outside into the remaining light of sunset.

David led her down the steps toward a small footpath she'd seen him use several times before. The wind smelled like fallen leaves and frost and it swept warmth and moisture from her face and hands as it blew by. Her steps seemed loud compared to David's though she had no idea how a man nearly twice her weight could make half as much noise over dry leaves and sticks.

He led her a short way into the concealing cover of the surrounding forest before he stopped. "We have to talk," he said, his voice grim and determined.

Noelle dreaded what he might have to say. She just wished she could finish her work and be on her way. Her poor heart was in jeopardy of being lost more with every passing minute she spent with David.

"Go ahead and talk, then," she told him.

"Someone has to stay with you tonight. I know things . . . got out of hand between us. I won't say I'm sorry, because I'd be lying." He pulled his hand away and took several steps, putting distance between them.

"I'm not sorry either, David. I said no regrets, and I meant it." It was a startling realization to know it was true. She didn't regret sleeping with him, regardless of the consequences. Life was too short and precious to waste even a minute of it.

His back was to her, and she could see the tension flowing down his arms and spine. "I don't know exactly what this thing between us is, but I wanted to make sure you knew how I felt. About last night, I mean. I felt . . ." He trailed off with a string of low curses. "I'm not sorry, that's all."

Noelle went to him, knowing she was playing with fire.

She laid a cold hand on his sleeve and he flinched. "We don't have to talk about this now. Things are still crazy, and we'd be foolish to make any decision based on our current situation. Let's just try not to think about it and get through this."

He whirled around so fast she jumped back in shock. His blue eyes blazed with anger and something more intense. "Try not to think about it? It's all I *can* think about! Every time I look at you, all I can think about is how it felt to slip hot and hard into your sweet body over and over again. I see your mouth and remember the way you moaned, the way you tasted. I see your hands and remember how they felt moving over my back, your fingernails clawing at me as you came."

His words lashed over her like a whip of flame—hot and bright and way too intense. Her body trembled, remembering all too well how it had felt as he'd taken her over the edge again and again. She wanted more. Now, here in the forest in the cold wind. She didn't care that there were people not far away. She didn't care that there might be spiders or poison ivy. All she wanted was to feel him inside her again—to feel the pleasure only he knew how to coax from her body.

She reached for him, but he took a step back. "You'd better be sure before you touch me," he demanded. "I don't have much control left, and if you touch me, it will all be gone."

Noelle was sure. She wanted him regardless of the consequences. Maybe it was self-destructive. Maybe it was even wrong. She simply didn't care anymore. Her attraction to David was too strong to fight.

With slow, deliberate movements, she reached out and

touched his cheek. The muscles in David's jaw bunched as he gritted his teeth. She could see a fine sheen of sweat break out over his brow.

And then all his control vanished. She could see it in his eyes, the way his expression changed from one of pain to acceptance. Victory.

He reached for her and pulled her in for a kiss. It was hard, demanding. She welcomed the thrust of his tongue into her mouth and returned his passion in kind. He gripped her hips, lifting her until she could feel his erection between her thighs. Noelle's world collapsed in on itself until it included only the space between them, the sounds of pleasure and the scent of David's skin and her own arousal.

She felt his hands squeeze her bottom, sending tremors of electric current along her limbs. She ripped her mouth away from his to find the salty heat of his throat. She loved the way he tasted. She licked and bit gently, right below his ear, where she knew it would make him growl in pleasure. She loved the feel of his body, the way his hands clenched on her bottom as she neared his favorite spot with her tongue.

He pressed her up against a thick tree to support her weight, freeing his hands to explore. His body held her tight, his hips pivoting slowly, grinding against her in a way that made her blood catch fire. "Need you inside me," she panted against his neck. "Now."

His long fingers made quick work of his jeans, then hers, stripping them off only one leg. In seconds, he had her legs wrapped around his waist so she was open to him, vulnerable. The cold wind chilled her overheated flesh, and she whimpered, needing him to keep her warm.

David lifted her up to position his erection at her entrance and slid her down slowly, filling her inch by inch. She was slick and ready for him, and there was nothing to bar his path.

Noelle could only groan as gravity carried her down to the inevitable conclusion of her ride. David stretched her body, stroking against every delicate nerve ending. Open as she was, she couldn't keep the grinding pressure of his body from stroking against her. Inside and out, he was setting fire to the most sensitive spots on her body without even moving.

David was breathing hard, his head thrown back to give her space to nibble and kiss the thick column of his throat.

"So damn good," he panted. "Being inside you."

Noelle made a rough sound of acknowledgment at his compliment and tried to wiggle her hips to release the pressure that was swiftly building inside her.

David grabbed her hair to lever her mouth into position for a deep, wet kiss. She tasted his desperation, his urgency, and it made her own swell. "I need you to move," she demanded against his mouth.

And he did. He lifted her until he was just barely inside her, then lowered her until she thought she'd die from the sensation of being filled. Over and over he moved her body, taking cues from her sighs and moans. She was getting close, and she couldn't slow it down.

Wind carried away the sounds of their lovemaking as Noelle's voice rose to a more demanding pitch. She wasn't going to be able to stop herself. Not now. Not while his hard arms were holding her, carrying her toward the heights of pleasure.

With one final thrust, she let go. Her orgasm swept through her system in a firestorm of pleasure so fierce it made her cry out. Her body convulsed around him, making her feel even more full, causing another wave of joy to streak through her nerves.

As the waves began to slow, she felt David tense and drive her down fully upon himself. He let out a guttural noise and she felt him fill her with pulse after hot pulse of semen.

Their breathing sounded harsh in the quiet night, but Noelle didn't care. Her bones had gone to Jell-O and her brain to pudding. She draped her arms over David's shoulders, trusting him to hold her.

Once their hearts had slowed, he disengaged their bodies and helped her slide the leg of her jeans and panties back on so she could sink to the ground to finish recovering. Already, she could feel the wetness of their release soaking through her jeans, cooling in the frigid air.

David adjusted his clothing, watching her with a guarded expression. She wondered if men felt insecure after sex the way she did. Or at least the way she used to. Right now, she didn't feel anything but powerful and sensual. She liked this part of being a woman—knowing she'd pleased her man, and if given the chance, she'd do it again.

"You okay?" he asked. "I, uh, had you pressed pretty hard against that tree."

Noelle felt her mouth curve in a smile. She could still feel the impression of the rough bark along her spine, and she loved it. "I know."

He ran a wide hand over his short, dark hair as if to straighten it, which was silly, considering it was too short to be easily mussed. "I had intended to bring you out here to ask you if you'd rather Caleb stay in the cabin with you tonight."

Suddenly, Noelle felt a little of that postcoital insecurity return. "Caleb?"

"Yeah, well, I changed my mind. After that"—he motioned vaguely at the tree they'd just used shamelessly—"I just don't think I could let that happen. At least without wanting to kill someone. I'm not typically a jealous man, but I find myself unwilling to share right now."

"Good," said Noelle. "I have some code to write, and I don't think the idea of Caleb watching me with those black eyes of his is very comforting."

"Damn right," agreed David.

Noelle straightened her coat. She kept expecting David to head back toward the cabin, but he was hesitating and she didn't know why.

Finally, he pulled in a breath and let go. "We did it again," he said. "Sex without protection."

"I know."

"Are you okay with that?"

"In a perfect situation, we'd have condoms and birth control pills. And a real bed. But this situation is far from perfect." She reached up and laid her hand against his face. His eyes shut, and she willed him to understand all the rioting emotions that were going on inside her. She couldn't bring herself to regret making love with David. She just couldn't. "We'll deal with things when there's something to deal with. Right now, I have to focus on my job. I'm close, David."

He nodded and took her hand in his. The look on his face was so serious it worried her. "I just want you to know that if there is a baby, I'll take care of him. Adopt him. Or her. I won't stick you with that responsibility if you don't want it. Okay?"

Noelle blinked. The man was really thinking ahead, but then she guessed it was part of his profession to do so. It was the only way to be prepared.

He was waiting for her agreement, she could see the anxious light in his eyes. She couldn't leave him hanging. "Okay," she said carefully. "If there is a baby, we can talk about how to handle it. I won't make any decisions without talking to you first." She didn't know if she could give her child up for adoption, even to that child's father, but it was almost as if he was excited about the possibility of becoming a father.

Something inside her melted as she realized that. Most men would just as soon leave a girl than be stuck with the responsibility of supporting a child, even just financially, much less being an actual father. But David had offered to adopt a baby that didn't even exist yet.

It was at that moment that she realized her mistake. Despite her keen intelligence and years of advanced education, despite her warnings to herself that she would keep her distance from David, despite the fact that his career and her principles could never mesh, Noelle had done the most stupid thing in her life.

She'd fallen in love with David.

Chapter Twenty-Three

David sat on the steps in front of the cabin the next morning, drinking coffee with Caleb and Grant in order to give Noelle time to work in peace. She'd said she was close to a solution and he prayed she was right.

The air was cold and crisp with frost and smelled faintly of pine and fallen leaves. There was little breeze and only the tops of the trees swayed as they were brushed by cold wind.

"I keep forgetting how much I love this place," said Caleb.

"Sure as hell beats the desert," replied Grant. "There's nothing worse than getting sand in your shorts."

David eyed Caleb, taking in his solemn face. Something about Caleb had changed since they had worked together two years ago. He was more serious than he used to be. Quieter.

David thought about what Grant had said about Caleb taking too many chances with his life. "Have you thought about a change of career? You're one hell of a carpenter. Why don't you take up cabinetmaking or something and make this place your permanent home?"

"That's an idea," said Grant, his eyes glittering with

excitement. "We could help you expand the place. Put on a real bathroom and maybe a bedroom. We could even see about getting power lines run up here so you don't have to use the generator."

Caleb didn't even blink. He sat there, coffee cradled in his huge hands, staring at the forest in that patient manner of his that made David want to shake him to see if he even knew they were talking to him.

"I bet you could get satellite TV up here," continued Grant. "Between that and a fridge full of food and beer, what more could a man want?"

One side of Caleb's jaw twitched, but he remained silent.

David knew Caleb well enough to see he was suffering, but from what, David had no idea. Whatever it was, the conversation was hard on Caleb, so it was time for a change in topic. Caleb would talk about whatever was on his mind if and when it suited him, which David hoped would be soon.

"One of us is going to need to make a trip into town tomorrow," said David.

"I'll go," said Caleb.

"I'll go with you," offered Grant, a little too quickly to be casual.

David frowned at Grant, who gave him an apologetic stare.

"I'm not suicidal," said Caleb. His mouth pressed flat into an irritated line. "Stop acting like I can't take care of myself."

"I know you can take care of yourself," argued Grant. "I also know that Monroe has labeled you as a man with limited self-preservation instincts."

Caleb's black brows rose at this news. "Has he? Huh."

David looked at Grant to see if this was one of the lean man's jokes. Grant had a wicked sense of humor, but right now, he was dead serious. "What the hell happened?" asked David.

Caleb turned his head and studied the forest. Grant's face darkened with anger. Neither man said a word.

A low buzzing sound came from Grant's pants, and he reached into his pocket to pull out a phone. Looking at the display, he let out a resigned sigh. "It's Colonel Monroe," he said as he pressed the button to receive the call. "Lieutenant Kent speaking."

Grant listened, then winced. "Yes, sir. The desert is damn hot. Sandy, too, sir."

David could hear the faint rumble of Monroe's voice.

"No, sir. Were we expecting Captain Wolfe on this op, sir?"

Grant shot David a frustrated look. "Yes, sir. If I see him, I'll make sure to pass on that you are looking for him."

The rumble coming from the phone got louder.

"No, sir. I'm fairly sure your boot will not fit that far up my—" Grant lifted the phone away from his ear and all three men could hear Monroe's deep, enraged voice booming out of the tiny speaker.

There was a vile string of curses followed by the command, "Hand Wolfe the goddamn phone, Kent!"

"It's for you," said Grant.

David took the phone and started talking before Monroe got the first word in. "Don't blame Caleb and Grant for coming here; I ordered them to leave their posts and give me a hand."

Monroe's voice was low and pissed. "The hell you did. I know those two men and neither one of them had to be ordered to give you a hand. The only reason they got away with leaving is because I wanted them to track you down. I knew they'd find you no matter how deeply you'd buried yourself. It worked, too."

"Yes, sir. I suppose it did."

"Why the hell haven't you been answering the sat phone?"

"I didn't want to be tracked. I don't like using this one either, so make it quick."

"Don't push your luck, son. You're still under my command for as long as she's with you."

David bit back a disrespectful phrase, just barely. "What do you want, sir?"

"We found the informant. It was one of the CIA agents. The Swarm has his son held hostage in exchange for information, though by now, I'm sure the boy is dead. We've had the agent under interrogation for forty-eight hours and I don't think he knows anything. He's just the Swarm's tool."

Shit. David couldn't bring himself to ask who it was for fear it would be someone he knew. Someone he liked. Maybe he'd even met the man's son. The thought was more than he could take right now. "Are there others?"

"Don't know. We were hoping to get the current locations of the Swarm out of him, but it doesn't look hopeful. We'll resort to more extreme tactics in a few hours just to make sure he's not lying, but I just wanted you to know that it should be safe to come back."

"We're staying put for now. It's safer here."

"You sure?"

"Yes, sir. I'd really like to be off this line, though. Who knows what sort of locating equipment they have."

"I understand. Is she making progress?"

"Yes, sir. She is. I don't think it will be long now."

"Check in again within two days, Captain."

"Yes, sir." David ended the conversation and powered the phone off. "Keep this off while you're here. I don't want to take any chances."

"Right. Will do. So, how fucked are we?" asked Grant.

David felt himself smile. "Not too bad. Monroe was hoping you'd come find me."

"That sneaky bastard." Grant grinned.

Caleb's eyes went hard and cold. He apparently wasn't fond of being manipulated like that. "If we're going to stay, we should plan that trip into town."

David heard Noelle's low mumble of incoherent phrases coming from the cabin. His heart warmed at the thought of having a little time alone with her again. Soon she'd be finished with her work, and they'd go their separate ways. He wanted to spend as much time with her as he could before that happened. "Why don't both of you go into town. Noelle and I will be fine here alone."

"I'm sure you will," muttered Grant with a grin.

"Jealous?" asked Caleb with a completely serious expression.

"Hell, yes. David went and got himself a brainy woman who's too cute for words while I haven't gotten laid in weeks."

"Weeks?" said David with mock horror, thinking of his two-year celibacy. "Poor baby."

"Fuck you, Wolfe. I don't have to take this abuse." Grant stood and headed for the tree line. "I'm going to go walk the perimeter and think about the woman I'm going to pick up while we're in town tomorrow."

"He will, too," grumbled Caleb when Grant was gone.

"Will what?" asked David.

"Find some woman willing to go for a quickie in a hotel with him. Or maybe just a public restroom. I swear the man can sense an easy target from a quarter mile. He'll be off getting his jollies and leave me to do the grocery shopping."

David laughed. He couldn't help it. He'd missed his buddies too much not to enjoy their quirks. "Since you'll be doing the shopping, I need to add a few things to your list."

"Like what?"

David felt his face heat. He was a grown man, but he couldn't help being a little weirded out about his relationship with Noelle. It was still new and uncertain and part of him still felt like he was being unfaithful to Mary's memory. He knew it was stupid, but he couldn't help it.

David took a deep breath and just spit it out. "I need you to pick up a pregnancy test."

Caleb's expression remained neutral, unsurprised. "I thought you looked like you were starting to show. I didn't want to say anything in case you'd just gotten fat."

David laughed and damn, it felt good. "Don't be an ass. This is serious."

"Okay. I'll see what I can do."

"I wouldn't bother if I knew how much longer we were going to be here, but we don't know and if we're here for a few more weeks . . . I just thought she might like to know. The idea really freaked her out."

"So, what are you hoping for? Negative or positive results?"

David knew what he wanted, but it involved a lot more than just a blue line on some test. In a perfect world, he'd have it all. A wife, kids, a nice, quiet life where he didn't have to worry about someone wanting to kill him or his family. In a perfect world, he'd forgive himself for Mary's death and be able to move on. But this was far from perfect and he had to face reality. "What I want is for Noelle to live long enough that the results of a pregnancy test matter."

"So, do you want me to pick up some prenatal vitamins, just in case? My mom always took those when she was pregnant."

"Good idea. She's either going to need them or feminine hygiene products."

"Damn," said Caleb, looking a little uncomfortable for the first time since he arrived. "I don't know anything about that."

"You have a sister, don't you?"

"Yeah, but she was still a kid when I left home. It wasn't really an issue. You were the one with a wife. Shouldn't you know about these things?"

"Mary always took care of that stuff herself. I never had to learn how to buy those . . . things."

They leaned forward, bracing their elbows on their knees for a strategy session. "So, what do we do?" asked Caleb.

"I don't want to ask Noelle what she needs. She's concentrating, and if I bring up the subject of whether or not she's going to need . . . feminine hygiene products, she might lose it."

"Right. We'll figure it out without her. We've planned missions that were harder than this, right?"

David gave Caleb a disbelieving look. "I don't remember any." He pushed out a breath. "Okay. I think Mary used tampons. Why don't you get those?"

"Don't they come in different sizes?"

"How the hell should I know?"

"I think they do. She looks like a small. What do you think?"

That thought made David remember just how tight and slick she'd been when he'd taken her last night against the tree. He cleared his throat and focused on the conversation before he became physically uncomfortable. "Maybe you should get a variety, just in case."

"I can do that."

"And some condoms."

Caleb did smile now. "Do you want those in size small, too?"

David shook his head. "Fuck you, Stone."

"Not even on your best day."

Noelle closed her laptop and straightened the chaotic pile of notes on the scarred table. It was after dark, and she could hear men's voices out on the porch, joking and laughing together. She could pick out David's voice, and every time he laughed, it made her smile.

It was a wonderful sound. One that she wasn't going to be able to hear for much longer. She was nearly done. A few more lines of code to debug, and she was sure her program would work.

After that, she knew David would take her back to Monroe and he'd go back to his life without her.

It was a bleak thought and one that she refused to dwell on right now. She had too much responsibility to let any part of her brain be occupied by borrowed trouble. David was still here and she would use what little time she had to make plenty of memories she could keep with her even after he was gone.

She poured four mugs of coffee and carried them outside, using an old cutting board as a tray.

As she pushed through the door, the men fell silent and all six eyes were on her. "What?" she demanded, squirming under all that masculine attention.

"We just didn't expect to see you detach yourself from your work," said Grant.

David stood and took the mugs from her, handing them out. "Everything okay? Are you stuck again?"

Noelle shook her head. "I'm just at a sensitive point and if I start wading through my code without a clear head, I'll end up doing more damage than good. I'll start again in the morning when my mind is fresh."

David sipped his coffee, staring at her over the rim of his mug. "That sounds suspiciously like you're planning on actually going to sleep tonight. And not at the table, either."

Noelle offered him a shy smile. What was it about the way he looked at her that made her go all syrupy inside? "I thought I'd give the sleeping bag another try. I'm less likely to fall off it than I am the stool."

Out of the corner of her eye, she saw Caleb nudge Grant with one thick arm. "We should get going," he said.

"Uh, yeah," stammered Grant. "We've got a lot to do tonight. You know, building a fire and . . . stuff."

Caleb shook his head at Grant's fumbled lie and finished off his coffee. "Night, Captain. Noelle."

Grant set his mug on the porch and followed Caleb back into the tree line, where they had camped last night.

"Why don't they stay in the cabin with us? They've got to be freezing out there."

David stood and offered her his hand. "I promise you they don't even feel chilly. We've been cold before, and this isn't close. Besides, they don't want to intrude on us."

Noelle's cheeks warmed. "Oh."

"But if it will make you feel better, I'll go get them and order them to sleep inside. They won't like it, but they'll do it."

"Uh, no. That's okay."

He was staring down at her, his blue eyes dark in the dim light of the porch. Only the soft glow from the lantern inside lit the space. He still held her hand, and he was standing close enough to her that she could smell his skin. He was just watching her, waiting for her to do something.

If she were a seductress, this is where she'd say something sexy and pull him in for a kiss. But she wasn't and she didn't really know how to tell him that she wanted to be with him again before they parted ways. She thought that he still wanted her. He was looking at her with hungry eyes, and he wasn't moving away. But he wasn't moving closer, either.

He was letting her make the next move. If this had been chess, she'd already have him naked, sliding inside her. Checkmate. But this wasn't something she knew, and her insecurity was driving her batty.

Noelle refused to be shy or girly about this. She knew what she wanted, and even if she wasn't sure how to go about taking it, she would at least let him know what she wanted so there would be no question. "David," she began, then faltered.

"Yes, honey?"

The sweet endearment made her shiver with warmth and gave her courage. "If you're not too busy and if you wouldn't mind terribly, I think I'd like it if we could go back into the cabin and make love."

A masculine smile curved his lips and Noelle found herself staring at them. Wanting. "I don't suppose I'm too busy right at the moment."

"No?"

He shook his head slowly. "And as far as minding terribly, well, you tell me." He pressed her palm along the ridge in his jeans, the hard, unmistakable proof that he wanted her.

Noelle's insecurity vanished. He wanted her. And she wanted him. She wrapped her arms around his neck, rose up onto her toes and kissed him. His lips were warm and firm and he tasted of sweet coffee.

His hands slid around her waist, gripping her, holding her close. She could feel his erection hard against her soft belly and it made her insides liquefy.

Her tongue played along the slick inside of his bottom lip, her teeth grabbing gently and tugging on his mouth. David groaned and cradled her head so he could kiss her more deeply. Noelle's head swam with sensation and she just let herself float in the midst of it. Nothing else mattered right now except David—his mouth on hers, his body pressed firm and hot against her.

Suddenly, he pulled away his eyes dark and hot on her mouth. His hands flexed, one against her scalp, the other along her hip. "Are you sure about this?" he asked.

"I've never been more sure of anything in my life. I need you David. Want you."

His nostrils flared as if pulling in her scent and his jaw bunched with tension. "God, I love hearing you say that."

She offered him a smile of feminine approval. "Let's go inside."

Noelle took his hand and led him through the door. David watched her as he stripped out of his jacket and vest, then continued undressing. Noelle watched with complete attention as he shed his boots, socks, jeans and shirt. He stood before her completely naked and aroused, completely immodest. His chest was covered with a dark swath of hair that narrowed as it led down his body. In the dim light, the muscles in his arms and legs were accentuated with deep shadows, making her fingers itch to slide over the masculine contours. His penis jutted out from a nest of dark hair, pointing proudly toward the ceiling, its tip glistening in anticipation.

Noelle's mouth watered at the sight of him.

David's voice was low and rough with arousal. "Look your fill, because as soon as I get you naked, we'll be pressed too close together for you to see anything."

He reached for her, but Noelle stepped back, dodging his hand. "Let me," she said, wanting to give him the same thrilling show he'd just given her. "I'm no professional stripper, but you'll have to forgive my lack of experience."

A low rumble of approval sounded from his throat and his eyes fastened on her fingers, which were opening the buttons of the flannel shirt she'd borrowed from him to keep warm.

"I'll take enthusiasm over experience any day."

She shed her layers of clothing, her hands shaking with excitement. Never once did David's eyes move away from her. He stood there, his feet braced apart, his hands fisted at his sides as if he was trying to keep himself from reaching for her. As she watched him, his body tensed, his erection twitched and Noelle stared in amazement.

"That's enough of a show," rasped David as he closed the distance between them and pulled her mostly nude body into his arms. Only her panties and socks remained, and when their bodies met, the silky brush of his body hair against her skin lit every one of her nerves on fire. His heat enveloped her, making her feel boneless, melting.

"Kiss me," she demanded, and he obeyed with a triumphant smile.

Noelle opened her mouth to his passionate onslaught, sighing as she tasted him once again. His arms were hot bands around her body, holding her upright in spite of her wobbly legs. The world tilted and Noelle relaxed, trusting David to carry her safely down to the cushion of the sleeping bags laid out on the floor.

The air was cold, but it didn't chill her, not while she was being held in the furnace of David's body heat. With the slippery sleeping bag at her back and David lying atop her, blanketing her body with his own, Noelle felt utterly safe and protected and wanted. It was a heady combination, one she relished with every bit of conscious thought that remained.

Her body thrummed, vibrating wherever his hands stroked. Noelle wanted to slow down so she could savor every moment, but her body had other plans. She ached with emptiness, knowing the only thing that could ease that ache was David. She shifted her legs, parting them in eagerness, but David didn't take the hint. He moved to her side, pulling away from her mouth with an audible kiss. "I want to watch you this time," he said.

Noelle had no idea what he meant. He always watched her. She cursed her lack of experience but refused to give up the heat building between them. She reached for him, trying to pull him back atop her, but, he didn't budge.

"Like this," he said, and shifted her body until she was straddling his thighs.

Noelle looked down at the marvelous expanse of man beneath her. He was laid out like a sacrifice, and Noelle wanted nothing more than to take what he offered. But instead, she held still, forcing herself to slow down. This was probably the last time they'd ever make love, and she wanted it to last.

The hair on his legs tickled the sensitive insides of her thighs, which were spread wide to reach either side of his body. She splayed her fingers over his ribs and leaned forward to reach his mouth. She wasn't quite tall enough to reach, so she settled for kissing his neck instead. His penis pressed hot and hard against her stomach, and the contact made David moan. Noelle's tongue swept out to taste his skin, dipping into the hollow of his throat in a wet kiss. She felt the sinuous length of the thin gold chain around his neck, but she didn't let herself think about why it was there.

"Mmmm." She made a humming noise, enjoying the salty taste of aroused man. "Do you taste this good all over?"

She felt him tense and reveled in the knowledge of her feminine power. Her lips trailed over one thick shoulder and she sank her teeth delicately in the hard pad of muscle.

David hissed, and Noelle gave a dark smile against his shoulder. "You liked that."

"God, woman! You're driving me out of my mind."

"Want me to stop?"

"Hell, no."

"Then you don't mind if I enjoy you? Explore you?"

She felt his chest move in a low chuckle. "I've never known a man who died from lust, but if I do, at least I'll die happy."

Noelle took that as consent and let her hands and mouth wander over his chest, down his abdomen. She loved the texture of his hair and the smooth heat of his skin beneath. He smelled like the forest at sunset, beautiful and wild and clean. The hardness of his body intrigued her as much as it excited her. She'd never known what such power felt like until his steely strength was flexed under her palms.

She continued her trail of kisses and touches and bites down his body until she reached the rampant length of his erection. His entire body was tense, held still as she studied him, taking in the sight of his need for her. She'd never before thought that the male body was all that attractive, but to her, David's naked arousal was beautiful.

She reached out a slim finger and touched him where the proof of his need glistened in the lamplight.

David pulled in a strangled breath, and his hips bucked up off the floor.

"You liked that," she whispered, watching as she spread that drop of moisture over the tip of his erection.

He was past actual words, but the grunt he gave conveyed his agreement as eloquently as if he'd started spouting poetry.

She wrapped her hand around his length, marveling at

the smoothness of his skin. Soft, like baby skin, over iron hardness. The contrast was arousing, compelling.

David's fingers slid through her hair along her scalp. His arms were shaking, as if he was struggling against the need to pull her head toward him. Noelle needed no encouragement. She wanted to taste all of him.

Without warning, she took him into her mouth, feeling the smooth slide of his flesh against her tongue, the salty taste and scent of his arousal filling her senses.

David moaned and his fingers clenched along her skull as his hips shifted in a chaotic motion. Noelle had never done this before, but apparently, her inexperience didn't matter.

He said he'd take enthusiasm over experience any day, and Noelle had enthusiasm to spare. She took her time enjoying him, figuring out what pleased him. He made these deep, husky moans of approval that made her blood sing with pleasure. Making him feel good like this was wickedly delightful, something she could definitely get used to.

His moans became more urgent, and she felt him tugging at her hair, trying to pull her away. Noelle released him from her mouth and looked up into his face. She could feel her lips, hot and swollen, knew that her enjoyment was showing plainly on her face.

"So beautiful," he murmured.

Noelle smiled, her newfound power giving her mouth a naughty slant. "So are you."

He wrapped his hands around her biceps and pulled her up his body until he could kiss her mouth. She sensed his fierce need for release straining his control, but his kisses were gentle, soothing, drugging.

Noelle gave in to her need to be swept away by feeling, closed her eyes and reveled in the way he made her body heat and her soul sing. He was her man, at least for right now, and she wanted to possess him, be possessed by him.

David pulled away from her mouth and lifted her up so he could sweep his hot tongue over the tip of her breast. Electric sensations zinged along her nerves, sizzling her blood and pooling low in her belly. Noelle pulled in a shocked breath, then let it out in a groan of raw need.

The short beard stubble along his jaw rasped over her breasts in a rough caress. He drew her hard into his mouth, using his tongue and teeth in a way that had her quivering on the knife-edge between pleasure and pain. It was too much sensation and still not enough.

Noelle used all her strength to pull away, scrambling to settle her eager body over the tip of his erection. She needed him inside her. Now. There was no longer time for slow, lazy loving. She needed him, hot and deep and hard. Her ache was too harsh to be appeased by anything gentle.

Without any help, Noelle shifted her weight and sank down on him, feeling the sweet pressure of being filled inch by hot inch. Her eyes rolled back in her head and she panted while she adjusted to the sensation of being stretched. David's hands held her hips in place, refusing to let her move. He, too, was breathing hard, and she could feel the tension of his body drawn tight beneath her.

"I'm never going to get enough of you," he said in a thick voice. "So damn good."

Noelle couldn't speak. It took all her concentration just to hold herself still. The urge to move was killing her, but if she fought his grip, she'd never have the strength to finish what she'd started. And she wanted that too much to let it go.

Slowly, his hands loosened, and he swept his palms up her body to cup her breasts. His thumbs rasped over her nipples and Noelle whimpered as those electric currents shot through her to where she was filled by David.

She braced her hands on his chest and started to move, slowly, carefully, feeling every slick inch of him against her sensitized sheath. Her balance was awkward, but she quickly learned how to ride him and let go of every remaining inhibition she had.

David helped her move, guided her body in ways she wouldn't have known would please her. When she thought he was seated in her as deeply as he could go, he'd pin her hips and rotate his, showing her that she had been wrong. He pressed his thumb against her clitoris, increasing the pressure with every stroke until Noelle could no longer contain herself. She gave in to her orgasm, letting it sweep through her in a relentless series of waves, one after another, while her body convulsed around David.

She felt him watching her but didn't care. There was no space left in her for embarrassment. This was pure pleasure and she gave in to every shimmer of sensation. The intensity of her climax waned, continuing in little ripples of her internal muscles. Beneath her, David groaned and tensed, pulling her to him in an unbreakable bond. *"Noelle,"* he shouted, and the first pulse of his orgasm filled her. He held her to him, gritting his teeth as his heat pumped into her.

Noelle draped her body over his, resting her head on his chest. She could feel his heart beating inside her, fast and in time with her own. She could hear it thud beneath her ear, a frantic pace that left her grinning in satisfaction. She was no seductress, but she'd made him feel good. That was all she really wanted.

David cradled her body in his big hands, smoothing his palms over her back and bottom. Even his calluses felt good against her skin. Between his warmth and caresses and the languid relief of their lovemaking, Noelle couldn't help but close her eyes and drift.

David shifted, and she realized that she'd fallen asleep. He rolled over, leaving her lying on one sleeping bag while he opened the second to make a bed. Noelle scooted over to where he patted the sleeping bag and he covered her with the second.

His expression was warm and tender when he tucked her in. He was such an easy man to love, the way he cared for her. She wished they had more time together, but she knew that wasn't going to happen.

Her body was sated and so tired from physical strain and mental pressure. Part of her wanted him again, but the rest of her was just too tired. "Are you going to sleep with me?" she asked him.

"Yes, but that's all. You need your rest." He blew out the lantern flame and padded back across the cabin, crawling in bed with her. "Give me your glasses."

Noelle handed them over, trusting him to put them somewhere safe where they wouldn't be stepped on. She needed to wash up, but couldn't find the strength to care that she was slick and messy from their lovemaking. Knowing him, even if she did wash, she'd end up messy again by morning.

He rolled onto his side and pulled her up against him so her back was cradled by his chest. "It's so good to be warm again," she said.

"I'll warm you up like that anytime you want, honey."

Noelle knew it wasn't a promise for the future, but part

of her wished it could be. Rather than being sad over the knowledge that they would separate soon, she decided to enjoy her remaining time with David.

She snuggled up against him, smiling into the dark when she felt his penis harden against her bottom. "I thought you said you wanted to sleep."

"I didn't say I wanted to, I said you needed to. And you do. Just close your eyes and pretend that you don't feel that."

Noelle laughed. "Yeah, right." She wiggled some more, experimenting with her newfound powers of seduction.

David's erection became less easy to ignore. For both of them.

"Stop that," he commanded.

Noelle disobeyed with delight.

With a growl, David rolled her under him and slid into her in one powerful thrust. He didn't give her time to warm up to her orgasm. He pulled it from her with a series of expert movements of his hips and wicked, knowing fingers and tongue.

Noelle had nowhere to hide from his demand, and by the time he climaxed deep inside her body, she was whimpering from a mixture of fatigue and pleasure.

She felt his satisfied smile against her temple. "You'll sleep now, I'll bet."

Noelle was out before she could find the strength to agree with him.

David held her for a long time before his limbs quit shaking. He slipped from the warm cocoon of sleeping bags to retrieve a washcloth. He wet it and held it over the stove until it was nice and warm. He'd made a mess of Noelle's sweet body, and she was too tired to clean herself up, so he did it for her.

She was so deeply asleep that she didn't even twitch. Poor thing. She'd been pushing too hard. He was glad she was getting a decent night's sleep tonight.

And she would. David was going to stay right by her side all night, holding her, making sure she stayed where he wanted her to. The fact that she was so soft and feminine and naked didn't make his task a sucky one. This was one job he was going to enjoy.

David pulled her back into his embrace, pillowing her head on his chest. Her warm breath swept out over him in a sleepy sigh of contentment.

He had no idea what he was going to do after this assignment was over, but he knew he didn't want to let Noelle go. Maybe it was just the fact that she was the first woman he'd been with since Mary; but then again, maybe it was something more. David wasn't sure, but he knew one thing. He wasn't letting Noelle go until he knew whether what he felt for her was as real as he feared it might be. Hoped it might be.

He'd lost one woman he loved, and he'd die before he lost another.

Just before dawn, Owen approached Brian where he slept at the base of a large tree. He had one more job for the boy. One final mission.

Before Brian could stir, Owen injected him with a heavy sedative. As soon as Brian felt the sting of the needle, his eyes flew open wide, but his awareness only lasted a second before the drug kicked in.

Owen lifted Brian onto his shoulder and shifted the boy's gangly weight to a more comfortable position. He had bait, now all he needed to do was to set the trap.

CHAPTER TWENTY-FOUR

Grant and Caleb had just left to patrol the perimeter one more time before running into town for supplies. There wasn't enough food to last for more than a day the way those two ate. David leaned against the counter in the kitchen, just watching Noelle. Since he'd woken her with his mouth early this morning to make love to her, she hadn't said more than a handful of words to him—most of those were really more grunts than words.

David grinned. She was so damn pretty when she was concentrating on her work. Her red curls kept spilling out from the knot she'd stuffed them into at the top of her head. She had some ink smudged on one cheek, but they were a healthy pink color rather than unnaturally pale. She kept frowning at her computer screen, then spouted out gibberish about simultaneous equations and vector analysis. She probably didn't even realize she was talking to herself.

David just lounged there, content to watch her. For the first time in years, the hollow, dead spots around his heart were coming back to life. It wasn't exactly a comfortable process, but it was better than he'd felt in a long time.

Since Mary.

Somehow, thinking about Mary didn't evoke the same

instantaneous pain it always used to. He still felt guilty over her death and had a burning desire to see every last one of the Swarm dead, but Noelle had done something to him that helped ease the searing pain he'd become so familiar with. She was helping him heal.

If he hadn't felt it happening, he wouldn't have thought it possible.

Noelle went completely still. "I did it," she said in a near whisper. "I figured it out."

David crossed the space in three long strides. He stared at the screen, not understanding a word or symbol he saw. "Are you sure?"

She looked up at him, excitement shining in her green eyes. David wanted to kiss her so bad he could almost taste her mouth. "Yes. I'm one hundred percent positive. Only . . ."

"Only what?"

She bit her lip as if trying to figure out what to say. "This isn't all of the text."

"Then how do you know you cracked it?"

"I could spend the next twelve hours trying to explain my solution to you, or you could just take my word."

David had a hard time sitting through an hour-long lecture. "I'll take your word for it."

"Did Monroe give you anything else? Any numbers or instructions?"

"No, nothing."

Noelle sat back and let out a frustrated sigh. "Then what I've got here isn't going to help much."

Disappointment and relief warred within him. It wasn't over yet, which meant she wasn't leaving him yet. "What do you mean?"

"It's kinda hard to explain without those twelve hours, but I'll try. Do you have a map?"

"Of where?"

Noelle shrugged. "It doesn't really matter. I just need it to show you what I mean."

David rummaged through his knapsack and pulled out a map of Colorado. Noelle went into the kitchen, dumped out a box of dried pasta into a bowl and tore the front off the cardboard box. There was a little clear plastic window that displayed the noodles inside the box. On that window, she drew an arrow and labeled it north. Then she drew another arrow pointing down and to the right.

Noelle spread the map out on the counter and placed on top of it the cardboard box front with the plastic window and the arrows she'd drawn. "Okay. The up arrow is north—just a reference—and the second arrow gives us our solution, which are map coordinates. The tip of the arrow is the destination this text was encrypted to hide. It's our target location for the weapons."

David frowned. "But you don't know the destination unless you know where to put the arrow on the map."

"Exactly. I know magnitude—distance in this case— and direction, but not the origin."

Frustration welled up in David's chest. "All this effort and nothing tangible to show for it. Damn, I'm sorry, Noelle."

"It's not a lost cause. There's got to be another piece of text somewhere, like this one, which gives us the origin. If we know that, we'll know where this text was telling us to go. Can't you ask Monroe?"

"I can try, but I'm pretty sure that he would have sent along anything he thought we could use. Is it possible you missed something? I mean, couldn't there be another bit of info in all that gobbledygook?"

Noelle chuckled. "It's not gobbledygook. It's a string of equations that share like variables. The solution to that series of simultaneous equations clearly leads to a fairly simple vector analysis. I made some assumptions along the way, and if I feed my algorithm different values for certain variables, then I will get a solution with a new magnitude and direction—a different vector, but it's all fairly simple now."

David stared at her. He could feel his IQ slipping as her words slaughtered brain cells left and right. "I'm sure it is."

She seemed agitated that she couldn't share this with him, but there wasn't much David could do about that. He just wasn't in her league when it came to this stuff.

"So, what do we do now?" she asked.

"First, you make a backup copy of all that stuff and show me how to use it. I want to get you away from this mess as quickly as possible. My gut tells me that as soon as we figure out the last piece of the puzzle, I'll be going wheels up immediately."

She looked away quickly as if wanting to hide her eyes from him. "So we'll be separating soon then?"

David didn't like the thought of leaving her behind any more than she did, but he knew it was her best chance for survival. At least until all this was over. He couldn't very well drag her into the remaining Swarm stronghold when he went to hunt them down. He needed to know she was safe. "Yeah. We will."

"Will I see you again?" Her voice was so small and vulnerable it made him want to pull her in his arms and promise never to leave her side again. Which was about the stupidest thing he could possibly do.

"You will. We have . . . unfinished business." David didn't promise. He didn't know if he'd survive this mission or not, but he knew that if he did, he'd hunt her down no matter how deeply they tried to bury her in any of the protection programs. She was his woman and he wasn't letting her go until one of them decided to call it quits. Besides, he might have a child on the way, and he wasn't about to walk away from that while he still drew breath.

She nodded, but he could see in her expression that she didn't believe him. David didn't blame her one bit. He had a hard time believing that he would come out on the other side of this mission alive too. Even though the odds weren't great, they were better than they had ever been before because Noelle had given him a reason to live, which was more than he'd had in a long, long time.

Caleb and Grant were nearly finished patrolling the perimeter David had set up to protect the cabin when Caleb heard a faint noise. He stopped, motioning Grant to do the same.

"You hear that?" asked Caleb, sniffing the air for the scent of animals—including the human variety.

The sound came again, louder this time—a faint moan coming from the woods. It sounded like a man.

Grant nodded and pointed to a thick growth of brush growing in the ditch that ran along the south side of the road leading to the cabin.

"Cover me," said Caleb as he readied his weapon and headed for the brush.

Caleb felt Grant standing guard at his back, knew his buddy would keep watch in case this was some sort of trap.

The breeze shifted, and the smell of blood filled the morning air, thick and heavy. Lots of blood.

Caleb leaned down and eased some branches aside. Under the dense overhang of twisted stems and dried leaves he saw an arm clothed in hunter's camouflage and a pale hand caked with dried blood. Cautiously, Caleb pushed away more branches until he could force his body through a tight opening.

The man moaned again, a low, pitiful sound. He was lying on his side with a deep gash a few inches above his right knee. Caleb could see bone. The heavy fabric of his pants was sliced open and soaked with blood around the wound. Just above the horrible cut, the man had buckled his belt tight around his thigh, making a tourniquet to stop the bleeding. A bloody axe lay on the ground a few feet away next to a partially chopped chunk of firewood.

The poor bastard had damn near chopped his leg off while gathering wood, and from the amount of blood staining the ground, it was a wonder he was still alive.

"Got a man down, here," Caleb told Grant.

"How bad?"

"Pretty damn bad," replied Caleb.

"Anyone we know?"

Caleb turned the man over so he could see his face. Shit. This was not good. "He's just a kid. Maybe seventeen. We need to get him some help."

"The truck is just down the road. Closer than the cabin."

"There's nothing in the cabin that can save this kid, anyway. He needs blood and lots of it. We've got to get him to a hospital." As carefully as he could, Caleb lifted the boy into his arms. The boy let out a rough groan that made Caleb's stomach churn. He didn't look good.

"Can you carry him?" asked Grant from the far side of the thick foliage.

"I'm on it," said Caleb. The boy didn't weigh much, but he was all arms and legs, and it seemed to take forever to work his way back out of the heavy brush without jarring his injured leg.

This whole thing made Caleb's stomach turn. He wasn't a squeamish man, but the sight of a kid cut up like this tore him apart. At least it hadn't been a girl. Caleb wasn't sure he could have handled that. Not after what had happened in Armenia.

Grant was still keeping careful watch, scanning the area with his rifle ready to go when Caleb cleared all the branches.

"Let's get moving," said Grant. "I've got a bad feeling about this."

Owen watched the two Delta Force operators until they disappeared around a bend in the gravel road. Brian wasn't going to survive long enough to get to a hospital—Owen had made sure he'd lost too much blood for that—but he'd served his purpose. He'd been excellent bait.

Owen made a mental note to thank Mr. Lark for sending the boy the next time they spoke. With those two commandos blown into tiny bits by the explosives he'd set in the truck, David and Noelle were going to be much easier targets.

Noelle knew her time with David was growing short, but she tried not to let it interfere with what she had to do. She showed David how he could input new values for the missing variables and how to interpret the results. She'd even made him practice.

While David used a satellite phone to contact Monroe, Noelle burned a backup copy of her work onto a spare disk she had in her laptop tote bag. Just in case it fell into the wrong hands, she put a password protection script on all the files. It might not have been the best security software out there, but it was decent, and it sure would slow down anyone who didn't know what they were doing.

Across the room, she heard him speak in a low voice over the phone. "No, sir. She's sure. There's got to be another script we didn't recover."

Noelle could hear Monroe's deep voice cursing on the other end of the line, even from across the cabin.

"Yes, sir. That's what I thought, too."

David's hand tightened on the phone as he listened.

"No, it wasn't a waste of time," he said. "Find the team that recovered the text and maybe they'll have a clue."

David's eyes closed for a moment, but not before she saw a flash of grief shining behind his lashes. "All of them? I thought Jasom lived."

He leaned against the counter, looking more defeated with every word. "Just what do you expect me to do out here? She's gone as far as she can with the intel we've given her. You want us to start making things up?"

David clenched the phone so hard she thought the plastic housing would crack. "No, sir," growled David. "That won't be necessary. Just give me the coordinates of where the team found the script and I'll go there myself."

The last piece of the puzzle fell into place in Noelle's head with a nearly audible click. "That's it, David. The origin. It has to be from the perspective of whoever wrote this ciphertext. Where was it found?"

"Hold on, sir," said David into he phone. To Noelle, he rattled off the coordinates that Monroe had just given him.

Noelle hurriedly typed them into her program and hit the run button. She held her breath, waiting. A few seconds later, the results shone bright on her laptop screen. David was looking over her shoulder.

When he saw the coordinates, he swore under his breath. Into the phone he said, "We're going to need cold weather gear, sir. We're headed back to Russia."

Just then, the tiny window in the door of the cabin shattered, David jerked and his head slammed hard against the blood-spattered wall behind him. The phone fell from David's limp fingers and he crumpled to the dusty floorboards with a dull thump.

Noelle screamed.

CHAPTER TWENTY-FIVE

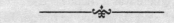

Caleb tried not to jostle the boy as he and Grant hiked back down the road to where they'd left the truck. This was the only road leading to his cabin, and with Grant's battered old Ford parked across it, no one was getting through this way—at least not without making one hell of a racket.

"He's not going to make it long enough to get to the hospital," said Grant.

Caleb glanced down at the kid. His breathing was shallow and his skin was ashen.

The image of Lana lying broken and bleeding in his arms flashed in his mind, making his chest ache with guilt. It had been almost a year since he'd carried her out of that cave, and there wasn't a day that went by that he didn't think about her. There wasn't a day that went by that he didn't hate himself for letting those bastards hurt her.

She'd lived. Maybe this kid would, too. "You're probably right, but I have to try."

"I know. We're not going to give up on him." Grant's tone was hopeless. Flat.

"You want to lay him out in the back or keep him in the cab?" Grant's rifle was in his skilled hands and his eyes were on the trees.

He could hit nearly anything he could see with that rifle, but that did little to ease the tension that had started growing between Caleb's shoulder blades ever since they'd found the bloody kid. "I'll hang on to him. Try to cushion the ride for him."

As they neared the truck, Caleb and Grant both slowed, surveying the area for signs anyone had come this way.

"Looks clear," said Grant.

Caleb saw nothing, but that nagging worry was still grating against him. "Yeah. Looks clear."

Grant gave him a sideways glance. "You got a bad feeling?"

"Yep."

"God, I hate it when you get those."

"Me, too. We'll drive up to the cabin to check on David and Noelle before we head back down the mountain. Let David know what's going on."

Grant opened Caleb's door so he could maneuver the kid inside the passenger's seat. The truck dipped under his weight, squeaking in protest. Grant hurried around the truck, still keeping his eyes on the trees. He slid in behind the wheel and stowed his rifle in a custom-made slot in the driver's side door.

The inside of the truck was as beat-up as the outside, with a wide crack running along the top of the dashboard, matching those in the aged vinyl seats. The knob on the manual window crank was missing and the lock on the glove compartment was busted so that it had to be held closed with duct tape. The truck smelled of sun-baked plastic, aging foam, half a million french fries and something else that Caleb didn't recognize—a harsh smell, like week-old sweat and a faint chemical odor that flirted with his memory, something he hadn't encountered for years.

Grant put the key in the ignition.

Homemade explosives. That was the smell. Holy shit!

Grant's wrist twitched as he started to turn the key.

"Stop!" shouted Caleb, and ripped Grant's hand away from the keys.

The kid didn't make a sound when his leg hit the dash because of Caleb's jerky movement. Not a good sign.

"What the hell?" snapped Grant, as he tried to tear his arm away. Caleb didn't let go.

"Get out of the truck. It's wired to blow." Cold sweat broke out along Caleb's ribs.

Grant opened the door slowly and eased out of his seat. Caleb leaned down, following his nose to where the smell was the strongest. It was awkward trying to lean over the kid, but he managed to get down far enough to see under the steering column. A bundle of wires led from the ignition to a squat metal can that still had some of the tuna label attached. Talk about homemade. He could probably disarm it, but it would take time. Time the boy didn't have.

Time David and Noelle didn't have. Someone was out here trying to kill them, and David needed to know it, pronto.

"We need to get back to Noelle," said Caleb.

Grant nodded and grabbed his rifle. "Catch up when you can," he said, and took off sprinting up the trail back toward the cabin.

Caleb eased out of the truck and laid the boy a safe distance away. There was nothing he could do for him now. Somewhere in the last few moments, the kid's heart had stopped beating, and without enough blood to keep it pumping, no amount of CPR would help. The boy was dead.

Caleb stood over him for a brief moment, feeling his blood cooling on his hands and clothing. So much fucking blood. So much innocence lost.

Caleb turned away, unable to stand the sight of yet another life ruined on his watch.

Shame gnawed at him, but he had a job to do, so he shut that part of himself down. If he didn't hurry, chances were David and Noelle would be added to that list, and he couldn't let that happen.

By the time Caleb was halfway up to the cabin he heard the crack of a rifle and prayed that it was Grant's rifle that had made the noise.

Noelle crouched beside David, willing her body not to seize up with fear. Somewhere in the back of her mind, she was still screaming, but the rational part of her brain kicked into gear and assessed the situation.

David's left arm was bleeding heavily, and Noelle said a quick prayer of thanks that the bullet hadn't veered more toward the right and everything vital. He was conscious, but groggy, likely from hitting his head on the way down.

She didn't dare move him, but she had to do something to stop the bleeding. She ripped off her sweatshirt, heedless of her glasses as they tangled in her hair. She tied the shirt around the wound, pulling it as tight as she could.

David groaned in pain and his eyes fluttered open.

Outside, Noelle could hear the heavy pounding of a helicopter's blades. The Swarm was coming.

Adrenaline surged through her blood, giving her speed and strength. She scrambled to slide the disk she'd burned out of her laptop and tuck it inside David's shirt. She only had a few seconds before they were here, and she needed to make sure the work she'd done wouldn't fall into the wrong hands.

Without hesitation, Noelle typed a command into her laptop, executing the clean sweep deletion program that would ensure everything on her hard drive would be scrubbed away without a trace. She didn't care about all the work she'd done being thrown away. She was only worried about David and making sure he stayed safe.

She shook him, wincing when he moaned in pain. Slowly, his eyes opened and she could see confusion clouding his blue eyes.

"David!" she said, filling her voice with every ounce of terror she was feeling. It got the desired reaction and she could see him forcibly throwing off the effects of his injuries. He looked almost lucid. And mad as hell.

"Do you remember what I told you the first night we made love?"

He blinked and she could see him struggling to focus.

Noelle leaned down to his face. Fear prowled along her spine with acid claws. She was shaking so hard it was difficult to move.

She grabbed his face in her hands and kissed him. It was a sweet, gentle kiss filled with everything there wasn't time to say.

Noelle pulled away and stared directly into his eyes. "Remember what I told you the first time we made love. It's important."

She heard footsteps approaching the cabin. They were out of time.

She threw herself over David's body and gave in to the torrent of fear and anger and guilt that had begun pounding at her the second she realized David had been shot. Tears streamed down her face in display of grief.

She pressed her fingers against his neck, blocking off the flow of blood going to David's brain. In a few seconds he'd pass out. Noelle prayed it would be enough to fool the men coming after her into thinking he was dead.

Three armed, masked men burst through the door, sending a spray of wood splinters into the air.

Noelle turned toward them, her face a teary mess. "You killed him!"

She pulled the gun from David's belt, stood and pointed it at the closest man. Before she could pull the trigger, one of the men aimed a pistol and shot her in the leg.

Noelle stumbled and the world became a giant black hole that swallowed her up in one bite.

Grant was too late to stop the man carrying Noelle from getting on the helicopter. He disappeared around the corner of the cabin with her limp body over his shoulder before Grant could take the shot. The two men who were struggling with David's body were another story.

He controlled his breathing as he peered through the scope on his rifle, targeting the head of the man carrying David's feet. Grant didn't have time to wait for his heart to stop racing, so he found the rhythm of the beats and made his shot between them.

Pink blood spray bloomed into the air from the man's head, but Grant was already finding his next target, who hadn't yet realized why the load he was carrying had suddenly become so heavy. A scant three seconds later, the second man crumpled to the ground in a lifeless heap.

The helo pilot must have been given orders to leave without the men, because it was already rising steadily, whipping the limbs of the nearby trees into a frenzy of motion.

Grant peered through his scope, targeting the pilot, but then hesitated. Noelle was on that chopper, and if he took it down, it might kill her. If that happened, David would never recover. Assuming he wasn't dead already.

The thought had Grant's lungs squeezing hard, blocking off his air. With a vicious curse, Grant ripped the scope from his eye and went to see if David was still alive.

The throbbing in David's head woke him. A sense of urgency called him out of the blessed comfort of unconsciousness. Then he remembered.

"Noelle!" shouted David, surging to his feet.

His head spun, and he could barely make out the little cabin among the dozen identical images swimming before his eyes.

"Easy," said Caleb. "Just take it easy and sit down."

Caleb's massive strength forcing David onto a stool left him no choice but to sit or fall down.

"Where is Noelle?" he demanded of all three Calebs who stood in front of him.

"We're going to find her, David."

Find her? She wasn't here? Fear and guilt threatened to drive him back into oblivion. Noelle was gone.

David clutched Caleb's shirt, not caring how desperate he sounded. "I have to go after her."

"We will," assured Caleb in a low, comforting voice. "But first we have to figure out where to go."

David's vision had cleared so that there was only one of everything again. The pain pounding at the back of his skull was still there, as was a deep burning sensation in his left arm. None of that mattered, and he couldn't let it slow him down.

"How long was I out?"

Caleb checked his watch. "Eighteen minutes. Grant stopped two of the men who were trying to pack you up and bring you along. Their helicopter left without them once the shooting started. Noelle was already gone, along with her computer and all her papers," continued Caleb in an even voice as if he were talking about the weather rather than the whereabouts of the woman David loved.

"Is she . . .?" David couldn't even bring himself to ask.

"If they'd killed her, they would have left her here and just taken her work. I'm sure they took her out alive."

Alive. Thank God.

"Noelle saved you when you got hit. She used her shirt to tie off your wound. She's one heck of a smart lady. If she hadn't stopped the bleeding, you'd be in bad shape by now."

David cursed. "Smart enough that she had to get tangled up in this mess to begin with. Maybe it's better to be stupid."

Across the cabin, Grant was on the phone, speaking in quiet tones.

Caleb crouched, squeezing his bulk into a fairly small package. David noticed there was blood on Caleb's clothes. Lots of blood. It was smeared all over him in splotchy patches, some that were already drying. "Did you get wounded?" asked David.

Caleb's jaw tightened. "It's not my blood."

Thank God.

"Did you see or hear anything that might tell us where they've taken her?" asked Caleb.

David concentrated on remembering what happened. It was hard to push aside his grinding emotional response to Noelle's danger—his fear for her, his guilt that he'd let this happen. She was so vulnerable, and if the Swarm did to her what they did to Mary . . .

"Focus, Wolfe," barked Caleb, giving David a little shake of his shoulders. "You've got to pull it together."

David knew Caleb was right. If he didn't start thinking with his head instead of his heart, Noelle didn't have a chance.

David pulled in a deep breath and tried to recall the last thing he could remember. "I was talking to Monroe about getting some more information. Noelle figured out what the text said, but it was incomplete."

"Grant's on the phone with Monroe right now. Do you remember anything else?"

David felt something swirling in his memory. A kiss, so sweet it nearly brought tears to his eyes. Noelle had kissed him before she'd been taken.

And she'd said something—something about the first time they made love . . .

David uttered an acidic curse. How could he have let this happen? How could he have let them take her?

Caleb's strong hand settled on David's shoulder in a comforting grip. "I know you're hurting now, but she needs you. You've got to think. What was she doing while you were talking to Monroe?"

David's head throbbed harder as he tried to remember. "She said something about needing the coordinates of where they'd found the text. She thought it might be the missing info. Monroe had just given them to me so I told Monroe to hold on and gave her the coordinates . . ."

"And?"

"And she typed them in and . . ." David could see the look of triumph on her face, the way she smiled at him so happy it made his heart sing.

"She ran the program and brought up the coordinates on her screen."

"Do you remember the coordinates?"

David shook his head as frustration burst through him. "We've got to figure it out before they do. I'm sure that's got to be where they're taking her. They won't kill her until they have the weapons and know they're done using her. We have to get there first and ambush them."

"How are we going to figure out where to go?"

"I don't know," spat David. "Her work is gone. She's gone!"

Caleb turned to Grant. "How long before our ride arrives?"

"They're closing in now," said Grant. "I've got the helo pilot on the phone. I'm going to go outside and guide him in."

David rose to his feet, being cautious so he wouldn't pass out again. Noelle needed him, and he had to do everything in his power to make sure he was able to help her.

Inside his shirt, he felt something slide down along his chest. He reached inside and pulled out a shiny disk smudged with two small, bloody fingerprints. Noelle's.

A spark of hope lit deep in David's heart.

"Is that what I think it is?" asked Caleb.

David nodded and a feral smile touched his mouth. He was going to find her. "I don't know how she managed to pull it off, but I'm damn glad she did."

Outside, David could hear the faint thrumming of a helicopter flying closer.

David grabbed his weapon and his duffel bag and stepped out onto the porch, ignoring his pain, silently urging the pilot to hurry the hell up.

CHAPTER TWENTY-SIX

Noelle woke up on some sort of military aircraft. The hard metal plates under her feet vibrated with the roar of the jet engines. Her ankles were tied to the frame of the seat she occupied. A harness-style seat belt was pulled snug against her torso and her wrists were tied together with flexible plastic handcuffs.

Her head felt like it was going to fly apart and her mouth tasted like it had been cleaned out with dead rat carcasses. She recognized this feeling—the aftereffects of the tranquilizer they'd shot her with—but this time it was different. David wasn't here to take care of her.

Noelle stifled her tears as she remembered David lying on the floor of the cabin, bleeding. Was he here? Was he still alive?

Needing to know, Noelle cracked her eyelids a little wider, gritting her teeth against the painful effects of the dim light filling the aircraft. For a moment, she would have welcomed her head actually exploding it hurt so much. She shut her eyes again and concentrated on not throwing up.

Slowly, the pain subsided to merely excruciating, and she tried again to look around her.

The plane was about twenty feet wide, filled with crates and electronic equipment, and she could only guess about their function. There were half a dozen men wearing black military clothing, but without any flags or symbols to give away their loyalties. They spoke in quiet voices she couldn't hear over the roar of the jet engines, so language was no help.

All she knew was that David was nowhere in sight, which meant she was on her own.

One of the men turned and saw she was awake. He was tall and blond and would have been handsome if not for the horrific burn scar that claimed half of his face.

He took a bottle of water from a compartment and came to stand beside her.

"Are you thirsty?" he asked in an accent that belonged somewhere in Wisconsin.

Noelle looked at the water bottle, which was still sealed. She nodded.

The man opened the bottle and held it to her mouth so she could drink.

He flipped open a small box he'd taken from his pocket and dumped out a couple of pills. "These will help with the headache."

Noelle turned her head, refusing the pills. She didn't trust these men, and she wasn't about to make it easy for them to kill her.

He gave a low, amused chuckle. "Suit yourself."

"Who are you?"

"You can call me Owen. We'll be spending a lot of time together, you and I."

Something in the way he said it made the hair on the back of Noelle's neck stand on end. "What do you want with me?" she croaked, making her throat feel like it was going to split open.

"What a foolish question from such an intelligent woman." He capped the water bottle and shoved it into the space between her thigh and the side of the seat.

He placed one hand on each arm of her seat and leaned down so she could see directly into his pale green eyes. There was no warmth there, no compassion. Only greed.

It was then that Noelle realized she was a dead woman. Maybe not yet, but as soon as they had what they wanted from her, he'd dispose of her without remorse.

"You're going to tell us what the Russian text said, and you're going to do it now."

Noelle's only chance was to stall them. As soon as David found the disk, he'd figure out how to find her. He'd find a way to stop these madmen. She was sure of it. "I don't know if I can. There was a power surge and my laptop started throwing off sparks. Have you checked to see if it's still working?"

He slapped her hard across the face. Noelle was so shocked it took her a minute before she even realized what had happened. The blow was hard enough that she could already feel her cheek swelling and taste the blood from her split lip.

"I don't think you fully grasp the magnitude of your situation, Dr. Blanche." He grabbed the back of her hair and jerked her head so she was staring straight up at him. The ugly scar on his face had darkened to an angry red. "We know everything about you. We know who your friends are. We have men watching your family. Do you really want them to suffer for your stubbornness?"

Her sister Lilly's face crystallized in Noelle's mind,

and she couldn't help the tears that slid silently down her cheeks. "I can't." She didn't explain that she couldn't risk the lives of others so that one person could live. Not even her beloved sister. Lilly had been raised the same way—never compromise your principles, no matter what. They'd both been taught that at their father's knee. They both knew the responsibility they carried because they were smart.

"We'll see," he said, and turned to retrieve a metal box that looked like a toolbox. From inside the box he pulled a syringe and a vial full of liquid.

Noelle trembled, unable to fight back the terror that swelled in her chest. What the hell was that stuff and what was it going to do to her?

He filled the syringe and casually injected it into her arm without worrying about disinfectant. It was just one more sign that they didn't care if she lived long-term.

Heat flew along her veins, making her shiver. After a few seconds, the plane seemed to swell and shrink repeatedly, throbbing with each beat of her heart. For some reason, that didn't seem strange.

The man stared at her, and then shined a small light into each of her eyes. "Don't worry," he said, his voice oily with a mockery of compassion. He stroked her hair with a gentle sweep of his hand. "It won't be long now."

David was nearly insane with impotent rage and frustration. He paced the room while the tech-heads worked to break the password protection on the disk Noelle had given him.

General Monroe watched him from the corner. Grant and Caleb had their heads bent together in a quiet conversation over a map on the other side of the sterile white room.

This small government-contracted lab was the closest place they could go with any sort of technical support—the only place nearby where they might be able to figure out where Noelle had been taken. Specialists were flying in to help, but they wouldn't be here for several more hours.

The white room was littered with wires and the entrails of open computer cases. Fluorescent lights hummed overhead while the muted clicking of keyboard strokes filled one side of the space. Three young men were frantically working to get to the information on that disk.

David wanted to put a gun to their heads to help encourage them to work faster, but he resisted the urge. Barely.

Monroe pushed to his feet, using a cane to help him balance. He'd taken a bullet to the leg during the firefight at the safe house, and although he would recover, he was getting old enough that he no longer bounced back like he used to. He looked tired. Old.

"Have you thought of anything, Captain?" asked Monroe.

David scrubbed at his face with his hand, trying to rid his eyes of the grit of fatigue. He'd had enough coffee to burn a hole in his stomach, but it didn't help. "There's something she said right before she left, but I don't remember what it was."

"What do you remember?"

David shoved some cables aside and leaned against the edge of a workbench lined with a blue electrostatic discharge protective coating. "It's, uh, personal, sir."

"Fuck personal. Spit it out, Captain."

David was hesitant to talk to Monroe about his relationship with Noelle. It wasn't that he worried about getting his ass chewed for breaking protocol. He couldn't care less about that. What he did care about was tainting what he and Noelle had shared by airing it in public. He liked remembering making love to her, knowing it was something only they shared.

Still, David knew that it might help figure out the password guarding the data on the disk, and that alone was worth tarnishing good memories. "She said something about the first time we made love."

If Monroe was surprised by that news, he didn't let it show in his face. "What about it?"

David slammed his fist down onto the workbench, making circuit boards jump. "Dammit, I don't know!"

"Try to remember. What were her words?"

David tried. His memory was foggy, but he could remember that kiss she gave him—the one so full of love it damn near made him tear up just thinking about it. "She said I had to remember what she said that night."

"What did she say?"

"A lot of things. She talked to herself while she was working. Most of it was garbage to me."

"What did she say to you?"

They hadn't shared many words that night. She'd woken him up looking at those scribbles on his arms. He'd tried not to give in to his lust, but he'd failed. He'd pulled her under his body and that look on her face—so open and eager—he was doomed. But, he'd made sure it was what she'd wanted. He'd demanded that she tell him it was what she wanted.

David stilled, seeing her face in front of him as if she were here. Her eyes were a deep, slumberous green. Her skin was flushed and her mouth was wet and ripe. "No regrets," whispered David.

"What?"

He looked at Monroe, shattering the sweet image of Noelle. "She said 'No regrets.'"

David flew across the room to the tech-heads. "Type in the password 'no regrets.'"

A short, pimply-faced kid who couldn't have been more than nineteen obeyed the fastest. Blue light flashed across his blemished skin, reflecting against the little round glasses he wore. "That's it. We're in."

David felt the rush of victory give him renewed strength. "Now, type these coordinates into her program and print out the results."

The tech did. David pulled the sheet out of the printer before it could finish spitting out the white space. The printer crashed to the floor behind him, but he didn't care. He was already out the door.

CHAPTER TWENTY-SEVEN

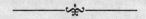

David saw the armed guards walking a perimeter of the old compound in Russia and knew he was too late. The Swarm had gotten here first.

Night cloaked the movement of his team. They wore black and had parachuted in over a mile away. That hike had been the fastest of his life. He could still hear a couple of the men struggling to quiet their labored breathing from keeping up the grueling pace he'd set. His arm burned where the bullet had hit him, but he pushed the pain away until it no longer existed.

Caleb and Grant flanked him, and he had never been more grateful to have them at his side. As it was, he was barely holding on to rational thought knowing Noelle was inside that building with the Swarm. All he wanted to do was rush in there and get her out. It was only the knowledge that his impatience might get Noelle killed that kept him restrained.

"I count fifteen," whispered Grant, looking through his night scope.

"Me, too," confirmed Caleb. "Heat signatures show another six inside."

David grabbed the scope that could see through the metal walls and aimed it at the aging building. There were indeed six figures inside. Two of them were moving. Three were standing in a cluster, and one was off to the side, seated and unmoving and smaller than the rest.

Noelle.

David realized he was trying to move in when he felt Caleb's big hand holding him down. "Not yet. We go in together or she doesn't stand a chance. Don't go getting stupid now."

Grant checked his watch and pinned David with a look of understanding. "Thirty-eight seconds, Wolfe. We all move in together then. You can wait thirty-eight seconds."

They were the longest thirty-eight seconds of his life.

Noelle was freezing to death—literally. She could no longer feel her fingers or toes, and the shivers that wracked her body were so extreme that she was sure they were damaging muscle tissue. At least she could no longer feel the stinging of the dozens of shallow cuts over her arms and legs.

They hadn't even hurt her to gain information. The drug they'd given her had made it impossible for her to keep silent about the coordinates she'd seen on the screen before the men attacked. She wished she hadn't had a good memory for numbers and that she hadn't been able to give them the coordinates, but in the end, she'd had no choice.

And still they had cut her. The scarred man said he just liked to hear her scream. She had a beautiful voice. Noelle had tried not to give him the satisfaction, but in the end, she'd failed there, too.

She was naked, gagged, soaked with a bucket of icy water and left bound to a metal chair in the center of a room that hadn't had a functioning heater in more than a decade. Her stomach cramped and she was so physically exhausted that even the involuntary shivers were beginning to subside. After so many hours, her body just didn't have the strength to fight any longer.

Only the thought of David kept her going beyond where she would have surrendered. If he was alive, he would be coming for her. She never doubted that for a second.

She forced herself to stay awake, looking for anything that would interest her enough to keep her mind alert. When David came, she needed to be awake and able to help him in any way she could. She was not going to go down without a fight.

Noelle looked around. The building was some sort of bunker made of metal plates that would have been easy to tear apart and transport elsewhere. The structure and everything in it was designed to be portable.

But as interesting as that might have been to her at one point in her life, right now, it was the only thing keeping her from focusing on the searing cold that sank into every pore. Already, she was feeling a heavy, sleepy lethargy she knew meant impending hypothermia. As deaths went, it was a horrible one—or would be until she just gave in to the urge to sleep. Then it would all be over.

Water dripped steadily from her hair into a shallow pool at her bare feet. Her eyelids slid down and she struggled to open them again. She told herself she had to stay awake. David was coming.

Faith in David was all she had left, and she was clinging to it with every ounce of strength she possessed.

Suddenly, the metal doors burst open, followed by a sharp staccato of gunfire. She couldn't lift her head enough to see who it was, but she didn't have to.

David was here.

Finally, David was able to act. Grant, sniper extraordinaire, was able to take out four men guarding the entrance before the rest of the group could even close the distance. David ignored the rest of the enemy guards outside, knowing they were the targets for his team. His goal was to get inside, eliminate the hostiles near Noelle and get her out. Caleb was right at his side.

Reports of downed hostiles filled his ear, but he tuned out the sound, putting all his focus into his part of the attack.

Caleb and David burst through the doors, shooting anyone who wasn't Noelle. Three men fell before the first enemy had a chance to return fire. One ducked for cover behind a metal partition and the third sprinted across the room, toward Noelle.

David saw her there, bloody, naked, tied to a metal chair. A pool of blood glistened under her chair.

David nearly lost it right there. It was like staring at Mary all over again. Beaten. Tortured.

Dead.

He nearly doubled over in pain, fighting off the urge to vomit. This couldn't be happening again. He wouldn't survive losing Noelle.

The day Mary died, a monster had been born inside him. Over the past two years, David had fed that monster a constant diet of guilt and grief and regret. The monster had grown, swelling inside David until there was little room for the man he used to be.

Noelle had somehow found that man and breathed into him a spark of life. But now, staring at her tortured body, everything human left in him died, screaming in torment. All that was left was the monster, prowling inside him, waiting for its chance to strike.

David forced out every shred of emotion left lingering in his heart. He couldn't stand to feel anything right now. If he did, it would destroy him—make him weak. He had to be cold. Hollow. A machine set to kill. He was going to take out every one of the bastards here and pray he died in the process.

A bullet whizzed by his head, and if it hadn't been for Caleb jerking him out of the way, it would have hit its mark.

"Get a grip," growled Caleb, using his larger body to cover David's from gunfire. They were pressed into a little alcove by the door, which was their only cover.

Caleb crouched, dragging David with him. "She's alive," said Caleb. "See her shivering?"

David peered around the corner, needing to see for himself. Caleb was right. She was still alive.

A sense of relief tried to take hold inside him. David squashed it flat, pounding it down mercilessly. He couldn't bear the thought of believing Noelle would be okay, then having her end up like Mary. He wouldn't survive that sort of pain again. It was all he could do just to keep breathing.

"I'm going after her," David told Caleb, his voice flat and hard.

"Right," said Caleb, knowing better than to try to argue. "On three."

Caleb gave David covering fire while David raced across the room toward Noelle. He'd never felt stronger or faster in his life. He lived for a single purpose—saving Noelle.

Behind him, he heard the pained grunt of the man who had taken shelter behind the partition. Caleb calmly reported another hostile dead over the comm unit stuck inside David's ear.

That left only one enemy in the building.

The blond man who had come David's way jumped out from behind a file cabinet where he'd hidden and used Noelle's body for cover. And in case that wasn't enough to stop them from firing on him, he lowered a pistol directly against Noelle's temple. "Stop," said the man.

David stopped, skidding over the concrete floor. Inside him, the monster howled in frustration.

He was going to kill that man.

David stared at him, waiting for his opening. Recognition flared bright in David's memory. The man was horribly scarred now, but David was sure this was the man who had held Mary captive. The same man who had killed her.

"I thought I'd killed you," said David. His voice was hollow, emotionless.

Noelle's eyelids fluttered in response to his voice but David refused to acknowledge it. He had to stay focused. She was going to be okay. He was going to make sure of it, no matter what.

The blond man smiled, causing the scar along his cheek to stretch into gruesome ridges. "Not quite. That fire you set nearly did me in, but I managed to escape, even with a bullet in my chest." He stepped to the side and crouched, putting himself more completely behind Noelle. David didn't have a clean shot. "I knew you'd come for the woman. You always come back for your women."

Noelle moaned and David gritted his teeth against the urge to reach out for her.

"You can't imagine how many times I've dreamed about killing you," said the man.

David felt nothing at the man's words. No fear. No anger. Only the frigid calm of knowing he was going to feel this man die. He was going to take his life with his bare hands and make sure—without any doubt—that he could never hurt another woman again.

David tossed his gun to the ground with a metallic clatter and spread his hands wide. "Here I am. Let the woman go, and I'm yours."

David could feel Caleb tense behind him. They'd been buddies too long for David not to know that Caleb was thinking he was being a complete idiot giving himself up like that.

A malicious grin lit the man's eyes. "Tell your gargantuan friend there to back off," ordered the blond man.

"Get out, Caleb. I can handle this."

Caleb took a step and David could now see him out of the corner of his eye. "Don't be an idiot, Wolfe. He's gonna—"

David didn't let Caleb finish. "I said get out! That's an order, Lieutenant."

"Not without the girl, Captain," said Caleb.

David forced out a frustrated sigh though he still felt nothing but the incessant prowling of the monster inside him and the pressing need to kill.

"Fine." He walked right over to Noelle, making himself an easy target. The scarred man's gun moved from Noelle to David, giving him the chance to get her away. He shoved her wheeled chair toward Caleb, trusting him to get her out safely. As long as she got out, David truly didn't care what happened to him.

Now that David was within easy reach, the scarred man grabbed him around the throat with one arm and pressed the cold muzzle of his weapon against the side of David's face.

David forced himself to feel nothing.

Caleb grabbed Noelle, chair and all, and picked her up as if she was no heavier than a sack of groceries.

The chair dripped red, which David could now see was more water than blood. Noelle had been hurt, but not as badly as he'd suspected. He wanted to feel relief, but couldn't. If he let go even that much, the torrent of emotions pounding for release would burn him alive.

Once Noelle was safely on her way out of the building, David deliberately let his monster free. It howled in delight and took over David's body, giving him nearly inhuman speed.

With one flash of David's elbow, the scarred man's weapon went flying across the room. It was only a matter of seconds before David had the man pinned on the concrete floor, with his hands around the man's throat, watching him die.

David felt nothing. No sense of victory, no joy. Nothing.

When David could no longer feel the beat of the scarred man's heart beneath his fingers, he let go. Just to be sure the man would not come back from the dead again, David retrieved his weapon and put two bullets through the man's head.

Only then did he turn to walk away.

Caleb hadn't left as he'd been ordered. He was standing guard over Noelle, using his body to shield hers, and his weapon was aimed at the dead man. He'd stayed in case David had needed backup.

Noelle's head hung limply from her shoulders, but she was still conscious enough to see him. Her green eyes were bright with fear and revulsion, staring at the man David had just killed. She'd seen the whole thing. She'd seen him kill with his bare hands.

Noelle hated violence, and after what she'd just witnessed, David was sure that she would have no choice but to hate him as well.

Fury rose up in him, but he stomped it down. He had to keep hold of his emotions for her sake. He had to get her out of here safely.

David crossed the room, watching Noelle as he moved. She was getting weaker by the second. He could see her strength draining from her with every shiver of her slim body. David refused to let himself feel anything. Not yet. Not until Noelle was safe and warm. He'd done it. He'd avenged Mary's death, but it brought him no joy. No satisfaction. He reached out for her and she flinched away from his touch.

It was confirmation of everything David had feared. She'd seen him kill with his bare hands to save her and in doing so, he'd lost her forever.

CHAPTER TWENTY-EIGHT

Noelle felt warmth close around her body. She couldn't open her eyes, but she heard familiar voices in little snips of conversation. She could smell David's skin as he warmed her, using his own body.

". . . she's freezing . . . get her warm . . . frostbite . . ."

"He's dead." That voice was David's, though it didn't sound right. It sounded flat and cold.

". . . injuries aren't severe . . . worried about hypothermia . . ."

Noelle struggled for enough strength to speak. "I'm sorry," she whispered. "I tried not to tell them the coordinates. I tried . . ."

"Hush, now," said David. He was close to her, speaking right next to her ear. His voice was still odd, but she didn't care. It was David. He was safe. "You didn't do anything wrong."

The warmth started to burn as feeling returned to her toes. Noelle stopped fighting sleep.

She woke later in a bed. There were hands all around her, a plastic mask over her nose and mouth. Everything hurt and she could feel needles poking her skin all over.

"Give her something for the pain," demanded David.

He was close, but she couldn't get her eyes open to see him. She tried to talk but couldn't figure out how to move the mask.

She felt the IV in the back of her hand wiggle, then whatever they'd given her for pain started working, and she went back to sleep.

The next time she woke it was dark. She was thirsty and her throat burned. There were faint noises around her of men talking in hushed whispers. "David?" she croaked.

The whispers stopped and she felt a warm, callused hand grasp hers. He was here. She was safe.

David refused to leave Noelle's side for two days. He was tired and hungry and ached from head to toe, but he couldn't bring himself to leave her. Not even knowing that as soon as she woke up, she'd look at him with revulsion.

Caleb stepped into the hospital room, his large body filling the doorway. There were no windows to the outside, for security reasons, and the only light in the room came in through tiny slits in the miniblinds covering the window in the interior wall that overlooked the nurses' station.

Caleb approached on silent feet, his black eyes taking in Noelle's condition in one thorough, sweeping glance. "She's better today," he stated as he stepped up to the bed, across from David.

"Yeah. I think she is. It's hard to tell under all those bruises, but I keep hoping."

"You should get a shower. I'll sit with her while you're gone, if you like."

One side of David's mouth twitched. "Is that your subtle way of telling me I stink?"

"A lot. If you want her to have anything to do with you when she wakes up, I suggest you clean the mud off your boots, shower and put on fresh clothes."

David looked back at Noelle. She was so still and pale under all the bruises that every time he saw her his gut twisted into a tight knot. He'd nearly lost her, and the thought still shook him to the core every time it passed through his mind, which was about every thirty seconds. He tried not to think about it, but the room was quiet, and her cuts and bruises were constant reminders of how close he'd come to losing her. How close she'd come to ending up like Mary. "I'll leave in a while."

Caleb nodded in acceptance and pulled up a chair to sit down. He settled into his seat with the patience of a man who had no plans of going anywhere soon. "What are you going to do now?" asked Caleb.

"What do you mean? I'm going to sit here until she wakes up."

"And then what?"

David looked up into Caleb's patient, black gaze. A bleak emptiness filled his chest. He knew what Caleb was asking.

David knew what he had to do. As much as it hurt him, he had to walk away from Noelle. Her doctor had confirmed that she wasn't pregnant. He'd demanded that they check, just in case. She'd started her period, so there wasn't even that excuse left to keep David from leaving. David had to give her a chance for a real life—one without the threat of violence looming over her every day.

She deserved to be happy. He wanted her to be happy. He loved her enough to walk away so that she could be.

David planned to go into hiding so deep that no one would ever find him again. Not even Monroe. He'd leave the country, crawl into some jungle so thick it would swallow him whole. Not even satellites would be able to see him. He'd disappear and Noelle would be safe from the taint of violence that still stained his soul.

"That's not what she wants," said Caleb, as if hearing David's silent thoughts. "That's not what you want."

"And you know me so well after being apart for two years that you think you know what I really want?"

Caleb nodded his dark head. "Yeah. I do."

"Okay, Mr. Observant. What do you think I really want?"

"Noelle."

"Well, of course I still want her. She's a beautiful woman."

"I'm not talking about sex. I'm talking about more than that. Commitment. Love. Forever."

"I can't. Not again. Not after what happened to Mary."

"Noelle isn't Mary. If you can't figure that out, then you don't deserve her."

"I didn't deserve Mary, either."

"She thought you did. She'd want you to be happy, you know."

"Yeah. I do. She loved me, but part of me feels like I'm cheating on her, betraying her memory somehow."

"You're only betraying her memory if you stop living. You've been dead for two years. Isn't that long enough to punish yourself?"

The only punishment that fit his crime was to die the same way Mary had—tortured, cold and alone.

David pulled the gold chain off his neck and dangled his wedding band in front of him. Light played over the simple golden surface, making his eyes sting with tears. He still loved Mary. He always would. How could he dishonor her by putting another innocent woman in harm's way because he was selfish enough to want a second chance at happiness?

He couldn't. He loved Noelle as much as he'd loved Mary. He never thought it would be possible to love like that again, but he did. It only made it that much harder to walk away from her.

It also made it that much more necessary.

"It doesn't matter what I want," said David.

"Fine. Let's just say you're right about that. What about what Noelle wants?" asked Caleb.

"Noelle hates violence. She saw what I did to that man who'd taken her, and I saw the way she looked at me when I reached for her. She pulled away. Flinched as if I'd hurt her."

Caleb stared at him with a look that told David he thought he was a total idiot. "Hell, I'd have pulled away, too. You have no idea what you looked like back there, do you?"

At David's bewildered frown, Caleb said, "You were covered in mud, your face streaked with paint. There were spots of blood on your clothes and skin and a feral gleam in your eyes that had even me scared you'd gone over the edge. You'd just killed a man with your bare hands and you looked like you were ready to do it again. She probably figured you'd gone a little crazy. Hell, I thought the same thing until you calmed down."

"She should have known I'd never hurt her. The fact

that she didn't only proves that she really does see me as a violent man."

Caleb rolled his black eyes and gave a snort of disgust. "She was out of her head, man—delirious from drugs and hypothermia and likely scared to death she was going to die. And she's a civilian. Give her a break, fuckhead. Unless you're just using that as an excuse not to try to make things work with her."

"Fuck you, Stone."

Caleb sighed and stood, his massive body towering over Noelle's bed. "Don't be dumber than God made you, David. You love her and if you're smart, you'll let her know before it's too late. Don't walk away. You'll be sorry." That last part sounded too much like the voice of experience, making David wonder just what had happened to Caleb over the past two years.

David stood and left the room, passing Grant on his way out. It was time to get moving. Noelle was going to be fine and he needed to be gone before she woke up. The least he could do for her was to be gone by the time she opened her eyes so she wouldn't have to see him again.

And he wouldn't have to say good-bye.

Noelle opened her eyes to find Grant and Caleb standing over her bed. "Where's David?"

Grant's jaw clenched in anger and Caleb regarded her with an even, black stare. "He's leaving. For good. I don't know whether or not you want to stop him, but you need to decide quick. He's got a three-minute head start, and once he's gone, none of us will ever be able to find him."

Noelle fought down a sense of panic. "Leaving? Why?"

"He doesn't want you to end up like Mary did," said Grant.

Noelle was still groggy, but she forced her mind to clear and take stock of what she'd heard. She knew David felt guilty over his wife's death and likely over what had happened to her as well. She also knew that he was a total bonehead to think it was his fault. "I can't let him go. I love him."

"You sure about this?" asked Caleb. "You need to think about what you're saying and be completely sure. Don't toy with him, Noelle." That last part was a warning, as clear and menacing as they got.

"Shut up! Which one of you is fastest?"

Grant smiled, vaulted over the bed in a casual, graceful leap and was out the door in a heartbeat.

"Help me up, Caleb." She used her best authoritative professorial voice.

"You're in no shape to be getting out of bed. Let Grant bring David back here."

"You really think Grant will be able to drag him back if he doesn't want to come?" She was frantic now, throwing back the covers, trying not to rip the IV out of her hand. "Caleb, I swear that if you don't help me up this instant, I'll use every single one of my massive brain cells to make you suffer for the rest of your life."

An admiring grin curved Caleb's mouth, and he started to obey. He helped her stand on unsteady legs. Noelle wasn't sure how she would walk, but she was going to figure out something.

Caleb stripped a blanket off the bed and wrapped it around her. "As much as David would enjoy seeing your naked backside, I doubt he'd enjoy sharing it with others. He's a little jealous when it comes to you, in case you hadn't noticed."

"Jealous enough that he's willing to leave me without even a good-bye kiss?"

Noelle started to unhook the tube from the IV, but Caleb stopped her. "You need that." He took the bag from the metal stand and handed it to her. "Here, you hold this, and I'll carry you out. Seeing you in the arms of another man isn't going to make David happy." The grin on his face told Noelle just how much the idea of upsetting David appealed to him.

He lifted her, blanket and all, and headed outside.

David had almost made it to his car when he saw Grant barreling toward him.

He guessed that Grant was coming to try to stop him from leaving, but a small, terrified part of him worried that something had happened to Noelle. He hesitated, and it was that hesitation that ended him flat on his back in the grass in front of the hospital parking lot.

Adrenaline flooded his system and he shoved Grant off in a rush of strength. His elbow hit Grant's nose in the process and blood dripped down onto his buddy's gray T-shirt.

If Grant noticed the injury, he didn't react. He just came toward David, his eyes glittering with joy. He slammed his body into David's, making air rush out of his lungs as he absorbed the force of the blow.

Grant and David had grappled often enough during

their training for David to know that they were evenly matched. Grant was a few inches taller but had nothing on David in the weight department. In a normal fight, David would have a fifty-fifty chance of winning. This was no normal fight.

Grant's hand found the bullet wound in David's injured arm and squeezed. Pain speared through David's body and he ground his teeth to keep from crying out. "That's for busting my nose. Again," said Grant.

"Stop that!" ordered Noelle imperiously.

David froze at the sound of her voice and looked toward her. She was cradled in Caleb's arms, swathed in a white cotton blanket, carrying her IV bag against her chest. Her face was bruised, and he could see it was an effort for her to keep her head upright.

"Get off me," shouted David.

Immediately, Grant let go and stood offering David a hand up. David glared at Grant and refused his hand. Grant just grinned. The bastard had always enjoyed fighting too much for his own good.

David's first instinct was to rush to Noelle's side, but he bit back the urge and planted his feet a good two yards away from her.

"I didn't tell you to hurt him, Grant," Noelle scolded. "Just to stop him."

Grant gave her a sheepish smile. "Sorry, ma'am. I guess I just got carried away."

Her green gaze fastened on David and it was like taking a punch in the gut. Betrayal shone in her eyes. "You were just going to leave?" she asked.

David wanted to murder Caleb, knowing he was the one who had told her that. It would have been so much better if he'd just kept his mouth shut. "I have to, Noelle. It's for your own good."

Her mouth tightened into an angry circle. "Don't you tell me what's for my own good! I'm a grown woman and fully capable of deciding what I want and don't want. If you're leaving because you don't give a shit about me, then go, but don't try to tell me that it's for my own good."

The effort of shouting at him sapped her strength visibly. She leaned her head against Caleb's chest and the surge of jealousy that ripped through David had him clenching his fists against the urge to slam them into Caleb's face.

"Put my woman down," growled David.

Caleb lifted a black brow. "She's too weak to stand. You want me to put her down, come take her from me. Otherwise, suffer."

David debated leaving her with Caleb, but he was so damn jealous he couldn't think straight, seeing her in another man's arms. It was stupid to think of her as his. After all, he was leaving as soon as he straightened things out with Noelle. He knew that eventually, some other man would find out what a treasure she was and marry her. He wouldn't be anywhere around to stop it from happening, either. It was best if he just got used to the idea of her belonging to another man.

Maybe even Caleb.

That was the thought that sent him over the edge, and he knew that Caleb had seen it in his face. David stalked over the grass and took Noelle from Caleb. He was careful of her battered body, but the glare he gave Caleb was a clear dismissal.

Noelle held herself stiff and uncertain, but David couldn't blame her. He'd hurt her feelings and probably a lot more than that.

"I think you owe me an explanation as to why you were leaving without saying good-bye," she said.

David refused to look down at her. He knew that look of betrayal was still twisting her face, making him ache deep in his gut for what he had to do to her. "Let's get you back in bed. We'll talk there."

"I'll stand guard at the door," offered Grant in a cheerful tone, wiping blood from his face. "Just in case he decides to sneak away again."

David growled, but made no comment. It was too cold outside for Noelle to be out here in just a flimsy hospital gown and a blanket.

He said nothing as he tucked her back in bed and hung the IV bag back on the metal stand. Once he was done, he put some distance between them, pacing at the end of her bed.

"Well?" she asked. Her voice was strained. Tired. Hurt.

David wanted to slam his fist into something—preferably his friends' faces. He felt trapped. Caged by guilt and responsibility. He knew what he had to do, it was just so damn hard to walk away from her now that she was awake, he wasn't sure he would be strong enough.

He didn't dare look at her, but focused on the square vinyl tiles at his feet. "We can't be together. It's too dangerous for you. You nearly ended up dead. There's no guarantee it won't happen again. Only next time, you might not make it."

"But I did make it. You saved me."

The image of Mary's body flashed through his thoughts. "It doesn't always work like that. It's safest if we're not together."

"Don't you think that should be my decision? I'm pretty smart. I have been known to make an informed decision on my own upon occasion."

"Not this one."

"Why not? Don't you trust my judgment?"

"It has nothing to do with judgment."

"Is this just your way of telling me that you're not interested in seeing me anymore? You fucked me and now you're done?"

Anger seethed inside him at her crude, completely mistaken words, eating at his control. "Hell, no!"

"Then if you're not just trying to blow me off, why were you running?"

"I can't let you get hurt again."

He finally looked at her, seeing every ounce of weariness outnumbered by two of determination. She wasn't going to make this easy on him, not that walking away from her ever could have been easy.

She regarded him with a hard stare. "And who's to say that if you leave I'll be safe? You yourself said that my life would always be at risk from those who want to use what I know. I'll always be in danger. It's something I'm going to need to learn to live with so I can protect myself."

"You'll be safer without me." His voice was sharp with resolve.

"So, what you're saying is that even though I'll still be

in danger, if you're not around, at least you won't be the one responsible if I get killed. Your hands will be clean. You won't have to worry about feeling all that guilt that you've felt over Mary's death."

Something primal and frightening rose up inside him and he could feel his eyes burning with anger. "You're not going to get killed! Ever."

"You can't guarantee that. No one can. In fact, I could get into a car to drive home and be smashed flat on the highway and there would be nothing you could do to stop it. Nothing! Just like there was nothing you could have done to keep Mary alive."

Mary. And now Noelle. Oh, God. He was never going to be able to stay sane under the weight of his crushing guilt. He had to get away. Shut down his emotions. It was the only way he was going to survive. "It's not the same thing."

Her green eyes flared with rage. "Bullshit! It's exactly the same thing. You weren't there and Mary was taken. What if she'd been killed in a car wreck because you weren't there to go to the store for her? What if she'd slipped on some ice and died from head trauma because you weren't there to walk her to work every day. You can't be everywhere, David! You can't be responsible for everyone. It's not your job to keep everyone alive."

Part of what she was saying hit home, but he refused to dwell on it. He had to make her understand. "I never wanted to keep everyone alive. Just the people I love. There aren't many of them. It shouldn't have been too much to ask."

"Are you saying that you love me?"

"No. I can't say that." And he couldn't. He couldn't admit to loving her and give anyone who might be listening a weapon to use against him—a reason to hurt her.

"I see. Well, I have no such problem." Her voice softened, though whether from emotion or fatigue, he couldn't tell. "I love you, David. I want to be with you regardless of the risk."

The words sang to his soul and made what was left of his heart ache in desperation to hear them again. She loved him. How could a man like him be so lucky? He didn't deserve her love. But, oh, how he wanted it. "Don't be stupid. Being with me is not worth that kind of risk. I'm not worth that kind of risk."

"You're wrong. Even knowing what I do now—knowing what would happen, if someone gave me the choice of whether or not to go back and do it all again—the time with you and the torture at the end, or no time with you at all—I'd gladly do everything the same way again. No regrets."

She wasn't lying. David could see that in her eyes. She meant every word she said.

It made his gut clench. It made him want to howl like an animal in the face of the bittersweet pain her words caused. How could she love him that much? Him, a violent man who had made so many mistakes? "You can't mean that."

"I do mean it. Those days we had together were worth every single cut and bruise, every single speck of fear that I suffered. And I only had a few days with you. Mary had years. If she loved you as much as I do—and I'm sure she did—she would have gladly accepted her fate as the price for the time she had with you. Maybe you're too dumb to realize it, but you're a good man. You're worth every bit of suffering."

"There's been enough suffering because of having me

in your life. Don't say you're willing to take that kind of risk again."

She reached for his hand, and it was only then that he realized that he was by her side, as close to her as he could get without climbing up on the bed with her. Her fingers were cold and he automatically wrapped them inside his hands to warm them.

Her voice was soft, but no less demanding. "Why? Because then you'll no longer have an excuse to run? Because you'll have to face the fact that I love you and am willing to be with you even if it means I die?"

"I won't let you die." It was a promise, a vow his soul forced him to give her.

"It's not your choice. It never was."

Could she be right? Could it be true that he never had control over life and death? He'd killed. He'd protected people from harm. Didn't that give him control? "God, Noelle. Don't do this to me."

"I'm not doing anything but showing you that your life doesn't have to be about guilt and trying to make up for a crime you didn't commit. You can have a second chance at happiness if you want it. All you have to do is take it."

The tiny part of him that was still human, haunted and hopeful wanted that more than anything. He craved a second chance, but did he deserve it? "I don't know if I can. What if it happens all over again? What if you die like Mary did?"

Her fingers slid over his palm, soothing him. The fire in her voice was gone, but her words burned all the same. "What if I don't? What if you let yourself love me and in forty years from now we're sitting on our front porch watching our grandkids play in the yard?"

"Oh, God," he groaned, nearly doubling over with longing. She was offering him everything he wanted. Love. A family. How could he turn it away? "Noelle, please."

Her voice was thin with weariness. "It's up to you, David. You can shut down and disappear, or you can let yourself live. Whatever you choose, I'll still love you. I'll never regret loving you."

He closed his eyes, willing away the hot tears that gathered behind his lids. He didn't want to cry. He hadn't cried since Mary died. He'd wanted to stay locked in his safe, emotionless box, but Noelle wasn't going to let that happen. She was tearing away every one of his barriers and forcing him to give his soul room to breathe. To grow.

Did Noelle really have no regrets? Could Mary have felt the same way as well? Would she have been willing to sacrifice herself for the love they'd shared?

It didn't seem possible. He wasn't worthy of that kind of love, but Mary had always given more of herself than he deserved. Just like Noelle.

He wished he could talk to Mary one more time and tell her how sorry he was that he'd failed her. There were so many things he wanted her to know—selfish things that would ease his guilt while doing nothing to bring her back. But Mary had always been able to read his mind. Maybe she already knew.

Maybe she knew that he'd done everything he could to get to her and it still wasn't enough. Maybe she knew that he would have traded his life for her a thousand times over if necessary. He would have gladly taken her place—been

tortured, frightened, helpless. He would have done anything. Anything.

As he looked into Noelle's eyes and saw her boundless
potential for love, so much like Mary's, he knew that
it was true. The Mary that he loved would never have
accused him of failing. She would have wanted him to be
happy. To be loved. To keep living even though she was
gone.

Suddenly, a quiet sort of peace settled over him. From
one heartbeat to the next, David felt free. Noelle made
him see that he'd been looking for what he needed in the
wrong place. He needed forgiveness, but not from Noelle
or Mary. He needed to forgive himself.

So he did. He let go of all the should haves and would
haves and what ifs and gave himself the benefit of the doubt.
Maybe he hadn't done everything right in his life, but he
always worked to get the important stuff right. He knew
without a doubt that when Mary had died, she'd known that
he loved her. He always made sure that she knew through
both word and deed.

Mary's death was in the past, and he was finally ready
to let go of all the pain and guilt and anger he'd kept
bottled up inside for so long. As he released all those feelings, he began to remember the good times with Mary—
the happy times that he hadn't been able to recall amid all
the guilt and shame.

They had loved and laughed and lived, and he would
keep those thoughts in his mind in remembrance of the
woman she had been.

He would live the life that Mary would have wanted
him to live. He'd let himself have the happiness he'd found
with Noelle. He only prayed that she would still have him

after he'd been foolish enough to think he should walk away from what they had.

David covered Noelle's hand with his, willing her to understand what he couldn't figure out how to say. "I'm not good enough for you. I'll never be good enough for you. But I want you anyway. I can't walk away from you. I want you to marry me. Not in a few years. Right now. I'll go into hiding with you. I'll give up my work. Compared to you, it means nothing to me."

Her eyes widened and he felt her hand shake harder against his palm. "Marry you? Now?"

"Don't say no. Give me a chance to make you happy. Let me keep you safe."

"Is that why you want to marry me? To protect me? I don't want to be a duty or a burden to anyone, especially not you."

"I do want to protect you, but that's not all."

"Then why? Why do you want to marry me?"

She was going to make him say it. He didn't want to. He didn't want to put his heart out there like that, all open and vulnerable for her to see. He wanted to keep that part of him safe. As long as he didn't say the words, if she refused him, he could walk away with at least his pride intact.

But as he looked into her eyes, he knew that if he didn't take the chance, he might lose her.

Fuck his pride. He wanted Noelle.

David took a deep breath, closed his eyes and took a chance. "Because I love you. I don't want to be without you. I want to go to bed with you at night and wake up by your side in the morning. I want to buy a little house somewhere and have a few kids. I want to sit on that porch with you in forty years and watch our grandkids play. I want it all, but only with you."

She was silent for a long moment, as if trying to decipher what he'd just said.

Her silence was making him worry, and like a babbling idiot, he kept babbling. "I don't care where we live. If you want to try to go back into teaching, I'll figure out a way for you to do it safely. I'm not sure exactly how, but I'll figure something out. If you want, we can—"

She grabbed hold of his shirt and yanked him down toward her, cutting him off. She kept pulling until his mouth met hers, and she kissed him like she had back at the cabin—so sweet and full of love that there was no way that even an idiot like him could miss it.

He pulled away, his pulse racing, his breathing faster from just a few soft kisses. Man, this woman went straight to his head.

"In case you were wondering," she said in a husky voice. "That was a yes."

"Yes? As in yes you'll marry me?"

"Yes. I'll marry you. And the rest of it, too. The kids, the grandkids. All of it."

David's heart swelled, forcing out all the guilt and insecurity of the past. He had all he needed right here in front of him. Noelle.

He bent down and kissed her gently, careful of her bruised face. She sighed and settled deeper into the pillow. He could tell she was tired, so he pulled away to give her a chance to rest.

"I'm going to go tell Grant and Caleb, but I'll be back in fifteen minutes to climb up on that bed with you and hold you. I'm not letting you get away."

She gave him an indulgent, tired smile. "I'm not going anywhere."

"You're one hell of a woman, Noelle."

"And you're one hell of a man, David."

David kissed her again, marveling at his good fortune in having her in his life. If Noelle thought he deserved a second chance, who was he to argue? After all, she was the smart one.

ABOUT THE AUTHOR

After spending too many years as an Industrial Engineer, Shannon learned to write from her husband, bestselling author Jim Butcher. She learned writing craft in order to help him with his stories, but found the idea of writing her own too compelling to resist. She lives in Missouri with her husband and son, where conversations at the dinner table are more often about things someone made up than about anything that's actually happened. Feel free to contact Shannon via her website: www.shannonkbutcher.com.

Don't miss the next
sexy suspense novel from
Shannon K. Butcher...

Turn the page
for a preview of

No Control

AVAILABLE IN MASS MARKET
IN 2008.

PROLOGUE

Armenia

Lana Hancock prayed for a swift death. The hood over her head made it hard to breathe, as did the smell of her friends' bodies. Through a tiny slit in her hood that her captors didn't know was there, she could see Bethany's lifeless eyes staring at her.

Lana tried to turn away, but even the smallest movement sent pain screaming through her broken limbs. The man who had broken them, Boris, came back into the cave, and she knew this was the end. Whatever her abductors told Boris to do, he did. She'd heard them order him to kill her right before they left, and she'd been lying here, waiting for the end for what seemed like days.

She was going to miss her family. Her friends. Her fiancé.

She wanted to see her nephew grow up and wanted to spoil him with loud presents that would drive her sister crazy. The little drum set Lana had bought him for his birthday was tucked in her closet. She hoped they'd find it and give it to him when her family cleaned out her apartment.

Boris pulled out his gun and crossed the dusty cave to where Lana lay. He was a skinny man with bright blue eyes and dimples that made her stomach turn. A sadistic killer shouldn't have dimples.

His booted feet stopped only inches from her face. Part of her was afraid, but most of her was simply grateful he was using the gun instead of the pipe again. At least this way would be fast. She hoped.

She saw a shadow cross the mouth of the cave, then another and another. Maybe her abductors were back to watch it happen. Maybe she was hallucinating. Lana couldn't bring herself to care. She was too tired. Too weak.

Boris reached down and ripped at the tape holding her hood closed around her neck. The movement caused broken bones to grind together, and her dry scream echoed against the cave walls.

She must have passed out, because when she opened her eyes, her killer was looking down at her with a concerned frown, patting her cheek as if to revive her. When he saw she was awake again, he nodded once as if satisfied and stood up again. Apparently, he didn't want to kill her if she was unconscious.

His gun was aimed for her head, thank God. Like the others he'd killed, it would be a headshot. Quick and painless.

A thick arm appeared from nowhere and wrapped around Boris's head, pulling it back while a second arm sliced his throat open with a knife. Blood spewed from the man's neck, and his gun clattered to the hard ground.

Lana tried to figure out what was happening, but she couldn't move her head. Couldn't keep her eyes open.

"We've got to get you out of here," said a deep, tight voice she'd heard somewhere before.

Pain sliced through her, and she realized she was being lifted. Her broken legs dangled painfully over a man's arms, but she kept herself from screaming. She couldn't alert her captors that she was escaping.

Lana forced her eyes open just as he carried her out of the cave. Light seared her retinas, but she welcomed it. Light meant freedom—something she thought she'd never again experience.

He laid her down and spoke in a quiet voice to someone nearby. "She's the only one alive."

"Not for long, she isn't," said a second man. "And not if they discover she made it out alive."

Lana's body throbbed in time with each beat of her heart. He was right. She wasn't going to last much longer. She could feel herself growing weaker by the second. Maybe she was bleeding somewhere.

At least she wasn't going to die in that cave.

"Our team took down three of them."

"How many were there?"

"I don't know. I only saw two, and not closely enough to ID them. I got orders from that skinny bastard, Boris. There could be another dozen for all I know."

"You took care of Boris?"

"Yes."

"Our men are in the hills. They'll find anyone who got away," said the second man.

"They'd better."

Lana wasn't sure what that meant, but she knew she

should. What they were saying meant something to her, but her brain was too foggy to figure it out. She was using all her strength just to keep from screaming.

If she screamed, they could find her.

A shadow fell over her, and Lana looked up into the face of Miles Gentry, the man her abductors had hired to bomb a U.S. elementary school.

Lana couldn't breathe. She wasn't safe. Not with him. He was a monster—a man willing to kill children for money.

He must have seen her fear, because he smoothed her matted hair back from her face and said, "Shh. It's okay. I'm a U.S. soldier. I'm not going to hurt you."

Liar! Lana tried to pull away from his touch, but her body wouldn't move, wouldn't cooperate.

"Back off, Caleb. You're scaring her," said the second man.

Caleb or Miles or whoever he was moved away. Behind him, from high in the rocky hillside, she could see twin flashes of sunlight reflecting off glass. Binoculars.

With a painful stab of clarity, she realized they were being watched.

She tried to tell the men, but her lips were swollen and stuck together with dried blood, and she couldn't seem to form a coherent word.

The wind kicked up, and dust choked her lungs. She tried not to cough. Someone pulled a sheet over her head to keep the dust out. It didn't help. She couldn't keep from coughing, and as soon as she did—as soon as her broken ribs shifted—the pain ricocheted inside her until all she could do was gasp for air.

All the pain and going without food or water for days was too much. She had to give up and let go. She couldn't take any more.

Lana's mind shut down, and she welcomed the oblivion as it came to claim her.

CHAPTER ONE

———— ❧ ————

Columbia, Missouri, eighteen months later

Caleb Stone had no business being this close to the woman he'd nearly killed eighteen months ago. Just the thought of having to face Lana Hancock again made him break out in a cold sweat. This assignment was going to be as much fun as taking a bullet in the gut.

Lana's office at the First Light Foundation was nestled in the middle of a run-down line of small, one-story leased office spaces, between a walk-in clinic and a print shop. The long, prefab building was cheaply constructed and badly in need of a fresh coat of paint. Early morning sun filtered through the line of trees adorning the front of the parking lot. It was late July in central Missouri, and even in the shade of the decorative trees Caleb's car was already beginning to grow uncomfortably warm.

He didn't shift to crack a window or turn on the air. With all the mistakes he'd made, he figured he was headed for hell anyway. Might as well get used to the climate.

Another car pulled into the lot and parked. It was Lana Hancock's white Saturn.

Caleb's body tensed and his stomach flooded with acid. This was not going to be fun.

She got out of her Saturn, putting Caleb no more than fifty feet away from her. It was too damn close, and every corner of his soul screamed for him to back away slowly before she got hurt again. But backing away wasn't an option. Colonel Monroe had ordered him to come here. The bastard.

If Caleb had thought for one second that Lana was in danger, he would have been the first one in line to play human shield, but that wasn't the case. Monroe was just being paranoid over a bit of random chatter the CIA had intercepted. Monroe was worried that the Swarm was back, but that couldn't be true. That particular terrorist group was gone. Caleb had been on the team that took them out six months ago. They'd made sure no one survived.

Monroe was convinced something was going on, so here Caleb was, up close and personal with the only living reminder of the worst three days of his life. Lana Hancock.

She looked a lot different now than she had the last time Caleb had seen her. She still had the same rich brown hair, but it no longer fell past her shoulders, tangled and matted with blood. She'd cropped it shorter so that it swung in a shiny wave that ended just above her shoulders. Her face was no longer swollen and bruised from repeated beatings, and he found himself staring at her, drinking her in, trying to replace this new, healthy image of her with the horrible one he'd held in his head for too many months. He'd been unable to see it when she'd been lying unconscious in that army hospital bed, but now he could tell how pretty she was, and the fullness of her mouth hadn't been totally due to swelling.

A man pulled his Honda into the lot and waved at Lana. She smiled and waved back, and Caleb caught a glimpse of deep, twin dimples in her cheeks. He'd never seen her smile before, and until now, he hadn't realized what he'd been missing. The only expressions he'd seen on her face were ones of terror and pain. He'd stayed by her bedside for three long days and even longer nights, and neither the terror nor the pain had lessened. When he'd been forced back to work, every day he'd expected to hear that she had died, but that word never came.

Even though he'd kept tabs on her recovery, this was the first time he'd seen her since, and watching her walk around was like witnessing a miracle. It soothed him and eased some of the tension that had been growing in him ever since he'd been ordered to come here.

Caleb watched with a mixture of respect and awe as she crossed the hot asphalt to her office. Her walk was smooth and steady, her hips swaying slightly beneath her faded jeans. If he hadn't known for a fact that it had taken her months to learn how to walk again, he'd never have believed it by watching her move. There was nothing hesitant in her stride, no hitch of pain or jarring movement. She was all rolling grace and swaying strength.

Her functional white T-shirt and matching tennis shoes were without frills, and there wasn't a single glitter of jewelry on her body or a speck of makeup on her face. Instead of a purse, she carried a green canvas backpack that looked like it had seen better days. But even without the bells and whistles, even though she was nothing like the women he usually dated, she still had more pull on him than all the women he'd known combined.

And if that wasn't fate's way of slugging him in the gut for fucking up, he didn't know what was. No matter how much she appealed to him, she'd probably rather spit on him than look at him. Which was probably safest for both of them.

Caleb forced his breathing to even out into a steady rhythm while he willed his heart to slow its pounding pace. He knew that seeing her again would affect him, but until now, he hadn't realized just how strongly. He'd never known anyone who'd come back after being that close to dying, and he'd known a lot of strong, highly motivated men.

Lana was one hell of a woman. If only he'd met her under other circumstances, things might have been a lot different between them.

If only. Caleb squashed that line of thinking before it could gain a foothold. If onlys could get a man killed.

THE DISH

Where authors give you the inside scoop!

♥ ♥ ♥ ♥ ♥ ♥ ♥ ♥ ♥ ♥ ♥ ♥ ♥ ♥ ♥ ♥

From the desk of Amanda Scott

Dear Reader,

Secrets! Lady Adela Macleod, heroine of **Knight's Treasure** (on sale now), hates them. Sir Robert (Rob) Logan, Scottish Knight Templar, has more than his share of them. But one of the most delightful challenges of writing a novel is creating obstacles for one's characters to overcome. In the case of Lady Adela, who has long borne responsibilities beyond her years and proven herself strong, capable, and intelligent in managing her father's large household and her younger sisters, the temptation to fling obstacle after obstacle in her path proved irresistible.

Abducted from the kirk steps by a ruthless villain before her first wedding (**Lady's Choice**), Adela finally marries as **Knight's Treasure** opens, only to watch her bridegroom collapse and die at their wedding feast.

Savvy readers, who recognized elements of Stockholm syndrome during Adela's abduction, will doubtless note symptoms of post-traumatic stress disorder as she comes to know Rob and, with his help, recovers from the shock of her abduction and her husband's death. Needless to say, although no one had heard of either the syndrome or the disorder in fourteenth-century Scotland, people suffered from their effects long before anyone had identified or labeled them.

Adela has little time to coddle herself, however, because even more powerful villains than the ones in **Prince of Danger** and **Lady's Choice** are after the Templar Treasure, and Rob's family guards yet another great secret, the discovery of which could alter the succession to the Scottish crown.

My objective was to make **Knight's Treasure** a fast-paced tale including mystery, murder, humor, and sensuous romance, and to cast a little light on two of Scotland's most fascinating historical mysteries. I hope you enjoy it!

Sincerely yours,

Amanda Scott

http://home.att.net/~amandascott/

♥ ♥ ♥ ♥ ♥ ♥ ♥ ♥ ♥ ♥ ♥ ♥ ♥ ♥ ♥

From the desk of Shannon K. Butcher

Hi. My name is Shannon and I'm a geek. It's been sixty-seven days since I last took apart something that wasn't broken just to see how it worked. I take it one day at a time.

As a teenager, I didn't have posters of rock stars or the latest heartthrob on my walls, though I do admit to a giant crush on MacGyver. Instead, I had diagrams of satellites in geosynchronous orbits plastered all over my room. I was convinced that I would grow up and figure out a way to collect solar energy from orbit and use a satellite to beam it to earth in some usable form, solving the world's energy crisis forever. Instead, I write romance novels, which is so close to my original life plan that it might as well be the same thing.

So naturally, when I started thinking of story ideas, the geeky parts of me had a lot of influence. As did my husband. He loves to watch The History Channel and I love hanging out with him, so I end up watching a lot of The History Channel too. One day, this show came on about the history of secret codes and the evolution of code breaking, and for the first time in a long time, I actually paid attention. A few days later, in that semi-coherent state between wishing I was asleep and actually being there, the idea for a different kind of code came to me. I figured that math is a universal language, so why not use advanced math as a basis? I had to do something useful with all those calculus and linear algebra classes.

I took that basic concept and asked myself what I'd do with the code. What if the CIA came across a bit of code that—if they could break it—would reveal the location of hidden nuclear weapons from the cold war era (another idea courtesy of The History Channel)? And what if they weren't the only ones who knew about it? What if there was a terrorist group out there that knew what the good guys did? Now it was a race to crack the code. Enter our heroine, Noelle, who, as the only person left alive with that ability, has suddenly become a target. And she doesn't even know it.

The bad guys are on their way to abduct her and now she needs a hero in a big way. I gave her David, who has the skills necessary to protect her, as well as some harsh life lessons that have taught him the painful price of failure. He's a tortured man with a guilt-ridden past, because, come on, who doesn't love that? And that's how NO REGRETS (on sale now) was born.

The rest of the story was a lot harder to figure out, but I knew that, in the end, I wanted the geeky girl to get the stud, because it's my story world and that's the way I wanted relationship physics to work. Clearly, I am not overburdened by reality.

So that's how the story began—with one geeky idea. Now, if you will please excuse me, I have a television remote to fix. I'm sure it's broken because we're still getting way too much History Channel around here.

Shannon K. Butcher

www.shannonkbutcher.com

If you liked this book and you like
Romantic Suspense . . .
You'll LOVE these authors!!!

KAREN ROSE

"Utterly compelling . . . high wire suspense that keeps
you riveted to the edge of your seat."

—Lisa Gardner, *New York Times* bestselling author

Don't Tell	*I'm Watching You*
(0-446-61280-4)	(0-446-61447-5)
Have You Seen Her?	*Nothing To Fear*
(0-446-61281-2)	(0-446-614483)

ANNIE SOLOMON

"A powerful new voice in romantic suspense."

—*Romantic Times*

Blind Curve	*Dead Ringer*
(0-446-61358-4)	(0-446-61229-4)
Like a Knife	*Tell Me No Lies*
(0-446-61230-8)	(0-446-61357-6)

*Want to know more about romances at
Warner Books and Warner Forever?
Get the scoop online!*

WARNER'S ROMANCE HOMEPAGE

Visit us at www.warnerforever.com for all the
latest news, reviews, and chapter excerpts!

NEW AND UPCOMING TITLES

Each month we feature our new titles
and reader favorites.

CONTESTS AND GIVEAWAYS

We give away galleys, autographed copies,
and all kinds of fun stuff.

AUTHOR INFO

You'll find bios, articles, and links to personal
Web sites for all your favorite authors—and
so much more!

THE BUZZ

Sign up for our monthly romance newsletter,
and be the first to read all about it!